The Border of Truth

The

BORDER

of

TRUTH

❧

A Novel

VICTORIA REDEL

COUNTERPOINT
A Member of the Perseus Books Group
New York

Published by Counterpoint
A Member of the Perseus Books Group

Books published by Counterpoint are available at special discounts
for bulk purchases in the United States by corporations, institutions,
and other organizations. For more information, please contact the Special
Markets Department at the Perseus Books Group, 11 Cambridge Center,
Cambridge MA 02142, or call (617) 252-5298, (800) 255-1514
or e-mail special.markets@perseusbooks.com.

Designed by Brent Wilcox

Library of Congress Cataloging-in-Publication Data
Redel, Victoria.
The Border of truth : a novel / by Victoria Redel.
    p.   cm.
ISBN-13: 978-1-58243-366-0 (alk. paper)
ISBN-10: 1-58243-366-6 (alk. paper)
1. World War, 1939–1945—Refugees—Fiction. I. Title.
PS3568.E3443B67 2007
813'.54—dc22

                                          2006032433

For my father

———— ∞ ————

On August 9, 1940, the Quanza, a small Portuguese steamship that normally ran between Lisbon and South Africa, was chartered to transport 317 passengers from Lisbon to New York and then Vera Cruz. The ship landed on August 19, 1940, in New York City, where 196 people disembarked. One hundred and twenty-one passengers were refused permission to come ashore. The boat continued on to Vera Cruz, Mexico, where thirty-five passengers left the ship before the rest were denied entry, their Mexican visas considered invalid. Eighty-six refugees remained on board. On September 11, 1940, the Quanza made an overnight stop in Virginia to load up on coal before it was to return to Lisbon, where the eighty-six refugees feared they would again be denied entry without proper visas and be returned to their various countries now under German occupation.

———— ∞ ————

SEPTEMBER 11

9:00 A.M.

Dear Eleanor Roosevelt,

Do you like stories?

So much of the story I need to tell happened in spring. A war story in spring seems wrong, I know. Yet so much of it is colorful, the tight buds of azaleas opening, wild rhododendron brushing hillsides white with flower, and the road out of Brussels bundled impossibly with carts and cars, trucks and bicycles, but scented with lilac and fields of freshly turned black dirt.

I wish I had many, many days to tell you this story, all the tender shades of green I saw—the first, pale, fuzzy twists of ferns, ramps we picked at the edge of a woods, the yellow-green of rolled hay, a dark line of cedar twisting up a driveway outside Paris.

But I suspect there's hardly even this full day before Captain Alberto Harberts turns this steamship from this port. We have come only to bunker coal. Harberts has detained passengers and even his crew aboard. There is no time for all I want to say. Anyhow, I know that a woman in your position doesn't have all day. So I'll try to be quick—though I have always been a little long-winded, something that Maman says will either make me a rabbi or a thief. Since when does a thief need many words? Perhaps Maman means a con man. Though having recently needed more just right words than I could conjure, I promise you, Mrs. Roosevelt, I am no one's con man.

I am instead Itzak Lejdel, born in Brussels, though lately I have had addresses in Paris, Toulouse, Perpignan, Lisbon, and almost in Vera Cruz.

I turned seventeen this spring.

Mrs. Roosevelt, before I go any further, permit me to double back and apologize for my English, which you will see is not perfect. I know it's not bad and according to my English teacher, Madame Dupais, I even have a flair for your language. Still, at this moment, I need to speak as perfectly as I can and while my French is better than my Flemish, which is maybe a fraction better than my German, I thought it was most polite and without the burden and time wasted on translators to address you in your own language. As for Yiddish, which was an option, I didn't think there's much chance that there are many Yiddish translators on the United States government payroll.

Truly I adore your English language. Madame Dupais taught us a mixture of high diction and the latest argot that would make us sound like the *real deal* in any bar in New York City. I was, let me brag for a moment, at the *tip-top* of her class. I was the *bee's knees, the elephant's ear.* *"You're the living end,"* Madame Dupais crooned when she overheard me practicing my Cary Grant with my copain, Henri. But this letter, finally, is too important to pick incorrect words or to wind up talking to the President's wife as if she were a cigarette girl on Tin Pan Alley.

But in any language I probably go about this sort of letter all wrong. My professors at the lycée—excluding Madame Dupais—would insist that the tone is already too informal (impudent encore, Monsieur Lejdel!), the substance vague, misleading (azaleas! thieves!) and bogged down with details that must be trimmed before the letter is sent.

And while I'm apologizing, let me say I'm sorry for this terrible, thin letter paper that, rotten and thin as it is, is all that I have on board. I would have liked that my presentation was a little more presentable for the First Lady.

Which leads directly to my third and grandest apology. What was I thinking, calling you Eleanor? It's one thing to write: Dear Hedy Lamarr or Dear Ginger. But you're the President's wife. The First Lady. Not that you need me to tell you this. Maybe it's just as well. They say our errors disclose us. Much to the dismay of Maman and my professors and even a few young women, it will not have been the first time I broke the rules.

My name, my situation, and what I need from you. A simple, direct plea: save Maman and me. That would be, no doubt, the proper letter. But Mrs. Roosevelt, how well does a list of rules and facts move our hearts? I think it is in the details that we are saved.

Here, you judge.

Our steamship, the *Quanza*, sailed from Lisbon, arriving in New York City on August 19. One hundred and ninety-six passengers—Americans and Europeans—went ashore in New York. The rest of us were turned away, our visas and documentation refused. Then to Mexico, where in Vera Cruz we were again denied entrance, despite transit papers I had secured for Maman and myself in Lisbon, proving that we must go through Mexico to find passage on a ship to Shanghai for which we also have visas.

Lisbon to Mexico to Shanghai! I know—cunning, yes, but still not a con man!

The *Quanza* has come to the port at Hampton Roads, Virginia, to load coal and bring the refugees back to Lisbon, though there is no certainty we will be granted entrance into Portugal.

Refugee. Suddenly this is one of my facts.

And that is practically the whole story when it comes to simple facts. Tell the truth, you weren't moved very much, were you?

Okay, there's another fact. On the ship, they call me the Poet.

But, really, I'm no poet. I think this must be obvious to you, even if sometimes I do go a little overboard with my descriptions. But let them think these pages that I curl over are poems, barely glancing up when they pass, knuckling my skull. "Itzak the Poet," they say, "Still with the poems. You don't think the Legal Advisory Committee could make a better use of your typewriter?" I don't budge. Every one of the All-Important-capital-A-capital–I-capital-C-Committees has tried to commandeer my Royale. This typewriter's a beauty. From cabin bunk to the upper or second deck, I carry my Royale, setting up a portable office. Let them think these are poems. Let them think I'm Itzak the dreamer. All along it's been letters, not poems. Mrs. Roosevelt, I'll admit you're not the first I've written a letter to on this passage. I've written Rosalind Russell and Claudette Colbert. Now may we talk about who is truly the cat's meow! I'd like to also write Ginger, Hedy, and Lana Turner. And Judy Garland. I'm a fan. Of all of them. Of actresses. In those letters I tell them how gorgeous and talented they are and that one day, in America perhaps, I hope to meet them, but until then, I am their eternal fan. Not that I wouldn't consider slipping a bit of poetry (Baudelaire, Verlaine, maybe the wild Rimbaud) into a letter to show my savoir faire. I've considered writing film stars for help. But I've decided, as Madame Dupais says, to *put all my eggs in one basket.*

Now, here on the *Quanza*, more than facts, what's left are rumors. For example, that certain legal petitions filed on behalf of the wealthier families will hold us in port. That a lawyer in Virginia has been hired and is trying to arrest the ship and buy time for his client's release from the ship. Rumor: that the client is Monsieur Rand. Rumor: that the client is Madame Cartier. Not a rumor: that the client is the third-class passenger, Itzak Lejdel.

And the big, big, big, biggest rumor is that you, Mrs. Eleanor Roosevelt, have been directly contacted.

That's why, bragging as this sounds, I think it important to write you directly and ask if you can help Maman and me off the ship?

There it is—I've written who I am and what I want.

Simple, clear facts, the lesson accomplished. Yet the facts tell us nothing. Or they tell a dreary story of stations and inspectors, the endless waiting on endless lines. Visas, papers, valises tied with rough, frayed string. Tell me, who wouldn't want that story to hurry up and end? But this is also a story with the long, grand hallways of European libraries. There is a fox stole and bright caged birds in my story. Here there are trains and disguises, the loosening of a woman's coiled hair. There are film stars and hiding in movie houses (and isn't everything better when the movies are involved!). There are deceptions, maps, and betrayals. There are long, ample kisses. In other words, here's a story of everything a boy might dream of knowing during the spring and summer he turns seventeen. But I hope this is not only a boy's adventure story or a flimsy poet's dreaming.

Mrs. Roosevelt, here's a fact that matters. I'm counting on you liking stories. I believe my life depends on it.

Yours truly,
Itzak Lejdel

Isn't this already what Sara wants? An early morning
walk through the park on her way to a full, uninterrupted day in
the library. Even the young man she passes playing Bach—a quick
shake of his shaved head to indicate—*no thanks*—to the dollar she
holds out, no cup for money, just playing for the love of it, the deep
notes of his alto recorder reverberating under the overpass—isn't
this even somehow part of what Sara wants?

And school's out. A forty-one-year-old woman still oriented to
the academic calendar. Sometimes she thinks she should have out-
grown the childish pleasure of school getting out. But forget it; it's
a thrill! *No more homework, no more books, no more students' needy
looks.* The long pleasure of summer. A grant to finish her second
book, a new translation of Walter Benjamin's essays, and with them
she wants to translate his correspondence to colleagues and friends.
She's moved by the letters, by the reflection in his careful hand-
writing; in his word choice there's a tone, a positioning of self at
once intimate and theoretical. Even the fine stationery Walter Benjamin chose, Sara's claimed in her grant proposal, seems important
in relation to the essays—a conversation, large and dear simultane-
ously, with both history and the intellectuals of early twentieth-
century Europe.

This morning it seems so simple what Sara wants. A summer to live entirely in the work and to ready herself for the other huge change in her life. The first round of adoption papers has been turned in. She's found a private agency specializing in placing children of war. Sara can barely talk about her decision to adopt without sounding like someone on a moral high horse—the babies and children in torn-up, land-mined countries. But it's not a soapbox; she's always planned on children, at the very least one child. She'd never imagined becoming a parent alone, especially having felt the burden of growing up without one parent. It's never been what she wanted for herself or her child. But now she's done waiting for the right circumstance when, let's face it, by now even Sara has to admit that she doesn't choose impossible lovers so much as lovers with impossible situations.

The path swings right, skirting the sloped wing of the Metropolitan Museum. There's a fork in the path, a stone bridge. She isn't even tempted to spend the morning wandering through Central Park, the bridge to the sheep meadow, to the zoo, or to the rambles. Maybe find what the birders have logged in the sighting book by the Boat House. It's not that she's afraid that she'll never translate seriously after she becomes a mother, but she's not exactly unhappy that there's a wedge of bureaucratic busywork before she can go get the child.

The park path opens onto Fifth. Two blocks to the New York Society Library, the city's oldest library, a secret, elegant place, paneled, with a turning staircase, a reading room where carefully dressed men and women spend mornings reading in wingback chairs, corridors hung with maps of New York harbor and portraits. Melville wrote in the Society Library. Auden, too. And even though she has access to libraries with far greater resources, this is Sara's library finally more than any of the great university libraries where she's been an undergraduate, a doctoral student, or, even now, a full professor. Hearing Bach before 9 a.m. A day beginning with such clear light. The focused work ahead of her, the seeds of her life with a child, the May park's ample promise of summer. She's had one kind of life for as long as she can remember and somehow it's all changing. This morning—whatever comes—Sara feels she wants it.

⌘

Caught. Verfangen. It's this word *caught* that has been worrying Sara for the last hour. She's considered *tangled* though she knows that election gives her little of the stuck-in-the-throat sound of *caught* so close to *got.* Used reflexively, *Verfangen—got caught.*

She goes back to the first sentence. *The angel would like to stay, awaken the dead, and make whole what has been smashed.*

If she had to pick out one sentence by Walter Benjamin, it would be this one, this sentence, that made her want to take on the whole translation project. Benjamin's *Angel of History.* The angel's face turned toward the past. Such longing in the sentence. *But a storm is blowing from Paradise and has got caught in his wings. . . .* This storm from Paradise that drives the angel into the future. It has always moved and frightened her, this image, the storm of the past caught in the angel's wings. She wants her translation to honor Benjamin's work. No, to equal it. That's the fear of the translator. To enter the work with a mind unequal to its maker. *Tangled. Tousled.* Ridiculous. Already fear has tempted her to ease the language, make it prettier! No, just plain *Got caught.*

With a tilt of her head Sara sees out of the library window to the Greek coffee shop at the corner. She's not entirely restless but maybe restless enough that she should get out for a library break, go get a coffee, stand in the May sun, and watch the avenue start to open for business. She could get two coffees and walk the few blocks over for a quick check-in on her father. Forget it, nothing's ever quick if she visits her father; she'll lose the whole day. He'll offer breakfast, a game of chess. He'll suggest they watch Myrna Loy in *Too Hot to Handle* for the umpteenth time and again complain throughout the whole film that his charming Myrna doesn't belong in such an idiotic film, even if she saves Gable's foolish reporter ass from being a complete and total nudnik. If Sara makes a preemptive declaration, "I'm only here for a short break from the translations, Dad," he'll ask again, "Who's this Walter fellow?"

She'll repeat the same truncated bio: brilliant literary critic, art critic, thinker, and translator. One of the key minds of the Frankfurt School. Killed himself in 1940 after crossing through the Pyrenees from Vichy, France, to Spain.

"Well, forgive me for saying this, but your brilliant man doesn't sound like he was using his smarts then," her father, putting down the paper coffee cup, says in German.

Now Sara's up on her feet. But there's nowhere to pace in this narrow research room with its six long tables. And she needs to move. Needs to pace.

Sara's come to this library since she was a girl, when her mother would walk her the few blocks from their apartment and they'd go up to the children's room.

"Choose carefully," her mother said. "Books change you once you let them inside your body."

"You mean my mind," Sara said once, her mother by then in the final stages of the cancer, the slow dying by which Sara knew her mother. Even now, more than thirty years later, Sara can hear the strict corrective tone she'd taken with her mother, the way she'd begun to scold her, as if she actually believed that her mother's slipping mind was something correctable. Sara wishes she could go back, lean a little more gently into her mother's words, go wherever they'd take Sara.

"No, darling, the body," her mother said, pulling a book off the shelf. Why can Sara still see it—the green cover of *Huckleberry Finn*? Honestly, more reliably than she can call back her mother's face, she can see the worn spine of the novel.

"You'll see one day where you feel *Anna Karenina* or *Hamlet*. This book I've always felt in my knees and low in my belly. Maybe it's all that low and lonesome Huck Finn talks about or maybe it's just a bit of seasickness from nights on the raft." Her mother gave a low throaty laugh and slid the book back, making sure it was exactly aligned with the others on the shelf.

Sara packs up, fitting her books and files into her bag. She's not quitting for the day, no way, she promises herself. She's got to move a little, clear her head, maybe walk up to 86th Street and then come back. She'll be ready then to tackle a letter, one of the 1940 letters to his friend and colleague, Theodor Adorno. Still, it's only good library manners not to monopolize a seat if she goes out. Instead of waiting for the wood-paneled elevator with its accordion pull gate, Sara runs down the stairs, her shoes clapping loudly on the marble.

The midday streets are busy, gates lifted, shops open. She catches her quick stride in the shop windows, her workbag knocking against her jeans. Sara passes the Italian grocer on Madison.

Apricots and cherries in wicker baskets. The same cherries she buys at her crowded West Side market, and yet she can't help feeling these look better, fresher, sweeter. She lingers at the window of Agnes B looking at a pink raincoat and it occurs to her that a pink coat from France, this exact pink coat from France, could change her life. She sees herself in the shop glass. Maybe a French coat is exactly what she needs. As a good luck charm. Who's she kidding? Sara knows she's blown it, today's chance for work, for coming close enough to Benjamin's mind. Not the letters, or the Baudelaire. She'll walk the city. With a new pink coat, to balance her boyish stride, she'll be the dandy. That's the closest she'll get to Benjamin or Baudelaire. She'll be frivolous. Isn't this what Walter Benjamin says about Baudelaire's vision of the modern world? *It moors him fast in the secure harbor forever and abandons him to everlasting idleness.*

She presses the buzzer on the Agnes B doorframe. The salesgirl smiles and waves as if she's been waiting all morning just for Sara. It should make her want to stay out, to turn away, but before she can, with a click, Sara's in.

SEPTEMBER 11

10:28 A.M.

Dear Mrs. Roosevelt,

Bombs woke me.

After the planes had passed, we stood out on our small balcony. I was in the middle, between Maman and Father, each holding tight to my hand as if I were still a small boy in the crowded park. But that night, listening for another round of planes, it was my parents who looked small to me. A head taller already than my father, it seemed I could hardly be the offspring of this little man and woman. My knees ached as they did most nights, as if that night before the bombs woke me I'd been yanked taller again. The fires could be seen at a distance from our apartment on Rue Rogier. From the look of it, mostly they'd hit bridges and railway stations.

Father bent over the balustrade. "It's all over," he said. "I think we should go back inside and sleep." Could he be serious? Brussels, our city, had been bombed, Mrs. Roosevelt, and Father was urging us back to sleep!

My father leaned farther over the iron railing, his fingers curling around a twisted iron vine. He was trying, I knew, to see into the courtyard where, at the far end, the chestnut tree branched over the entrance to his small glove factory. Even if he hoisted himself out at the foolish angle I'd dared so many times as a boy, my bony hip catching against the edges of the rail, my father could never prop himself out quite far enough to see the factory door.

"I should check," Father said. "It's not good if the leathers start stinking of smoke."

I knew the inside of his workshop by heart. At the front of the shop, close to the long-paned windows, was the heavy cutting table where Charlotte's shears lay each night, leaning against whatever thick bolt was ready for the next day's cutting. I wanted to ask if he thought Charlotte was safe in her room with the one window that looked over the river, but I didn't want them to know I'd been there eating the jam cakes she served me at her green table. I thought of the electric metal glove molds at the back tables, like a row of hands held in a wave or a salute. Early mornings as a child, after the stoves were lit and the machinery switched on, the room still too cold for anyone to take off a coat and put on the blue shop coat, I loved to hold my fingers spread against the square fingers until, finally, the metal almost burned me. Sometimes, leaving the shop, I'd turn and give a sharp salute and pretend the metal hands waved back a goodbye.

"It matters? It doesn't matter," I said. "They're gloves. We're going."

The city was bombed. There was no choice. In six days I'd turn seventeen. In six days I would have to become a soldier of the Belgian Army. Or a dodger of the Belgian Army. That sounded like someone fast, a dodger. But standing on the second floor with these little people buckled to me and my legs aching and sore, I knew I could barely run.

"Maybe not so quickly. Where are we going? How are we going? Everything seems—" my father said, but I cut him off, saying, "No Papa. Quickly is how we're leaving."

Maman tugged at my arm. "Shh."

"We'll leave tomorrow," I said, refusing to turn to her. "I'm going in to pack."

Most days I could only take my parents for a few minutes before one of them said something and I'd feel mean inside and like I needed to get far away. But that night, going in from the narrow balcony, I didn't feel mean. Listening from inside, their worried voices hushed and small like little animals chittering in the forest, I should have felt lonely for the life I was leaving—days at the lycée and the early dark afternoons arguing with friends at cafés. I should have been sad for all the Saturdays I wouldn't bicycle with a girl out to Viviers or the chance again to see Odile in her swimsuit at Coq Sur Mer. But I was happy. The air was burnt and there was a pink cast to the night from the distant fires. But still you could smell spring. The night was like a night in a poem, maybe a Baudelaire poem where everything's flowery and smoky and wrecked.

I had no idea where we'd go. Or how. My father didn't know how to drive; we had no car. We'd ride bicycles. Somehow we'd leave. I didn't care if we had to walk.

I was tipsy with leaving.

This sounds horrible to say, but right then I was happy for Germany and their smart German plans. It served us right, all the stupid singing confidence about the flimsy Albert Canal or the

Maginot Line. I shouldn't admit it, but I felt I was on the German side. The Germans were getting me get out of Brussels, off the Rue Rogier. I was happy.

Yours truly,

Itzak

P.S. Okay, bombs didn't really wake me. The truth is, Mrs. Roosevelt, I'd been up reading my new issue of *Le Film Complet*. It's a weekly from Paris with not only French stars but your Americans too. My knees keep me up at night. Anyway, it's the best time—the middle of the night, half awake, to fall in love with movie stars. I love their gowns. The tilt of their heads and the lacquered sweep of their hair. I adore Norma Shearer. Did you see *Marie Antoinette*? And Irene Dunne. I'm crazy for Carole Lombard in *My Man Godfrey*. You've got to have seen that. I'd give a lot to be William Powell with Carole making za-za eyes at me. I also get some of your American magazines. Like *Movie Story* and *Screen Album* and *Modern Screen*. They don't have Carole Lombard too much in the magazines anymore. Most issues have Gable alone or with a starlet like Joan Crawford or Loretta Young. But I'm still a loyal fan of Carole's. I hope this doesn't sound too foolish, but sometimes turning the thin pages and looking at the actresses, I dream I can feel their hair in my fingers.

Maybe it's not a big thing. Saying I was asleep when I was awake. But I just want things A-okay between us. I don't want you ever doubting the truth of what I say.

HER CHIN PRESSES against the underside of Marco's arm. The man can sleep. In the beginning she thought Marco was just stubborn, willfully rejecting touches, pretending he didn't like the feel of her hands slipping up his leg to hold him. Now, a year later, she almost gets it. No pretend, no rejection. No subtext to keep her a little distant. The man can just sleep. A baby's sleep. A sleep Sara's never slept even as a baby. Certainly not as a child wandering in at midnight, finding her mother worrying over medical books in the kitchen. Or after, in the years when it was just Sara and her father left in the apartment, she'd wake and hear one of the old movies. Her father patted the sofa next to him when she'd appear in the doorway. He never sent her back to bed. Not even on school nights.

"Dad, not Carole Lombard again," she'd say, looking always first to measure her father's sadness.

"Come on, ma petite chouchou," he'd say, settling her against his arm. "You know that as far as I'm concerned there's never enough Carole Lombard."

Marco turns, pulls her close so that his mouth is buried in Sara's neck. His hands make their way along and down her stomach. The man can even make love asleep. And not badly, not gingerly, not even selfishly. For a skinny man, he's strong and insistent, a surprising lover, his whole being a taut muscle. It took a while to let it be okay, his thinness against her fuller body.

"I want you," he says, annoyed when she points out the impossibly thin downtown girls who live on his street. "Anyway, if I wanted scrawny I'd just get another underfed Ecuadorian cholo like me."

"Hey," Sara says, still refusing to trust this sleeping. She pulls her fingers across the tendons of his neck and down along his ribs. Feels the held, sputtering breath of his sleep. Hasn't it always been like this?—Sara keeping vigil over men asleep or awake. It sounds a little martyrish, she knows. But it's also just the truth. It was only after her father finally drifted off that Sara could ease out of his large, fatherly arms, shut off the TV, and find her way back to bed.

"Hey," Sara says again. "I'm going back to the library. I'm going back to work." She's saying it more for herself than Marco. She could stay like this all afternoon, watching the way his lips push out with air. She puts her mouth along his hair; the glossy feel of it slips against her face. She loves his handsomeness. His mixed elegance, Indian and European. He shakes and rolls to the edge of the mattress. At some point after she's gone, he'll shake himself up and get right back to his music.

"It was the most beautiful melody I'd played all day," he says when she calls later to see if he even remembers that she'd surprised him with a midday visit. "Like water in the mountain streams." It's amazing how he gets away with his exorbitant talk. How she's come to even enjoy his willful devotion to large poetic phrases.

"And where was I?" she teases.

"Oh darling, all day in your library, of course, being the serious girl you are." Even his voice is smoothly handsome, extravagant. "But you, my darling, were every wonderful wet note."

Sara leans to kiss her father's head. "Come. Let me get you outside, Dad. Let's air you out." Two o'clock, he's still in his robe, sitting on the edge of his bed. His shoulders slope, the robe sags open to show the flat buttons of his pajama top. Not thinner or heavier. Just old. Older. He looks surprised, as if he's just taken in that Sara's actually there, in the room with him. He finds her hand. Tender, he's always been a tender father, protective, and a proud papa—my daughter the professor, he still crows, though she's been tenured for years.

"Where could we go?" he says, as if even the idea of outside is mystifying. Maybe too vast. Maybe hardly there at all.

"Anywhere. It's just good to go out."

Her father stares at her. She sees him preparing, squinting with determination. As soon as he repeats "Sara," she knows he's readying himself to deliver one of his declarations.

"Sara, you might think I'm just a big worrier with hardly anything worthwhile left in this brain, but, take my word, with what's in the world today, what we're about to live through, trust me it's good to have cash in the house." His face is wet with tears. She's not surprised; her father's always been an easy cry.

"What are we about to live through?" she asks, not expecting an answer. She can see he's drifting out into wherever his mind goes now. It isn't that he's become forgetful or that he's losing access to parts of his mind. Rather he seems deeper, even more committed to the privacy of his mind.

"Take my word," he says and puts his other hand over Sara's.

As much as she's ever gotten—*take my word*. His word about what? About Sara, about his wife, about his old movies, about his work, he loved to talk. When it was just the two of them left in the apartment, Sara waited to eat dinner with her father, no matter how late he got home. She dined on her father's descriptions of the fluctuations of the market and the habits of every day-trader in the futures ring.

"It's learning to read their anxieties that puts a good meal on this table each night," her father joked. "And if there's one thing I've learned to do in life, it's read faces."

As a teenager all Sara had to do was get him started on OPEC and oil prices or the TV schedule for the Million Dollar Movies and she was guaranteed to skirt his protective fatherly inquisition about her weekend plans.

But whenever it came to anything about her father's life before his marriage, he was silent. She knew he was born in Belgium. That he came with his mother to America. Like so many immigrant Jews in the 1940s, they lived somewhere out in Brooklyn. Sara knew his mother didn't last long in America. But all Sara knew was that soon her grandmother died of the war, like the war was influenza or heart disease. There was never a single story about his childhood in Brussels, nothing about his street or school, no childhood moment with his mother or father, not what happened to his father, why he didn't come with them to America.

When she was assigned a fifth-grade paper on family history, her father refused to be interviewed. This was in the long year before her mother died. Her mother could still muster the strength to prepare dinner for the three of them each night, as if she wanted to nourish them until her last moment. That night there was leg of lamb, spinach, and potato gratin. There was wine, candlesticks—an overly elaborate affair for a school night. Sara wanted to hurry and finish her homework, but she could see how much her mother wanted them to linger over their meal.

"Take my word, it's not an interesting story," he said.

"But it's my assignment," Sara argued, knowing there was no point arguing with her father. "I know all about Mom's family. But I'm not allowed to just do one side of my family."

He lifted his glass of red wine. "Why don't they better spend the time teaching the history of this country? You're an American."

"But what do I do for this homework, Dad?"

Later that night she heard them in their bedroom. She'd never, or practically never, heard her parents fight. She started to go in to stop them, but when she got to their half-open door, instead she knelt on the beige carpet.

"She's directly asked you," her mother said. Sara hated hearing the effort in her mother's voice, the way the illness had taken away the soft easy rhythms of her speech.

"But she's just a child," her father said.

"I need to trust that you will talk to her." Her mother's voice was stern, unlikable. "How can I trust you'll ever answer her honestly?"

"Isn't this enough?" Sara heard him and knew he was crying. "Isn't what we're going through now enough for her to have to bear?"

"Over my dead body, promise me."

"Don't say that." Her father could barely speak. Sara felt furious; her mother was so tough tonight, so quick to speak about her death, so cruel to her father, who by now was weeping with painful gasps. The homework really didn't matter. It wasn't worth it. She'd make up a history for her father.

"Look at me. It will be my dead body," her mother said. "When she asks next, promise me that you'll tell her. I need to know that while I'm alive." Sara stood from the carpet, scuffed her feet against the rug to erase the mark her knees made in the plush pile. She hated her, her mother, the harshness, the *look at me I'm dying* insistence, as if dying gave her special rights.

If her mother was going to die, she wished her mother were already dead.

She made her own promise then, there in the dark hallway. Not to ask her dad. Ever. To let his silence rule. To take his side.

Now Sara slips her hand from her father's and pulls open the drapes. The bright day seems startling. Again she couldn't stay put, keep herself focused in the library beyond noon. It feels pitiful to be the unfocused translator of Benjamin, a man who despite frequent, serious bouts of ill health seemed capable of hours and hours of uninterrupted work. Even during his two months in the internment camp at an abandoned chateau where he slept on a bed of straw, Benjamin managed to read, write, and give lectures and philosophical training. He wrote letters worrying about his page proofs for the Baudelaire essay. He even started a scholarly journal with other writers interned at the camp.

"Dad," Sara says, "how about I walk you to the coffee shop for a late lunch?"

"I don't need your walking outside," her father says, adjusting his robe. "I've got to get back to my papers. I've got work."

SEPTEMBER 11

11:15 A.M.

Dear Mrs. Roosevelt,

"Eleanor Roosevelt is our best hope." Or, "Eleanor Roosevelt is our only hope."

You should know all anyone on board talks about is you. Leon Frankle spreads his scrawny, big-shot arms wide against the ship rail, saying, "My brother, Samuel, in Chicago, practically owns Eleanor's ear."

"Ouch, that must hurt," I mutter, bending farther over this typewriter.

Leon Frankle insists there's already been an important meeting, a meeting—capital I, capital M—with you and his relatives in Chicago. Do I believe this? Do I believe anything that comes big-shotting out of his mouth? I wish you could see the way he tries to look like he's something, his mousey hands rummaging in and out of his pocket like there's A MOST IMPORTANT MEETING going on right there in his lousy trouser pockets.

"My brother in Chicago," Frankle says, "has explained to Eleanor Roosevelt exactly what kind of important people are on this ship."

I'd like to think he's thinking of me. But I'm guessing he's talking about first-class passengers like Rand or Cartier or Dalio.

Wait, wait, wait a moment! How did I not tell you this yet? You won't believe this. Marcel Dalio, you know whom I mean, right, *the* Marcel Dalio, is here, here on the *Quanza*. You know him? The French film star. In *The Grand Illusion* he was the rich prisoner. And was in last year's film by Renoir, *Rules of the Game*. Stuck like the rest of us. A film star on my ship! That's what I mean about my being lucky! He's on board with his wife, Madeleine LeBeau. No more than nineteen to Dalio's forty years. She wanders the ship wearing a straw hat with ribbons. A face, what a face. And she's beautiful and blond. As my friend Henri would say, ooh la la. A real catch.

Then there's Theodore DeJong. He sits most of the day in a slat-wood cabin chair, a white linen scarf knotted about his neck. One leg crossed over the other. He barely moves. Maybe only to recross a leg. I swear, I don't even think he's gotten up to look at this port where they've docked us. Rumor is he's the guard and secretary to a Polish Prince, Prince Stanislaus Gielski, who's already safe in New York. Here's another rumor—that the Prince had tea with you, Mrs. Roosevelt. If that's true then let me ask you, is the Prince a tiny prince? Because I've got to tell you, I don't know how such a small fellow as DeJong could be anyone's bodyguard.

But you are the star, capital S, of this ship now. Someone's even put up a picture of you by the first-class dining room. It's cut out from the newspaper. "Mrs. Roosevelt Champions Children's Rescue from Britain"—that's what it says beneath your photograph. We haven't had newspapers on board since we left New York. I'm going to admit it was the first time I'd ever laid eyes on you, Mrs. Roosevelt. You're wearing a light-colored suit and cloche hat.

Truth is, I've got the committees to thank for even giving me the idea to write to you. It's not that I'd never heard of you, but I guess I'd just thought of you as the President of America's wife. Are you surprised—a boy who knows a cloche from a pillbox? Remember, when you know gloves, you're bound to know hats. What kind of boy knows gloves and hats? The kind whose father leaves Brussels with a trunk of gloves and turns around and goes back to Belgium for more gloves. I've noticed you're not wearing gloves in the photo. I just happen to have quite a few leather gloves here—kid, pig, calf. I have a fine pair of calfskin with raw silk cuffs. Can I make you a gift? I'm not pretending to be a big shot. I'm just a third-class passenger. It's a small factory workshop. Charlotte, Father, Didiot and his foreman, Phillipe, in Brussels and a smaller finishing shop out in Villevorde.

But you can trust me; I've got quality gloves. I'd go with the kidskin with a gusset of pigskin. Beautiful and they hold up well.

Yours truly,
Itzak

P.S. There's the Legal Committee, the Food Committee, the Relatives and Friends Committee, the Correspondence Committee, the Ship Committee, the Visa Committee and, as I've mentioned, the Eleanor Roosevelt Committee. There are new ones every day. But just so you're up-to-date, these are the current committees organized aboard on our ship.

SEPTEMBER 11
12:45 P.M.

Dear Mrs. Roosevelt,

Maybe you'll think it's crazy getting into the back seat of a Citroen with two people you don't know driving up front. But please remember, just the night before we were stranded without a car or a plan. It wasn't crazy; it was lucky.

It was Henri who announced that luck, capital L, had shown up. "Can you believe it, Izzy? They knocked on our door. Izzy, can you believe it? They've come from Charleroi. No money or petrol. But the car works, Iz." Henri managed to run and talk all the time while keeping a cigarette dangling from his lips. With my bad knees I could barely keep up.

But wait, I'm rushing down the street with Henri to get to the car that appeared out of nowhere and I haven't slowed down to introduce you to Henri. My apologies.

Henri Goldenman has been my best friend since our parents threw us on the floor and said, "Play, boys." Our parents, they're best friends, too. They say that together Henri and I make one decent boy. To look at us, we're Laurel and Hardy. But if I'm Stan by size then I've got to steal Ollie's line: "It's a fine mess you've got us in." Henri always finds the fun and the trouble and then gets me caught in it. He's got enough laughter in him for two of us. But running the ten streets between our apartments, it was Henri who repeated over and over in an astonished, serious voice, "Iz, Can you believe this luck, Izzy?"

We passed the rail station where small fires burned on the track. Other than that there was no sign of last night's bombs. The vendors were out. Women with baskets of lilac. Farmer's chickens poked from crates. Boys played on the rails, jabbed at the fires with sticks.

The Goldenmans' car was packed, suitcases and boxes strapped up top. Madame Goldenman layered blankets across the car seats. My father—I don't know how he was there before me—helped Monsieur wedge a soup pot under a box. "Maybe," my father said, "We better stay put. How do we know what's what? We'll be safer here." He pulled the rope's slack.

"Stay? Stay?" I shouted. "Here's what's what!" I pointed back at a thread of smoke from the rail station. It's not right, I know, Mrs. Roosevelt, shouting at my father. But last night I considered leaving on a bicycle. This morning, when there were fires and no trains leaving Brussels, luck had arrived and I wasn't going to ignore it. Suddenly it was like I was in my own adventure film. Just when the lead actor is cornered, about to be sent off to the Army. A knock on the door. Voilà, the getaway car. Out of nowhere it shows up. He'll be saved! He'll get out! Out of Brussels! Out of Belgium!

And here my father dawdles with rope, saying we should stay put!

"Where? Where are they, Max?" I pushed close to my father, calling him Max and not Papa. "Not only does a car appear, but a person who actually knows how to drive a car. There's no more staying put.

Haven't we been trying to plan a way out? You think I can go to the army? If you're going to be an idiot, Max, I'll make them the offer."

"Max, he's right. This is your chance," Monsieur Goldenman said quietly to my father. My father fiddled a little longer with the rope and then walked away without turning to look at me and went to meet the couple waiting inside the Goldenmans' apartment.

Our offer was simple. In return for riding in the back seat, we'd pay for petrol, lodging, and food. We'd go to Paris. The Goldenmans were going to Paris, too. Our cars would travel in tandem.

Henri said they came from Charleroi, but when I saw the man and woman I decided they must be from Liege. Not that it really mattered, Charleroi or Liege. They could have been from China! Henri said they worked in a factory, and I knew he was also wrong about that. She wore porcelain clips fixed in her black hair, and there was a metallic color to her eyes that made it hard for me to return her look. His face was tricky and unkind, his hands small and well kept, and he shook Max's hand in a way I thought was dicey. Their names, they said, were Gustav and Marie Bruchel. I didn't like either of them. I decided they were not to be trusted.

Marie and Gustav bent close to discuss the offer. They spoke in Walloon. This only strengthened my suspicions.

"We eat and sleep the same as you. No differences," Gustav said, turning back to French.

My father shook his hand. "Of course, of course, Monsieur Bruchel. And after Paris," he said, suddenly all hesitation gone. My father seemed happy, as though we'd just decided to go off on holiday. "Maybe we'll all stay together after Paris."

Then my father reached into his pocket and brought out beautiful blue Spanish leather gloves. He made a big to-do about giving

Marie a pair of his finest, most elegant gloves. But what was my father thinking? I could see these narrow gloves would never fit her large hands. Here was proof that my father, a man who could glance at your arms to declare your hand size, a man who could shake a customer's hand and register specific adjustments—a longer fourchette, a wider inseam for a misshapen knuckle—here was proof that my father was no longer thinking exactly right. I understood then that my family was actually leaving and that my father was not at all prepared.

Yours truly,
Itzak

P.S. Let me show off for a moment. When it comes to gloves, you're a size 8 1/2. If you don't have a pair handy and you want to check, first measure around the fullest part of your palm and then measure from the tip of your middle finger to the base of your hand. The larger of the two measurements will be your correct glove size. Got it? 8 1/2. See. What did I tell you?

P.P.S. I've decided that as soon as I step off the ship, I'm changing my name. I've learned Isaac's the American style. I'm all ready to be American. Why wait until I'm off the ship? No more Itzak. Call me Isaac.

Sara smiles at Diana, glad to see that the other single mother is still attending the pre-parent group. It's the third combined old and new parents sessions, so they don't go around again with their names, but that's okay since Sara has devised a name for everyone in the room. There's the We-Just-Want-the-Chance-to-Share-Our-Love couple, who won't quit holding hands, and Weeper, the woman who can't say "child" without starting to sob, and her mate, Twister, who Sara thinks might actually twist and bounce himself today right out of his chair. There's Repeater 1 and Repeater 2, couples back for their second babies, and the Freak Outs, who definitely freak Sara out with their spare-no-detail-horror-tales about failed inseminations and botched adoption efforts. Sara remembers that Diana works in finance and that she came from a big family from Massachusetts where they've all been planning to go en masse, a huge family trip, a pilgrimage with Diana when she goes to pick up her baby.

Georgette, the adoption counselor—whom Sara has double-named Little Miss Muffet on account of her poofy-sleeved dresses, and also Madame Long-and-Winding-Road, for her grim accounts of the adoption process—is going over the next documentation that the agency requests. The agency has more documentation than Sara can believe; she's constantly receiving urgent forms that look exactly like forms she's already filled out. By now she considers she might be adopting a whole orphanage. Maybe another agency, one that didn't specialize in adoptions from disaster zones, would be less bureaucratic, but Sara's come this far, too far to consider anything but going forward.

"Just as the child you'll adopt has a story, so do you have a story," Georgette says, and Sara considers renaming her Dr. I'm Earnest. "Your history, your family history is something you're going to share with your child. It's important that you understand your history, where you came from. Who were your great-great-grandparents? I'm always surprised that some of our clients can't even tell you what their grandparents did for work. It's as important as knowing the family medical history," she says with a busy-bee tone that makes Sara instantly rename her Dr. Buzz-Buzz.

"Why would my history necessarily become the child's?" Sara is horrified to realize that she's actually spoken out loud and that Buzz-Buzz is taking a breath, getting ready to give a long-and-winding-road answer. Sara figures she better finish out the thought.

"I mean I hardly think that my first job as a mom is to impose all my family's history on my kid. I'd like to give us a chance to create something." Sara hears that she sounds defensive, that she's not even saying what she exactly means or that she even entirely agrees with what she's saying. She has no idea what her grandparents did for work.

"What about the children's situations? Their stories?" Weeper asks, strangely dry-eyed. "How much will we be able to learn about their birth families? Will we actually know if the birth mother or the father is alive?"

"Well, in our situation," Repeater 2's wife says, "we actually plan on visiting the town where our daughter was born when we go back for our next child. But we've been told that most of the town is un-recognizable. It's been rebuilt since the war."

"This documentation is for you and for us at the agency." Now Buzz-Buzz is back in the official dress of Madame Long-and-Winding-Road. "It doesn't go to the host country. It's for us, here. And for you, of course. The point is your story will become part of your child's story. And your child's story becomes part of yours. But your relatives and their lives will become your child's family. So it matters to think about who you are, where you've come from. It isn't imposing. It's how you begin constructing family. But I've got to help us keep moving forward or else we'll wind up a discussion group instead of a group that has some real work to do before they become parents. Has everyone set up an appointment for the one-on-one and started processing the first round of official documentation that goes to the host country? These are extremely laborious papers and the slightest error can set you back six months or more."

Sara feels the collective shudder that goes through the room go through her too. Sometimes the others look more certain than Sara thinks she is. A six-month setback almost sounds like a benefit. Some days it's a gift, this path to a child. But today it feels a little foolish, even a little pathetic to take on parenting alone. She looks around to calibrate her anxiety against the others. She's not exactly feeling sorry for herself, but, aside from Diana, they've all got two people to shoulder the ambivalence.

When the group gets up, Sara makes her way over to Diana. Suddenly she feels shy. Why has she been thinking just because they're both here without a partner means they're going to click?

"I was really relieved by your question," Diana says with a smile.

"You were? Really?" Sara hears how incredulous she sounds. Like a school kid getting a right answer. "That's a relief. I feel a little like an alien in the room."

"Yeah, like I really want a family history of generations of addiction and rage to become my adopted child's legacy. It's like: welcome, you just got lucky—here's the family album from hell," Diana says.

Sara looks at the fullness of Diana's smile, the way it really looks like an easy smile despite what she's saying. This is the same family that's all going off together to help Diana bring home her child. Like a schoolgirl wanting to copy a new friend, Sara's tempted to chirp, "Me too, my big, crazy family!"

"I don't have enough family to even have a history," Sara says, struck by how bleak this sounds. "I guess no one will know if I just make things up."

<hr>

The spirit, wary of the future, looks into the distance. Sara writes it down, first in German and then in English. It's the third sentence of a letter Walter Benjamin wrote to Max Horkheimer, his dear friend. Horkheimer was already living in the United States. In the prior sentence Benjamin writes, *I often ask myself whether and under what conditions we will see each other in the foreseeable future.* In the rest of the letter he attempts to sketch out the three parts of a section of his book on Baudelaire. It is only at the end of the letter that Benjamin returns to a personal note. *I do not have to tell you under what circumstances I worked on this project the last two weeks. I was in a race against the war.* . . . *I have made every effort to keep any trace of these circumstances out of the work, even its external aspects, and have been in Copenhagen for ten days in order to see a flawless manuscript is produced.* . . . *I do not know what my plans are,* he writes in the final paragraph. *I would therefore be very grateful if you could give me the names of Danish, but also Swedish and Norwegian, friends—if you have any—to whom I could turn.* The letter is dated September 28, 1938—two years before Walter Benjamin crossed the border into Spain.

SEPTEMBER 11

3:15 P.M.

Hello, hello, Mrs. Roosevelt, it's me, Isaac.

Have you thought about those gloves?

I'm not joking that I've come to trust gloves and hats. Take Toulouse. At the Portuguese Consulate it was a hat, finally, that did the trick.

Maman and I waited in the Portuguese Consulate for two long afternoons. The waiting room was large with open, unshuttered windows and three clacking ceiling fans, but it was unbearably warm and with all of us crowded on the sticky benches or standing in silent clusters, it seemed there was not sufficient air. We waited for two full afternoons before our names were called. Maman and I were shown into the Consul's office.

"Monsieur," Maman began, edging closer to his heavy wood desk. The man—he was the very caricature of the bureaucrat, the porcine, petit bourgeois—hardly raised his snout to look at her.

"Madame, let me make this quick. There are no visas—transit or otherwise—at my disposal." His fat lips chewed his words like they were spring truffles. There was a wet sheen above his lip and on the bulb of his nose.

"Mais Monsieur," she said, pushing closer. Her hand moved to touch the brass paperweight as if holding that heavy object would help balance her. "We were told that you could," Maman said.

The snout raised a little, but only a little, to interrupt. "Well, I am telling you this now, Madame. There has been no shortage of people who were told no shortage of incorrect information. I have no visas to give them nor you."

"But, Monsieur, we were told," Maman repeated. Her fingers brushed across loose papers and folders, as if she were ready to straighten up the Consul's desk. Something had to be done. In the game of visas you must understand that securing Portugal might help claim a transit visa for Spain. France to Spain to Portugal or Morocco or Mexico or Shanghai. The strategy was to create options. I stepped in, took Maman's hand, but she yanked away from me like I was a restless child distracting her from urgent business. I made a bit of a scene. Nothing extreme, not too loud or physical, though I would have done anything to get us quickly out of his office. I trusted Maman's easy embarrassment to work in my favor.

"Izzy, have you lost your mind?" she managed to ask me once we were back in the waiting room. "Two days we waited to get into his office. Have you lost your mind?"

Indeed if you'd seen me out in the center of the waiting room, you might have agreed with Maman. I was smiling, a little Fred Astaire satisfied smile, head up, puffed chest, shoulders pressed back as I let go of Maman's hand and with a turn and a kick strutted my way over to the Consul's secretary.

Let me say with some discretion that, due to long hours of waiting, I'd had an opportunity to notice the evident talents that recommended this woman for the position of the Portuguese Consul's secretary. Her clothes seemed to be all darts and buttons fastened mostly to show what they could not entirely contain. If the Consul was a caricature of one kind, then the secretary, seated at her desk adjusting the seams of her stockings, was her own quite remarkable kind. As the expression goes—a pair straight out of central casting.

I bent close, my elbows leaning on her metal desk. "Mademoiselle, is it always this warm in Toulouse? It seems hardly bearable to wear any cloth against the flesh. Or might there be a time, perhaps an early spring night when a woman might be comfortably in need of a fur?" Behind me I could feel Maman bristling, restless with fury.

"Hot or cold, doesn't a woman always need a fur?" the secretary answered, making me almost think she'd been given this script in advance. From there we chatted about furs. I don't know a thing about furs. But I do know my leather, and that appeared to work fine. I asked questions. She fancied fox and mink. Thought rabbit and seal respectively cute and drab. Loved the elegant look of a fox paw. Her name, I learned, was Veronique.

I said, "May I call you Veronica Lake?"

She pulled her blond hair over one eye, tilted her head, and said, "How's that?"

"Veronica," I asked, "is the Consul an agreeable man?"

She laughed and her hair shook back into place. "I'd say that, like most men, given the right circumstance, he's most agreeable."

I pulled back and let my head tilt, hopefully a bit rakishly.

"I bet, Veronica"—and here I had no choice but to take the full risk—"that you are a person who can provide the nearly perfect circumstances that make Monsieur the Consul most agreeable."

Maman drew a sharp, astonished breath. The room behind me became even more intensely quiet, not a movement from those waiting on benches.

Veronique gave a bold laugh. "I'm not sure about nearly perfect, sweetheart. I'd say when I provide a circumstance it's entirely perfect." She was indeed all fast-tongued Veronica Lake.

"Of course, I apologize," I said, fearless now, my tone soft and conspiratorial. "My mother and I, we'd love to give you a wonderful gift. A stole, perhaps a fox stole. A gift of appreciation for making possible an agreeable circumstance where Monsieur the Consul would sign a transit visa for us."

Veronique stood. She kept me riveted in her gaze. In that moment it was clear that I'd miscalculated. A slap, a hurl of insults, perhaps even shrieks to call in the gendarmes might close this movie scene.

"And also a fox hat." I rushed because there wasn't a clear way of backing out. I needed to keep speaking. "I believe something with a little height and tilt would be a good match to the stole and most agreeable for your face. And of course a good pair of kid gloves. Perhaps, Mademoiselle, you'd prefer to make your own selection of pelts. We could provide for that as well."

She leaned close, and I waited for what she might hiss at me. Instead she placed a kiss, a light, delicate kiss on my jaw.

"You and your mother are most kind. I do think choosing for myself will be best, though I appreciate your notice of my face," she said, her mouth lingering against my cheek. She straightened, patted down her blouse, and in an official and measured voice said, "The Monsieur says your papers will be completed and stamped by six. Do come back then. Perhaps we will both be able to surprise one another with our skills."

And that, Mrs. Roosevelt, is what I mean about the power of gloves and hats.

So this is how by that evening we were in possession of Portuguese transit visas. But I'm rushing ahead. I shouldn't be telling you about Toulouse, forget about Spain, when we're not even out of Brussels! Getting everything out of order; it's no way to tell a story, is it?

And please, I'm not comparing you to a secretary in Toulouse, Mrs. Roosevelt. I'm just talking gloves, if you know what I mean.

Your most loyal,
Isaac Astaire

P.S. Do you actually think that Isaac is a good name? I mean, why only go to Isaac? I could be Thomas or Charles or John or Steven or Frank or Fred. I could be Richard. I could be whatever name you think is the best American name for an American man.

NOW NEITHER TALKS about it.

When she first told Marco about the adoption, he refused to believe her. Then he told her she was ridiculous, indulgent, an American in the stupidest fashion. He'd said, "Nothing more ridiculous than a guilty American." At the worst of the fight he'd yelled that she was a hobbyist, a dilettante, a colonizer, a Mother Without Borders.

"How can you do this to us?" he'd asked, his lips moving across her cheek. It was hours later, the two of them having fought and made love and then, exhausted and with no resolve, done both again.

"Do what to us?" she'd said, pulling away from his lips. "What's the us? You're the one with the wife; remember her? The good wife with your three children waiting back there in your perfecto Motherland. What am I doing? You tell me."

⌗

But it's all Helen wants to talk about with Sara.

"You know, some people try to do it in this weird order: love, marriage, child. Even crazily enough, a child with the same man that you sleep with."

They're in Banana Republic. Helen pushes hangers on a sales rack, holds up a red shirt, and Sara sees Helen's head tilt and her body go into a pose, stomach pulled in, as she looks in the full-length mirror.

"Remind me, is this abuse why you're my best friend? Helen, not everyone finds a great husband like yours." Sara can't help but notice the exhaustion in her friend's face, the way Helen has started wearing matte lipstick and too much under-eye concealer. Sara wants to take her finger and smooth the chalkiness, but she can feel the bristle in Helen today, the urgent way her friend keeps pulling out clothes, frantic for something to want to buy.

"For starters, most people try to find someone who's not already a husband, Sara. Is it so impossible for you to ever find a lover who isn't already married to someone else?" It's classic tough-love Helen talk. She doesn't bother to wait for Sara to answer but delivers a steady set of blows. "Tell me what the difference is between any of them? Marco, Omar, even that what's-his-face had a woman he lived with. Have you just decided it's easier to find a kid who's available than a man who is?" It's not that every blow doesn't ram right into Sara. It's not that she likes putting up with Helen's judgment and displays of self-righteousness. But it's part of what she's loved about Helen since they were grade school girls together; the more Helen loves someone, the less she can suffer any foolish action or thought. Even if it's hard to take, Sara loves knowing that she never has to guess what Helen feels.

"I don't know what's easy, Helen. Is easy even what we're after?"

"Easy's good, honey. I'm really not trying to rough you up," Helen says. "It's just painful seeing you choose something incomplete over and over and over."

Helen holds up a ruffled flower shirt. "Is this good or too much?" Before Sara can decide if she has the heart to say it's clownish, Helen's jammed it back on the rack.

Sara stands behind her father. He hasn't turned around to smile at her coming into the room. Or even to acknowledge her right behind him. She doesn't expect him to; he's set a problem for himself on the chessboard. He's so still she could almost think he's fallen asleep over his game. But she knows he's not asleep; he's watching the board, moving pieces across his mind. He does this for hours. "It relaxes me," he says, but Sara never thinks he looks relaxed. More like he's keeping vigil. "Do something," she'd say to her father when she was a child and they were playing chess together. She'd toss in her chair, kicking her legs over the arm. "Come on, this is boring. Do anything." She'd go make a tray of snacks for them and still her father would sit. "Hello," Sara would say, pressing a sliced apple to his lips. "Are you alive?" Her father would glance up with a victorious smile. "Notice how it unsettles your opponent when you slow way down, Sara."

Her father's hand moves out, hovers over his queen, then withdraws.

Sara doesn't recognize this board he's playing on today. It's a small, wooden, folding box; the chess pieces are painted metal. It looks old, used, but hardly ornate. The painted chess pieces are chipped; at best there's just a sheen of color on them.

"Where's that from?" Sara asks, though there's little chance he'll answer when he's working a problem.

Surprisingly, her father tilts his head to look back at Sara. "I don't know, it surfaced."

"What do you mean surfaced? From where?" She knows everything in this apartment, every cup and ashtray, practically every wooden hanger and fork. If her mother hadn't bought it thirty years ago, Sara had. Her father buys nothing. He hasn't wanted to change one thing in the apartment since his wife died. He even put up a fight when Sara insisted they recover the threadbare living-room sofa.

"How would I know?" Her father looks at her as if she's asked him what's going on in Timbuktu. He faces the board and then his hand moves decisively to position the queen.

—⁂—

At first it was almost a relief. No, it *was* a relief, to clean the house of all the machinery of late-stage cancer. The morphine drip, the needles, the hospital bed dismantled and picked up by brisk servicemen. The room turned back into a proper living room, furniture rearranged into familiar, comfy positions.

Sara took to making the house a house again. Their house. Hers and her father's. Like a fervid housewife, coming home directly from school—no time for middle school band, no after-school sports—she was too busy running a household. Each morning she left a shopping list for Carmen, the woman her father had hired to keep the place clean and help look after his daughter. But Sara didn't want looking after; she didn't have time for it. She began cooking, pulling out cookbooks, careful to avoid recipes her mother had marked, her father coming home to beef Wellington, chicken Marseille, Sara sending Carmen to specialty stores for pancetta and chunks of Parmesan cheese.

"I'm getting spoiled; every night is like a state dinner," her dad said, watching Sara spoon a dollop of whipped cream on his butterscotch pudding. "Mom would have been proud. A little amazed to see her little tornado become a regular hausfrau, but she'd have been proud, Sara."

She wished he hadn't said it, the part about her mom. And at first mostly they didn't speak of her, either talking of school or her father's work or maintaining a silence both of them respected, as if silence protected them from sadness, as if they thought they were each protecting the other.

It didn't stop with food. Sara became her father's film companion. Garbo and Dietrich, Barbara Stanwyck, and, of course, the little missus, Shirley Temple, for them to watch on Sunday mornings. Don't get Sara started on Katharine Hepburn in *Alice Adams*. She can recite along with Olivia de Havilland as Maid Marian in *The Adventures of Robin Hood*. She jokes that she's practically a gay man the way she can rant on about Bette Davis and Joan Blondell in *Three on a Match* or argue the merits of Hedy Lamarr and Charles Boyer in *Algiers* versus the French original, *Pépé le Moko*. At fourteen Sara got teary right along with her father when Jean Gabin looks at a Metro ticket, reciting the stations of his longed-for Paris.

"I knew that guy, Dalio," her father said once when there was a tight shot on the informer.

But the next time when they watched *Pépé le Moko* and Sara said, "That guy, how'd you know him? What's his name again?" Her father said, "Oh, he was a just another good French actor."

"When's the last time you were there? In France?" Sara asked her father when the movie ended. "Describe Paris. Did you love it?" Her father kept his eyes fixed on the television. "I can't remember," he said. "I was there once on the way to somewhere else."

My Dear Mrs. Roosevelt,

It took six days. Six days stuck in the backseat of the Citroen; six days on clogged roads, each day the road more completely clogged with more people walking, more cars, more bicycles, more donkeys, more carts and wheelbarrows than I'd ever imagined. Six days to go from Brussels to the French border when, you must understand, the entire distance between Brussels and Paris is perhaps 240 kilometers, and maybe the border is less than 100 kilometers. It seemed astonishing that there were all these people out on the roads. The priest walking with his suitcase, the children dressed in winter coats perched like crowns in donkey baskets, the man and woman like Sunday lovers sleeping under the shade of the new leaves of a chestnut tree and old men wobbling on bicycles while steering handcarts. Yes, I'd wanted to leave Brussels. Yes, I'd yelled at my father. The attack was handy. I saw it as urgent—an urgent opportunity. But, truthfully, had I believed the situation demanded immediate flight?

"I need to stretch my knees," I said when I couldn't take another minute crammed in back, the five of us strapped to whatever news we could pick up on the radio when we could pick up anything more than static. Most of the time I could actually move faster walking once I'd quit the car.

"Go find where the Goldenmans have run off," my father said, pointing up the grassy slope. He was desperate that the two cars never lose sight of each other.

The French soldiers kept coming, moving north against our tide. The radio proclaimed that the French were joining 600,000 Belgian soldiers. The Germans would be stopped from entering our cities. "Keep them back! Scare them home!" we shouted the first days, as the French Army trucks headed north. When they came, everything was forced over to the embankments, our endless crawl brought to a full stop. Soon only a few children waved, though even they seemed more dutiful than cheerful.

From the hill I looked down on Gustav and Marie's car, my mother's linens trunk tied on top of two valises. All our belongings lashed together looked flimsy, ready to topple. When I'd found Maman on the last morning in Brussels emptying the linen wardrobe, I said, "Enough. We don't need every last pillowcase." She cut me off with a sharp, "Itzak, enough from you! There are things I know." Now, for the first time, on these unbearable roads I wondered what she knew. What did Maman and Max expect in Paris? For the first time I considered that they had plans of their own that I was not privy to.

"Izzy! Izzy, here!" I heard Henri, my fool of a copain, shouting and I spun around to find him. But it was impossible to spot Henri in the congestion of people. "Hey, hey, hey, over here, Monsieur Izzy, don't you see me? Look!" I saw him at the hill's crest doing a little cabaret shuffle, dancing in circles with his sister Jeanette looped in his arms. Henri was having his usual fun. I'd fumed and squinted and frowned through our childhood with Henri clowning beside me.

Henri rushed down the crowded hill to me. Jeanette seemed to fly behind him like his cape.

"How slow can you go?" he said, throwing an arm around my shoulder. "Are you on holiday? Does that Gustav actually know how to drive?"

I wanted to joke, but it came out in a snarl. "Oh, we've been off at a bistro having cassoulet. Now I'm strolling before my nap."

"Well, my good friend, voila, share this smoke." Henri pushed his cigarette to my lips, and before I could decide if I wanted to storm off, if I wanted to turn and lose myself in the press of others trudging to the border it seemed we'd never approach or just slam the car door and sulk in the backseat, I took Henri's cigarette between my lips.

Henri put his arm around my shoulder, knocked his head against the side of my head. "Don't worry, Izzy, soon we'll be in Paris."

An army truck rolled past, the flaps pulled up and the men inside sleeping or staring off almost asleep.

"They're going to get destroyed," I sneered. A second truck passed and we could hear a few voices singing one of the popular songs about the lazy dumb Germans who could never touch our Albert Canal and Maginot Line. We stood watching the troops on foot, the proud slant of rifles and their hobnail boots ringing against the road. We were all the boys we'd ever been together, Henri and I, playing our stupid war games. We'd played all the sides of our last war, fighting along the back alley between the row houses, hiding out in father's glove shop under the drape of fabric, planning missions. We'd been an army of two bragging about our heroics in the Belgian Army. There'd even been evenings just this winter when, walking home after flirting with girls in the café, Henri would clip me on the shoulder, whispering, "Quick to the left! A bon homme!" and in an instant we were hardly sophisticated young men but practically back in our short pants, hiding in a doorway listening for enemy boots against the cobblestones.

"Destroyed," I said again.

"Well, then, it's just you and me in Paris." Henri leaned against me. "So many grieving women to console. Our task will be noble. And tell me, what's she like?" Henri pressed in closer. His free hand curved a female form in the air. "What has Marie said to you? She has some, shall we say, abundance."

"I hear that, Henri." Jeanette poked her head between us. "You are disgusting."

"I don't trust either of them," I said. I didn't want to say anything about her, the way that despite not trusting her I'd sat in the backseat looking at the line of her long neck. At the base of her neck and head there was a tear-shaped groove, like the indent a finger might make in clay. I wanted to reach forward and touch her. I was sure my finger fit there perfectly. "No, I don't trust her at all."

"Why? What happened?" Henri gave Jeanette a shove from where she'd wedged herself between us.

"Ah, Henri! I see your terrible cruelty!" a voice called through the crowds. Monsieur Goldenman sidestepped his way down the slope. He balanced a plate piled with slices of cake. I was glad for his interruption. I didn't want to have more of Henri's questions.

"Madame says there are two for you, Izzy," said Monsieur Goldenman. My appetite was their family joke. Skinny Itzak's enormous appetite. Many nights Monsieur Goldenman stood looking at the positions in Henri's and my chess game. He made little sounds, his tongue pressed against his cheek. He'd hold back, but eventually I'd hear a long release of breath and then, "Henri, Henri, will I ever come home to find that this scoundrel friend of yours hasn't cleaned out my pantry and mercilessly trounced my own flesh and blood in the same afternoon!"

Monsieur Goldenman held out the plate. I was hungry but determined not to seem too eager for the cake. But I was more determined to keep off any conversation about Marie Bruchel. I hadn't lied. I didn't trust her. I didn't think I liked her. And I certainly didn't like that I wanted to lay my finger against the skin at the base of her neck.

I took a piece and ate it in a few quick bites. Madame Goldenman's cake was always delicious.

"Come, Itzak, have your second piece. First we find you a car; now we feed you cake. What would you do without the Goldenmans? Of every street in Brussels for these two to show up on, they end up on my street in front of my door. Such luck, we should stay this lucky. Where are your parents? We should stay together. We're pulled over just up ahead."

I hated the triumph in his voice. I didn't want to be indebted to the Goldenmans. Not for luck or cake. If it sounds ungrateful, well, I was. The convoy of soldiers had ended. People were trying to push a broken-down car out of their way. I could see Gustav and Marie's car advancing slowly. How was this lucky? I didn't want to be stuck in the back of a car that could barely move out of first gear. I started off down the hill and when I was a good distance away I turned. Henri and his father hadn't moved. Mr. Goldenman, like a waiter, stood holding out the plate with my second piece on it.

Yours truly, your new American,
Sam Lejdel

SARA SPENDS THE day moving her hands over maps of Europe, tracing Walter Benjamin's movements in the last months of his life. She imagines him in Paris, after the Netherlands and Belgium have been attacked, trying to close down his apartment, dispersing his papers to friends who might safely hold them, walking for the last time under the shop arcades in the city he loved. His beloved city is swarmed with refugees. He knows that as soon as he leaves, which he must, he'll become a refugee. Isn't he already? Her finger follows the route of a train to Lourdes. Sara sees Benjamin step off the train, barely managing his two bulky suitcases. She locates all the small towns of southern France where Benjamin is known to have been in those few months. Later, after he leaves Marseilles, he has only one suitcase to carry on the trail up from Banyuls-sur-Mer. Where did he pare his life down even further? Stash that last suitcase with friends? Sara turns to a physical map of southern France. The distance between Banyuls and Port Bou on the Spanish side is nothing, less than a pinky nail between them. She tries to imagine the colors three-dimensionally, where the map shows steep green and dark blue contours, dark shadings, the rugged vertical rise of difficult mountain crossings.

There have always been rumors about Benjamin's death. Sara thinks it a waste of time but, anyway, she's kept up with the discussion, even the latest article that claims it was Stalin's agents, not a morphine suicide. An alleged missing manuscript in a suitcase that Benjamin, exhausted during the long escape through the Pyrenees, never let anyone carry for him, is proof of foul play. Where did it go? What was the nature of the manuscript? A radical critique of Communism? Did Henny Gurland, the last person with him, take the manuscript? Did she alter his suicide note? Why? Sara can't take it very seriously, the controversy, the doubters amassing evidence for doubting. She sees the frail Benjamin in a small pensione in Port Bou, dispirited, penniless, and ill. He's made it through the rugged mountains, barely kept up with the group. Indeed, he'd fallen behind, spent a night freezing and alone. Now in Port Bou he's been told there's been a change in policy. Suddenly Spain will not honor his Spanish transit visa without a proper French exit visa. Come morning, they'll send him back to France. Why is it so hard for admirers of Benjamin to imagine that he just can't conjure the internal resources to keep responding to increasingly complicated circumstances, that he can't manage another internment, that he can't feel hope for the luck that this edict will shift again, as it does, by morning. Sara knows it's not a matter of intelligence and passion depleted. His heart is literally exhausted; it seems too hard to figure out everyday how to stay alive. There are no more changes of address possible.

At the end of the day Sara takes the marble staircase instead of the library's small front elevator. Sara looks at each framed print on the wall. View of New York from the East River. Settlers trading with Natives. Maps of Manhattan in 1716. Maps of the New York Harbor. She stops and looks at the small map of the stairwell itself. Each floor is designated. Third floor: children's room. Fifth floor:

staff only. Sixth floor: typing rooms. She looks at the orange dot with its *you are here* arrow marker. There's enough comfort in the certainty of the statement that Sara stops on the next landing and the next to look again at the next orange dot.

∽

"He's fine. It's you, Sara. You have to accept he's getting older," Carmen says, holding open a garbage bag while Sara tosses in magazines. Sara's stayed at her father's trying to help Carmen work, to make some order with the avalanche of her father's papers. There's no order to any of it, current bank statements buried under tax records from 1995. He's kept everything—sometimes a rubber band bundling a year of receipts and checks and statements. Lists of names. Monthly statements from brokerage firms. Magazines and newspapers stacked like a barricade against one wall. More often it's just heaps. He's napping and the two of them are working on the sly. "He doesn't want to go nowhere. Even he doesn't want to leave his room too much. He just wants to move around papers. And then nap."

Carmen says they can count on a good hour and a half. Sara sees it won't make a dent. Sara's been arguing that they should just toss the entire room. But almost as proof that there might be hidden fortunes, Carmen opens an envelope and finds old photographs.

"That's your father when a boy," Carmen says. It's a picture of a young man, on a beach dune. He's wearing short pants and knitted kneesocks.

Sara goes through the pictures. Except for her father's, she doesn't recognize any of the faces. Her father, maybe fifteen or sixteen, leans, in one photo, against another boy, both of them in fedoras smoking cigarettes. Three pale women in square swimsuits stretch out on a picnic blanket. There is another photograph of her father crowded in among boys and girls at café tables. In one a pretty woman strikes a pose, blowing a kiss.

"This is your grandmother and grandfather?" Carmen says, handing Sara a photograph with scalloped edges. Her father has his arms around a squat man and woman who stand almost a head shorter than him.

Sara looks at the grave, unfamiliar faces. "I don't really know."

"I'm certain," says Carmen, tying up a plastic garbage bag filled with old copies of *Business Week*. "You've got the eyes same as your grandmother."

Her grandmother, this woman? No, Sara had been told there were no photographs. "We left in a rush," he'd answered dismissively, the time Sara had dared to ask. "Photographs are not necessarily the first thing you think to take."

"Well, what about you and Grandma here, in Brooklyn, before she died?" she'd ask. But her father looked at her as if taking a photograph was a luxury and Sara felt spoiled for asking.

Now Sara moves through the pictures quickly, as if they're a flipbook that will reveal even a momentary narrative. Her father's never done anything with these photographs, never showed them or organized them in a small album, as her mother had done so carefully with the few existing pictures of her childhood with Sara's maternal grandparents. Sara would almost rather not look, as if she's bound to get caught. She slips the photographs into her bag.

"Carmen, when did you come here exactly? From your country to the U.S.?"

"It's a long, long time now," Carmen says, and Sara hears the shift in Carmen's voice, a little clipped, defensive, and final. Carmen bends over a large black garbage bag. "I think this is enough for today. We better not clean too much or it will upset your father."

SEPTEMBER 11

6:30 P.M.

Dear Mrs. Roosevelt,

For no good reason other than the blue of this late afternoon sky in this shipyard, I'm now caught up thinking about our delicious August holidays at Coq Sur Mer. There are many other pressing matters; I should be telling you about what they're saying this evening on the ship. But look, maybe they're right about me being a dreamer—this end-of-summer blue sky has me practically tasting my Odile's lips.

It might help you to look at a map and locate Coq Sur Mer, our family's holiday spot right on the North Sea. Each summer a gang of us, boys and girls, ride bicycles and have picnics, and all summer we wonderfully fall into trouble and love. Even this shore, with its broad loading docks and tankers, has me remembering the wooden rowboats we piled into. Eight of us jostling the boat, the gunnels tilted until we almost capsized. Then six of us teamed up and we pushed Henri and Jacques off the side. The rest of us boys followed, leaping from the boat, shouting great declarations of irreverence and loyalty to our ship, which we had named the *Terror*. Our dives became more elaborately acrobatic and competitive. The girls clapped and cheered us on. The fat old proprietor was back on shore, shouting for us to quit the funny business! Stop this minute! He was not responsible for our injuries! He hobbled about, and from the distance he looked in his bright green shirt and pants like a balloon being blown about on the shore. The girls blew him kisses and waved. One girl, you can easily guess that it was the always daring Sylvie, did a cartwheel dive into the lake with her dress still on.

When we rowed back, the girls crowded close to the proprietor, saying next time they promised to do better controlling us ruffians. Sylvie in her wet jumper stood close to the old man and put her wet arm against his green shirt. And though he was trying to stay gruff in his warnings, he was most obviously charmed. The others went on to the café while Odile and I stayed back on the grass. We watched the proprietor lock his boats for the night. The old man kept stopping to look at us. He seemed pleased to have us see him pull the long chain through each boat's loop. He shook the chain and it clattered against the wooden hulls. Then he fastened the metal lock and left. We kissed and kissed long enough for my lips to have a pleasant puffy feeling from long kisses. I love to kiss (doesn't everyone, Mrs. Roosevelt?) and loved best to kiss Odile. I watched the way her eyelids parted slightly and I could see a white rim inside her eyes. I felt that evening she was particularly abandoned to our kisses, a kind of freedom that held a promise of more nights. She pulled at a lock of her hair that had gotten caught in our mouths and I saw that instead of brushing it away she took more of her hair up in her fingers, lightly twirling or tangling them through her brown hair. It made me jealous.

"Shouldn't you touch my hair instead of your own?" I whispered. Odile pushed out of my embrace. She looked at me as if I were a stranger who had startled her from sleep. "I'm joking, Odile; it's a joke," I said, trying to fold my arms around her.

Odile's eyes filled with tears. "A stupid joke. I want to go to the café," she said.

Not only because I'd never seen eyes fill that way—with not a single tear breaking over the lower lid and onto her cheek—and not because her blue eyes seemed bigger wavering under the watery surface but because I was stunned that anything I did mattered enough to make a beautiful girl cry, I said, "I love you."

"That's stupid," she said and let me kiss her again, which I did and then did again just before the café where our friends had joined up with others and were trading songs—funny songs, school songs, and even a few rough ditties. But they were different kisses. When I opened my eyes, her eyes were open wide.

Odile was quiet at the café. I decided that despite her suggestion to join up with our friends, she'd actually wanted to be alone with me. I leaned close, asking if she wanted to leave. She snapped, "Why would you think that?" Soon she joined in with a boy who was singing an endlessly long ballad about a prince who couldn't find his castle. Though I knew Odile had never met this boy, their voices sounded practiced together. Odile, like me, was from Brussels. The boy was from Antwerp. He was tall and handsome in the rough way I'd learned that some girls liked. Her eyes were closed as she and the boy sang the chorus. Her face tipped up as she sang. It was astonishingly beautiful, white, the palest white though the rest of us were burnt or even peeling from days of picnics and swimming in the sea. I stood up to leave. If Odile felt me stand up, she showed no sign or concern that I was offended.

I wasn't sure what to do with myself. I couldn't just sit back down, so I went to the bar and ordered a coffee, though I don't even like coffee. I stood against the bar with a cigarette while I drank it down. I could see out to the jetties where young boys fished and other boys pitched rocks into the water. It seemed the night might never go entirely dark but the blue just deepened and deepened. I was trying to will Odile to look over at me. If she looked over— even if she pretended to look past me—it meant I was forgiven. Or at least might have a chance with her again. Then I'd take her down to the shore and we'd walk out as far as we could on the long stone jetty. We'd poke at barnacles or the shell fixed to the rock. I wouldn't even try to kiss her. I'd let her kiss me—which she'd boldly done before.

"This song should be reason enough to abolish all princes and all monarchies. Maybe music should also be outlawed. Can't you do something?" asked Sylvie, who had come up to the bar with one of the six boyfriends who'd followed her like a litter of puppies all week.

"At least maybe you can get your girlfriend to skip every other lousy verse," said the boy, clearly for Sylvie's benefit.

I laughed loudly, happy to have a reason to look occupied. But Odile wasn't looking at me. When the song ended the boy from Antwerp rushed over, lifting Odile in his arms and giving her a kiss to both cheeks and then one to the top of her head. Everyone cheered and clapped. Odile blushed, which was a brilliant contrast to her pale skin. The boy put her down and pressed his hands to her cheeks. It was then only that she looked over at me. She wants me to come over, I thought. Instead I leaned close to Sylvie and her boyfriend and in too loud a voice said, "Well, we survived that one."

In a few days all of us had gone home. Oddly, the inseparable gang of summer now greeted one another on the crowded streets of Brussels with only quick and often indifferent nods.

I wish I'd gone over and told Odile how beautiful her voice sounded. I wish I'd even shaken the hand of the boy from Antwerp. In January when I had my second chance with Odile, neither of us mentioned the way our summer came to a bad end. I wish I'd had the courage to say I was sorry, then, instead of only worrying about my chances at kissing her. Though I'd be a liar not to say her face was deliciously cold against my ungloved hand.

Well, Mrs. Roosevelt, thanks. I know I've got other, more pressing stories to tell. And I will, a little later, when I don't feel quite so lonely. Sometimes I think we need to tell our stories more than anyone needs to hear our stories. Maybe just so that anticipation or happiness can be reached for again. But other times it is almost as if the story itself wants repeating. So that the strand of hair caught in a kiss or the turn of a beautiful face isn't lost forever. So that, especially when it comes to beauty, we're not alone and left with the burden of remembering.

Again, thanks for listening.

Always yours,
Jack Lejdel

"I HAVE SOMETHING for you," her father says, handing Sara a red embroidered silk pouch.

"It's not my birthday," Sara says. Every year on Sara's birthday her father gives her a velvet box or a Chinese silk pouch like this with a piece of her mother's jewelry inside. In this way, with a strand of freshwater pearls, topaz earrings, amber beads with an agate clasp—never too fancy—her mother, dead now more than thirty years, has shaped Sara's taste.

"You think I don't know when your birthday is?" Sara's father shakes his head teasingly. "I gave these to Simone. When you were born."

Sometimes the way her father says *Simone*, her mother sounds more like one of his movie stars than his wife. Sometimes the way he speaks of her, perhaps standing in front of a florist shop, pointing at the bunches of lilacs, and saying, "Simone loves these. She longs all year for the month they're in bloom," his wife sounds like someone still waiting for him at home.

"I've been waiting for a grandchild. This adoption business isn't exactly the way I expected it. I can't say I understand what you're doing. But if you're certain, Sara, if you're really ready for this, then you know I'm right here."

She unknots the small purse and reaches her fingers in. Turning the bag over, Sara shakes out small gold hoops with faceted oval sapphires that dangle and slip along the rounded gold.

"Simone told me I was to give these to you when you were having a baby." This idea that her father is still carrying out her mother's wishes, that they still have secrets and surprises for Sara, astonishes her. "Your mother said that as an infant you used to love to reach for them; you were excited when Simone shook her head at the way the stones caught the light, but they were small enough that you could tug but you couldn't pull them off her ears."

Her father latches the old vinyl suitcase where he keeps Simone's jewelry in a small locked box. Sara knows the suitcase intimately, could still reel out an inventory of its contents from the countless times as a child she sneaked into her parent's room and pulled it out from under his side of the bed, where it waited like the hospital overnight bag for an expectant mother. Each time she'd loved the mystery just as the latches sprung, as if this day lifting the hard top there might be something missing or something new. But each time the contents were the same: a pressed tin box that Sara knows holds velvet and silk pouches with her mother's jewelry, a leather sleeve with current passports, three envelopes of money, two index cards with a typed list of official-sounding business names and numbers, her mother's thin photo album, and a bundle of letters and cards her father and mother sent each other for birthdays and anniversaries, tied with a green ribbon. There's a map of the New York ports and folded road maps of the Northeast. Each time Sara pulled the money out from the envelopes, counting the same thousand dollars per billfold. Sara has read the letters and endearments between her parents so many times, she can, years later, almost recite them like a poem memorized for school.

"Oh, those are truly beautiful," her father says, seeing Sara's tried on the gold hoops. Sara reaches into the velvet pouch again. In each pouch her mother left Sara a handwritten note, little missives sent through time to celebrate birthdays, graduations, and now this acknowledgment to a daughter almost as old as she'd been at the end of her life. Some notes have been instructive, funny, irreverent. Some have just aimed at the hope of joy in Sara's life. Others were like little riddles Sara had to solve. They've all brilliantly avoided the maudlin, though her mother's words are so direct and tender. More than once Sara tried to find the key to the locked box so that she could read through all the notes at once, memorize them, and then control the impact when she reads a new note and the quirky specificity of her mother's personality hits Sara like a full body blast. Every bit of the message, Sara knows her mother has considered, the yellow slip of paper instead of a boy blue or girlie pink, and the direct opening lines of the note: *my darling child, first of all—not necessary to be a hero. It's just fine to get drugs in the labor room. Whatever they tell you a pacifier's not a crime and if you breastfeed, after two weeks introduce one bottle and keep it up. By the time you'll want an afternoon or evening's freedom, you'll be delighted that you can walk out the door.* Sara reaches up to fool with the sapphire dangle. She glad there's only her father to tell about the adoption. *As for everything else—not to worry. Don't be scared of making mistakes, Tootsie-pie. You'll be a great mom. Trust me on this one. I promise you.*

Tootsie-pie, there was the shrapnel this time. Not the *my darling child,* or even the assumption that, of course, Sara would give birth to a baby. Sara had forgotten it, that name, *tootsie-pie,* and with it comes the smell of her mother's hand lavender cream and almost, just almost she can hear it, the slight upturn in her mother's voice as she leaned over Sara's bed and said, "Hey, hey, Tootsie-pie, it's wake up time."

Sara goes to the closet mirror. She shakes her head trying to see what light catches in the faceted stones. *Trust me on this one,* her mother had written.

"Dad," Sara says, her head bobbling to keep the sapphires moving, "Before you put the suitcase away, I need Mom's family album. Apparently to get this baby, I have to have something to say about my past."

⚬⚬⚬

Crimped hair, hats pinned at funny angles, wide shoe buckles. At first that's what Sara noticed in the photograph album her mother showed her. When her mother pointed to a photograph of men and women at an outdoor table lifting glasses in a toast, Sara looked at the rug set outdoors under a patio table and wondered about it.

"That was the last afternoon," her mother said, touching the face of a child. Sara looked at the big bowl of fruit in front of the child. She wondered if the child liked any of that dull fruit. She asked her mother, "Was it always black and white back then? Was the whole world that way?" Her mother laughed until there were tears in her eyes. It took a childhood of afternoons looking through the album with her mother, her mother pointing at a man with a thick mustache and a woman in a belted coat and a stacked fur hat for Sara to understand. Even then, what did she understand? That man and woman had put her mother on a boat and sent her to England to live with an aunt. "For safety," her mother said, but Sara thought of the rowboats in Central Park and wondered why a parent would put a little girl alone on a boat and call that safe.

"Simone, for God's sake. She's too young," her father said, walking into the living room where Sara snuggled in the big reading chair with her mother. Her mother gave a silent shake of her head and turned the album page, saying, "Look how glamorous your grandmother looked." Each time Sara looked at the photograph she counted the twenty-two buttons on the gloves that went all the way up the woman's arms.

"I was so young," her mother said. "For a long time, living in Leeds, I couldn't recall anything about my parents. Even when I tried. A song my father sang to me about dragonflies or the way my mother pressed her lips together after putting on lipstick. It hardly seemed like anything, hardly enough to call parents."

When her mother spoke about her parents, Sara tried to always have some part of her body—her arm, her hair—touching her mother's. She made herself look at the woman's face. The woman had her mother's full lips, the same sleepy look in her eyes.

"But when I had you, so many years later, Sara, it seemed to me my mother and father were always in the room with me. Like I see you, I could see them and they were talking, talking, talking. I loved it, even if I thought I might be going a little crazy."

Later, in the end, when Sara had to hold the album, her mother said, "You'll see, darling. You'll have your children and suddenly, like it or not, the dead all come to talk with you and tell you what to do."

SEPTEMBER II

9:15 P.M.

Dear Mrs. Roosevelt,

What would you take, Mrs. Roosevelt? If you had a day, an hour, if the building were on fire? What would you take? It's almost a philosophical question, don't you think? Though not an inquiry I encountered at the lycée. Of course, there are practical choices—the official papers, visas, letters of transit, all the documentation from Ricardo in Mexico and the name of his contact, Manuel, in Paris, cash stored in hatboxes, under floorboards, divided into three money belts. This new compact Royale typewriter, there was never a question of leaving it behind. And now my only chance of being saved is poking with my stupid two-fingered typing at these keys. Yet why did I take the pencil sketch of me that my friend Sylvie made one afternoon at the Café Le Monde? Maybe you think it was a romantic gesture, that Sylvie's another sweetheart. But, honestly, there's nothing between us. Nothing like my creamy-faced Odile whom I had the luck to kiss again in January, her face so cold in my hands and her mouth so warm. Let me stop that right away before I get lost in that story. Sylvie had drawn me with my hat angled sharp across an eye and in the corner she'd written, *Toujours le Bon Vivant*. She was teasing, but I can't help hoping that I do look rakish and handsome. But given everything left behind, why'd I slip it into an issue of *Movie World* and pack it away between my suits? Maybe some would think it crazy to take a magazine. But there's no point questioning why a fan like myself took along an issue or two of *Movie World* and *Le Film Complet*.

What would you take, Mrs. Roosevelt? It's worth giving it a thought. But look, right now I've got to take a break and walk the decks. I sound like a regular sailor talking like that. But with these aching knees and the damp September air, moving helps.

Your most loyal sailor,
Itzak

P.S. At the risk of offending you, I need to say that I'm not convinced the cloche you're wearing in the newspaper photo is the best hat choice for you. A simple turban or even a fedora might better suit you. I saw in Paris a nifty off-the-face tricorne designed with the pompadour in mind. Half red and half black, it was extremely stylish.

Yours truly,
Jack

She's come to this shop on Amsterdam Avenue to find out what it will cost to re-cane her frayed dining-room chairs. It's Sara's Saturday reward for two days of good concentration on the translations. Hardly a roll, but she's happy to be in a rhythm, even a little in a rhythm. She thinks it's superstitious to connect the good work with seeing the young man in the park again playing Bach, but there it is.

It delights her, this shop, old world, one of the last stores in the neighborhood that isn't just a copy of a flagship store with displays chosen by someone in an office in Cincinnati. It doesn't have a catalog or a website. In fact, there's nothing new to buy. It is simply a chair-repair shop, up a narrow flight of stairs, chairs hanging from the ceiling, from poles, from hooks. Chairs like chandeliers. Chairs stacked on the wooden floor. Three levels of chairs and great floor-to-ceiling windows that swing out to the street with chairs hanging on hooks in the windows. Sometimes there are a few never-picked-up chairs for sale.

It's breathtaking.

Even the difficult owner delights her. The owner is quirky, his prices shifting, his mood gruff then flirty.

"You can't afford to re-cane these chairs," he says to Sara. And when she asks will it be cheaper to go into one of these big stores and buy new chairs, he says, "You don't look like the kind of woman who wants to live with new chairs." She finds his scruffiness adorable, an old hippy craftsman. "I'm expensive and the mall chairs are shit; what's the choice?" he says, looking so directly at Sara she feels it in her chest. She looks down. He holds a pencil in his left hand, letting it tap against a notepad. She likes his hands. He's not wearing a ring, but Sara knows that doesn't mean anything.

She says she knows just how expensive he is; she's actually had a chair repaired by him before. "It was almost worth it," she says, giving herself a little edge in the volley.

"What's your name?" he says, looking at her as if she might be the chair he worked on.

"Oh, it was years ago."

"Okay," he says, "but what's your name?" And when she tells him, he looks at her harder than he's already been looking and says, "Leader. I remember your blue chair."

Sara tries to hold the directness of his stare. Like it's a contest she's committed not to lose. She's flattered he's remembered her. Doesn't want to be flattered. Then, suddenly, there's someone, a woman, next to her, tapping Sara on the shoulder. "Excuse me," the woman says. "Your name. Leader. Is your father Itzak?"

Sara doesn't want to break the fix of her eyes, to be distracted from the chair guy, to lose. She gives a quick look at the woman.

"What?" she says. "Itzak? No." She'd noticed the woman peripherally in the shop, poking among the aisles of rockers and ladderback chairs.

"Your father's not Itzak Lejdel?" the woman says, and Sara sees she's disappointed.

"Well, it was, yes, he was. Itzak, and Lejdel, I think," Sara says, although she can't really remember knowing his first name was Itzak. His Hebrew name? Her father's name is Richard. Richard Leader.

"Itzak Lejdel. I thought there was a chance when I heard you say Leader. My father never went for calling him Richard. It was always Itzak," the woman says, like she is saying the name of someone famous. "This is amazing. My father is Henri Goldenman." She stands back, clearly waiting for that fact to register hugely in Sara.

Sara doesn't know what to say. She hasn't heard that name, Henri Goldenman.

"I've heard so many stories about your father. This is incredible," the woman says, smiling. She's standing close to Sara, and Sara feels her almost vibrating. "You've heard of my father, right?"

"This is incredible," the woman repeats this time to the chair man. "Our fathers were boys together. Best friends. In Brussels. Can you imagine? We're meeting in this shop in New York City. They left together. Our families left Brussels together. Then some things happened, you know."

Sara looks from the woman to the chair guy, who is smiling, his body pressed against the wooden counter.

The woman touches Sara's arm. "Oh, right, I forgot to say I'm Rochelle. Rochelle Goldenman. I can't believe this, the absolute crazy luck of this. I've got to sit down to take this in," she says, falling into a split leather armchair.

"Sara Leader," Sara says, relieved she can simply say something she actually knows.

Rochelle looks knowingly at Sara. "Sara, yes, I know, like your grandmother, Sahra."

Sara wants to turn back to the chair guy. Just flirt a little more, get a quote to re-cane her chairs, go back to her errands. It's too unwieldy. Someone has said her father's name, Itzak. And now this woman, this Rochelle Goldenman, some Upper West Side lady in a repair shop, knows her grandmother's name.

"Sure, Rochelle," Sara lies, "of course I've heard of your father. This is amazing. How lucky. What a coincidence. Henri Goldenman."

She's never heard of Goldenman. She thinks of the photographs in her pocketbook. She could pull them out. Maybe Henri Goldenman is the other boy in the fedora. But even after seeing those photographs, she had never thought of her father having any friends. She can't even imagine him as a boy, as a young man. What things happened? But it's not curiosity she feels; she feels caught. Kneeling on the carpet before her parents' door, she'd made a promise not to ask questions, to take the side of his silence. But the baby thing, this adoption, is unraveling that. She's supposed to have the history she's never had. What are the chances of this? It's freakish, really. She's three blocks from her apartment and there's a woman who knows about her grandmother, about Brussels. Suddenly she can almost hear that her mother wasn't being cruel to her father so much as wanting to take care of her, of Sara.

"So how is your father?" Sara asks, trying to look as if she's almost up-to-date on his whereabouts.

"He died. Two years ago," Rochelle says, lowering a bit in the leather chair. Sara nods an "I'm sorry" and looks over at the chair man, who is grinning, fascinated and charmed that reunions are taking place in his shop.

"Look, are you free?" Rochelle asks, clearly excited. "When you're done here, want to get a coffee?" The question comes at Sara like a blow. She's curious, yes, but not ready to break her promise to her father. It was not her mother who was there every night. Her mother left, disappeared. And when she did she left Sara and her father not so much waiting for her to return as waiting to join her. If her father wanted silence, he must have had a good reason.

"I'd love to," Sara says, "but I've got to work. I have a deadline. Let me have your number and address." She takes the pencil from the chair guy's hand and he slides his pad across the counter. She looks hard at the letters as she writes them so that neither Rochelle nor the man can catch the easy lie on her face. "Can I call you? We'll do it soon. Definitely."

Sometimes still, like tonight, Sara calls her father and they watch TV movies over the phone together. Her father says, "You're just in time. Turn to the Movie Channel. It's *Casablanca*." They can both just about recite every line from *Casablanca*. When Yvonne says to Rick, "Where were you last night?" she hears her father take a breath before saying, "That's so long ago I don't remember."

"Oh Rick, what a big mistake. Look at those oh so kissable lips," her father says after Rick dismisses Yvonne's, "Will I see you tonight?" with a curt, "I never make plans that far ahead."

"Dad, you know what happened today?" Sara wants to ask him about the woman she's met, about his friend Henri.

"Shh, come on, you know the rules. No talking, no side conversations. It's *Casablanca*."

SEPTEMBER 12

6:05 A.M.

What news this morning, Mrs. Roosevelt.

We've had a jumper! At first I thought it was yet another rumor.
There's been no shortage of jumping talk since Vera Cruz when one
of the crew, an African, swam from the boat. Not a few of us have
boasted about following his example. There's also been talk of trying to steal off in the night in one of the lifeboats. Rumors and talk,
rumors and talk. We could rename this ship the *Rumor*.

But now, indeed, in the middle of the night Monsieur Wolff
jumped from the *Quanza*. He's the last person aboard you might
think would or could jump and swim against the rough, cold cur-
rents. And make it to shore. A small, bespectacled, German man,
he's not the most durable-looking fellow. Unlike the African in
Mexico, Wolff's been returned to the ship.

I'm trying to stay uplifted, but I admit that things early this
morning don't look too hopeful here, Mrs. Roosevelt.

Maybe it's rumor, maybe not, but according to the News Committee, Captain Harberts has banned the lawyers and immigration
inspectors who attempted to come aboard. He claims that since the

ship is not officially in port and isn't paying tonnage tax, we passengers don't have rights. Even the crew is not permitted to leave the ship for shore leave. There's another rumor—care of the Legal Committee—that Harberts has pushed the Rands into signing an official paper that states that they did not give their consent to the lawyer who is suing the ship. There are rumors that Jules Wolff was given a meal of eggs and was allowed to call his relatives in Brooklyn before being returned to the ship. I don't know what to make of any of this. But I know two things. I know that if there were a Rumor Committee it would have the full ship's membership. And I know that as much as it might seem that I'm writing you just because I like to tell stories, I really urgently need your help today.

It occurs to me that you might go directly to the President and mention to him that there's a young man on a ship called the *Quanza* who has really bad knees and practically can't walk. Maybe rather than discussing a refugee visa or political refugee status, you might say, "Franklin, there's this young man, like our sons, Franklin, and his legs are killing him."

Just one guy with bum legs to another.

It might reach him. He might really consider a boy's plight. I think it's worth a shot, Mrs. R.

Yours truly,
Isaac

SEPTEMBER 12

6:45 A.M.

Forgive me, First Lady,

More than a bad idea, that was just plain stupid, telling you what to tell your husband. And him, Franklin, not just any husband, not like my scatterbrained father, Max, but Franklin's the President of the United States of America. Okay, I admit I'm a little bossy. I tell Maman all the time what to say to Max. She needs the help. On our first night inside France, Max announced that he was going to take a train back to Brussels to get cash and a few more things from home.

"I've got a firm idea." That was how Max put it. Max had concocted a whole story about Monsieur Gochet from the bank. Max believed that when Gochet saw that Max was among the loyal citizens and not one who'd fled Brussels, Monsieur Gochet would ignore the moratorium on withdrawals, allowing Max to take more money from his accounts.

"Are you an idiot?" I shouted. Okay, I shouldn't call my own father an idiot, but what should I do when he says, "I'll go take care of the factory machinery and then meet up with you in Paris."

More and more my father spoke in ways that indicated that he thought we'd been rash to leave. Why leave our good apartment and sleep in fields or scrounge and pay for rooms on farms? Why trust strangers when Brussels had many good people who knew us? According to Max, we had security at home. We had a business. Devoted employees. Who was this Mexican contact we were counting on in Paris?

It is true that after all the days on the road, after seeing soldiers returning from the north in medical trucks or alone on foot, having fled their divisions, even I thought longingly of our solid, spacious apartment on Rue Rogier. But the next day I turned seventeen; I was obligated to the Army. Returning to Belgium was not an option I could entertain. There were countless moments I wanted to leap from the car and take off on my own. But I knew that our family needed to remain together moving forward, always forward.

"Say no, Maman," I said. Mrs. Roosevelt, Maman is not the strongest woman in the world. She managed our home partly, it always seemed to me, because the daily providing for a family gave her a reason to stay healthy. She's a quiet woman, delicate, prone to illness. Since we'd left Brussels she'd seemed frail. She sat in the car with her suitcase half-filled with the family photographs (Tell me, would you at the last minute grab photographs?) practically buttoned to her body. She could barely permit herself to lift even one hand off her suitcase.

"I've got two workshops. I've got employees. We have an apartment. This isn't just a magic trick, Itzak, walking away from our life. I can't walk away from Brussels without settling my business. You'll stay with your mother."

"What did you think you were doing a week ago?"

"Look, Itzak, I never was certain our leaving was the best choice. The roads are a little clearer right now. I'll go back. Instead of listening to who knows what on the radio, I'll actually see what's going on in our city. Who knows, maybe I'll wire you to come home. Or at least when I meet you in Paris, we'll be in a much better situation."

"Maman, say no. Please." I said it softly.

Maman rubbed her hands across the pebbly grain of the leather valise. She reached and took my father's hand. "No Max, please, you can't leave me."

"Sahra, it's fine. Izzy will be with you all the time. He's a man now. He'll look after you."

"I might be picked up for desertion. Then what? Maman will be alone," I said to Max.

"No, Max," my mother repeated. She practically whispered, never even looking up at him. "You can't leave. You are my husband."

I knew that for that moment I had won. We were still together in the cramped back seat. I'd kept him with us. Going forward together.

Yours truly,
Victor the Victorious

THE CHOICES ON this new round of adoption forms are dazzling, disquieting; her answers unnerve her.

She wishes she were a better person.

Just when Sara thinks she'll die if she has to fill in the same information on yet another version of the same form, there's a new form with new, terrifying questions that make her long for the comfort of dull repetition. Check acceptable boxes for medical diagnosis. Some she's never even heard of. She understands hepatitis, allergies, asthma, diabetes, even defects of the heart. But reactive detachment disorder? Failure to thrive, what exactly does that mean? And can Sara live with that? She's been thinking about the terror inside Kazakhstan, Sierra Leone, Bolivia, Peru, the disfigurement of towns, the landscape, the destruction of social order. Giving her child a chance to thrive. But what to do about checking boxes for facial irregularities or spina bifida? The ravages not of war necessarily, not even of poverty, but of biology.

She's horrified by the glaring borders of her compassion.

Over the phone the social worker says, "Go easy. Just be honest. The point is to look at yourself, to make choices as you make a family, to see what you're ready for as a parent. Really. Feel your way into this, with your heart, not your mind."

The limitations of her heart make her like herself a whole lot less.

She can't help wanting to count on her mind; she's an academic. Research is how she manages things, even her anxiety. Especially her anxiety. She finds herself studying the history of adoption in America and the more recent concerns about foreign adoptions, baby trafficking, and women getting paid practically nothing to have babies for export. Indigenous craft, Sara thinks to herself. And what kind of buyer am I? A collector? Where can a child come from? How can a child look?

She doesn't want to be the person she mostly is.

She wants to close the image of Marco out of her mind. The way last night in the shadowy light of his draped room he looked at her and said, "Even your ideas about parenting are so American. You want a baby, I'll give you a baby."

She wanted then to stand up, say, "What are your righteous ideas? That every winter you go back for a little visit to the campo and leave your wife with another baby to nurse while you come back to New York to play world music to adoring Americans hungry for something authentic?"

Instead she succumbed to stupid rage, finding nothing more eloquent to shout than, "You're a phony," until he wrestled her close to his bony chest and whispered, "I'm sorry, Sara."

———

"Sometimes with all these adoption forms and meetings," Sara complains on the phone to Helen, "it feels like the only work I'm already doing is baby work."

"Oh please, Sara," Helen says, "then don't do it. Before I say something unkind, I better hang up."

Okay, so maybe she's a little out of line, but Sara has had to produce so much documentation that it really does feel like she could use her entire fellowship just becoming a mother. Letters on her behalf, questionnaires, criminal checks, a medical, all this even before the home visit. She likes the stability of this private adoption agency. Definitely established, even fussy with all their coordination groups and social workers and facilitators, their reassuring lifelong commitment to families—it makes her feel supported. But after the last pre-parent group, Sara can't help but think that an Arizona lawyer would be faster. She'd get a call and—snap, snap—be on a plane. Like that. Mexico. Paraguay. El Salvador. Romania. No one to meddle with her once her baby is home. There's no shortage of lawyers who advertise: simple, fast adoption, our specialty. But what's their specialty? She's read testimonials from women who, having lost families in war, then had their infants stolen. A new trade. Babies from poor mothers, disappeared babies? A new worldwide commodity. He was talking about prostitutes, not mothers, but it was Benjamin who said "*in big cities, the woman appears not only as a commodity but, in the most graphic sense, as a mass-produced article.*" Even if she isn't managing to translate the essays, Sara keeps bumping up against Benjamin and Baudelaire, their vision of the modern world glaring, dehumanized, writ large.

Sara hears a racket on Helen's side of the phone, Helen's three kids doing something that hardly sounds human. Shrieking, more shrieking, then Helen shouting, "I'm not even counting to ten before you guys have lost every privilege until you're fifty."

"What happened? Are they killing each other?" Sara says.

"Oh, you know. Nothing," Helen says coolly. "I'm just here having the same kind of busy-mother day you are, Sara."

"This will be part of your story," Sara's mother said. They were on a bench at the entrance to Central Park. Too hard for her mother to get far into the park anymore, but from here they could see a rectangle of lawn, boys practicing soccer, the pierce of the coach's whistle, a shouted command, and the boys forming new positions on the field. Women crossed on the paths, jogging women, women in tailored suits on their way to important places, women caring for other women's children—all moving through the park. Sara's mother looked shrunken and small on the bench.

"What? This bench?" Sara sneered, surprised by the meanness in her own ten-year-old voice. She touched her stack of books from the library they'd just come from. Her mother saying, "Let me choose one for you that I so loved." Sara rubbed her finger along the spine of the top book and, without looking down, tried to guess which book it was.

"Part of what story?" she said, looking where her mother was looking—at the boys taking angled shots at the goal, or was it past the boys to the hill where people lay out sunbathing? A young woman rolled down the hill, a whirl of red dress against the green lawn. A man leaned over drum skins, his large hands teasing out a rhythm. "What's their story?" Sara asked, trying to get her mother to play one of their favorite games. It had always been a way they loved watching the world go by. They could sit in the window of a coffee shop and invent the lives of passing strangers—where's she rushing off to? Party? Art opening? Where's he coming from? Job interview? Patenting his new invention? What's in his bag? Cupcakes? Maps to the ruins in Mexico?

"Mom, I think that lady in the yellow jacket has skipped lunch on her break from the dentist's office and is going to the museum to spend her lunch in front of Degas' ballet dancer."

But her mother's eyes were closed. Sara looked at the way the lids shifted. There was something scary and reassuring about the fluttery vibration.

"Mom, I think that guy reading the paper is actually making up a story about us."

Her mother's eyes stayed closed. Shut tight. And the movement under the lids had slowed. It looked like her mother couldn't open her eyes even if she tried. Sara felt a panic seize up in her throat. And anger. And then despite every determination not to cry, Sara was crying.

"Mom, stop making me do all the work alone. What story are you talking about?" She squeezed her eyes against her tears, trying to keep them inside her face. Her mother still didn't open her eyes or make room in her arms for Sara the way she always did when her daughter needed the slightest comfort.

"This story, Sara," her mother said in a distant whisper. "That I went and left you with all the work still left to be done."

SEPTEMBER 12

8:00 A.M.

Dear Mrs. Roosevelt,

A victory, even a little one, Mrs. Roosevelt, makes us bold, and having kept Max from rushing back to Brussels allowed me to snarl "no" a bit fiercely when Gustav suggested it was time to think about pulling the car over in a field.

"We need at least to put the cars where they won't be seen." I was firm. They had all better understand I was not a child in this car.

"This field looks as good as the last, "Gustav said, pulling off the road. It was dark and we had just missed hitting a small animal in the road. Gustav cursed. In the dark of the car, I'd seen Maman's eyes widen and then shutter closed. Each night we traveled the narrow dirt roads, stopping at farms and offering money in exchange for a room and a place to hide our cars. Few people left the main roads; we found it gave us better chances. We'd grown used to reluctance, the "sorry, no petrol" or "sorry, no bread" that cautiously shifted when we inquired if perhaps there might be just one last loaf or spare room in the garage if we made them a special offer. Sometimes there were rooms for the night in a farmhouse, but most nights the women slept in the cars and the five men slept wherever we found to settle down.

The Goldenmans beeped their horn and pulled beside us.

"Gustav," Marie said firmly. "Keep going. Itzak's right."

Then there were words in Walloon between them, Gustav's phrases angry and clipped while Marie kept flicking her hand, her fingers making quick stabs at the air. Suddenly Gustav jammed the gears and the car lurched forward.

Down the road we found an abandoned farm with a small shed and the ruins of a stone granary. Though the farmhouse looked abandoned, we decided it was safer to stay outside in the shed. It was our first night in France and we wanted to keep our circumstances simple.

We moved wooden crates to fit both cars side by side, but only Gustav and Marie's car fit inside the shed. We parked the Goldenmans' car behind the shed. Maman and Marie untied and took down all the bedding. As I've said, each night the women slept in the car; the men made makeshift beds outside. But tonight Maman said, "Iz, stay in the car with me." My mother, I suppose, wanted to shelter me, have me sleep again as a child curled in the warmth of her arms. But I was too large, and in the end, Maman settled against me, my arm around her. Because we were hidden inside a shed, we kept the headlights on and I took out a film magazine. I kept turning pages of the magazine, my eyes cast down. But instead of looking at it, I watched Marie taking her hair out of the chignon. I watched her pull the long pins, collecting them in one hand as she unfastened the coil of hair. I thought then of Odile, how I'd been so jealous of her own hands. And the boy I'd been that last summer already seemed young. Marie's fingers were so particular and intent and I was excited a little by my invasion of her privacy.

Then suddenly, she'd turned around, her fingers lost in her hair, and spoke to me.

"Itzak, you were right tonight. Sometimes Gustav is a simple fool."

I'd been caught. Stupidly I turned the page as if I'd really been reading. "I suppose," I said trying to keep my voice steady, uninterested. I tried to meet her eyes, which were relaxed and had none of the steely stare I'd come to think of as her gaze.

"Well, goodnight," she said and turned the knob of the light, and the shed went dark.

I lay in the dark listening, but there was no rustle or any noise to catch hold of. I didn't know what I was listening for. But when I heard it, some material sound—blouse fabric in motion, or was it the lining of Marie's skirt?—I admit I'd been listening in the dark for a sound of her in the front seat. I waited for some next sound, her stockinged legs shifting on the front seat. Anything. I thought I might even hear her hair against the seat. Maman's breathing was nasal, not snoring, not really, but short raspy draws. Thinking about Marie, Gustav's wife, and having Maman there, right next to me, made feel ridiculous, made me wish I'd slept outside. My legs ached. I shifted mother off my arm, disturbing her—"Izzy?" she stirred.

"I'm just stretching. It's okay, Sahra." She resettled against the door. I'd started calling my parents by their first names. Since Brussels. No one had mentioned it. My calling her Sahra was, you must imagine, the least of Maman's worries.

I stood from the car. There was an old smell of grain in the shed. And chickens. The air came up cool and sheathed my body. In the dark I circled the bulky, overgrown shape of the car. I stretched my legs as I did in school before a sprint.

"My legs ache, too." She was right there leaning out the car window. I jumped. Marie. I hadn't heard her sit up, not even a rustle. Her voice was slow but had no rough edge of sleep to it. "After a day's work, I beg Gustav to give them a rubdown."

I refused to be startled. "You work in Charleroi?" I said and kept stretching in the dark. I didn't want her to think I'd stop because of her.

"Not mostly."

"Mostly?" I challenged.

"I work wherever there's work."

"Where's that?" I took the heel of my foot in hand. I hoped she could make out the line in the dark, that she'd see my flexibility and balance.

"What exactly do you think we do, Itzak?" I was startled now by the direct sound of my name in the dark. My foot lowered, wobbling a little on the uneven ground. "You think we're in a factory, Itzak. Long hours in the factory and then perhaps we have a little plot of land? Some leeks and onions, carrots? That's right?"

I didn't know how to answer. Or what I could answer. I had nothing tricky to say. I tried to remember more about her and thought of her porcelain clips, her long fingers.

"I don't know what you do," I said finally. And when she didn't say anything, I asked, "Well, what is it then?"

She kept to the silence. I could see her arms folded in the rolled-down window. The tented mass of her hair.

"I wasn't trying to insult you," I said.

I could hear her breath. "Ropes, horses, fire. We've done all of it." Her voice challenged me. Even in the dark, I could feel the burn of her eyes. And her smile, full and insistent. She was having fun. She was working me. And there wasn't any letting her or not letting her.

I wanted to get out of the shed. Have a cigarette. But I wanted more to hear her speak in the dark to me. I didn't know where Max and Gustav had settled their blankets. Had Max held out his hand for Gustav to give him the keys for the night, saying, as he said each night, "So we can all sleep peacefully?" Henri and his father were most likely sleeping with them, and I thought it would be best for me to take a pillow and find the other men.

"We take what comes. Mostly what comes is circus, Itzak."

I loved the way my name sounded when she said it.

"The circus." I worked hard not to let my voice lift into a question.

Then she was laughing, not against me but, also, not with me, saying, "I've traveled with the circus for fifteen years. How else do you think I've gotten so good at this business of sleeping anywhere?"

That was my first night in France. May 15. I fell asleep thinking about touching Marie's leg. The next day was my birthday.

Yours truly.

Iz

P.S. Update from the Rumor Committee on Jules Wolff:
Much claiming that Wolff:

1. Had a heart attack.
2. Spoke with officials on shore who say we are to be sent this evening to Venezuela or Lisbon or back to Mexico.

3. Gave an interview to reporters before he was sent back on the ship.
4. Gave a lawyer 1,000 dollars to secure his removal from the ship.

Also a rumor capital-R that there are other meetings going on and certain crucial conversations with the Captain that only first-class passengers are permitted to attend. (Am I surprised?)

SEPTEMBER 12

8:50 A.M.

Dear Mrs. R.,

Quick, quick. Boat moving. No longer Hampton Roads. Down to
the coal pier of the Virginia Railway at Sewalls Point. They say this
is a good sign. I'm not sure of what. Something to do with the
lawyer I told you about who is suing the shipping company.

Find me there. Sewalls Point. We're not leaving yet!

Yours, I

SITTING AT THE long table with her French and German and English dictionaries and Benjamin's books, Sara feels more like a sentimental schoolgirl than the tenured professor that she is. Despite herself, she's crying. A woman crying into her books. She can't bear the loss, again, she can't bear the loss. In his final note he wrote, *There is not enough time remaining for me to write all the letters I would like to write.*

She sees Walter Benjamin in New York.

And more than one Walter Benjamin. First a man bent over papers at the Café Reggio on MacDougal Street, his shirtsleeves rolled up, showing a wide, thickly haired forearm. On Park and 94th carrying flowers wrapped in green-and-white paper, Walter Benjamin stands talking to a woman in nursing shoes. On 23rd street Walter Benjamin wears his overcoat in the middle of July. Despite herself, Sara believes it really is him. She wants to catch up to him. *I often ask myself whether and under what conditions we will see each other in the foreseeable future.* Sara hurries until she's abreast of the gray wool–coated Benjamin. She's almost too nervous to look. Walter

Benjamin right down to the suitcase, though this suitcase is on wheels, the strap wrapped around Benjamin's wrist. Sara thinks about the unfinished manuscript inside, perhaps a few books, letters, photographs of his wife and son, a change of clothes, a folded yellow wool blanket. She smells Benjamin's pipe. In a late letter, just two months before his death, Benjamin wrote to Hannah Arendt. *Mrs. P. found her husband again. It seems he was in rather bad shape.* In the note he left with his suicide, he wrote, *There is not enough time remaining for me to write all the letters I would like to write.* In Spain he was told that despite his Spanish transit visa, the borders had been closed and he would be returned to France. The next day, without any more explanation than was given for their closing, the borders were reopened. Of course, here, in New York on 23rd Street, when she's right beside him, it isn't Benjamin. It's a young man, his sloppy shuffle like an old man's infirmity. He smokes a corncob pipe. He juts his head to glare at Sara. He's even younger than Sara first realized. More kid than man, he has a steel ring in his nose.

"I thought you were someone, excuse me." Sara says. Comical, really, the translator who can't translate walking the streets of the city and finding Benjamins everywhere.

Less than comical, pathetic.

He puffs smoke from his pipe, his face narrowing. "I am someone," he says and speeds up, away from Sara, his suitcase wobbling behind.

⎯⎯⎯∞⎯⎯⎯

"Oh, I'm so sorry," Georgette says. "Both your grandparents?" Sara watches Georgette's face arrange itself into the compassionate how-horrible-I-didn't-know shape Sara sees whenever she tells people. But she doesn't usually tell people. It's horrible, sure, but it's not a horror she feels close to, can locate inside herself. Saying *Buchenwald* or *the Camps* has never felt personal. But immediately Sara can see it's useful in this one-on-one meeting; this piece of information somehow gives her status with the adoption counselor. Georgette begins to arrange papers on the desk: there are four folders labeled with Sara's name. Sara sees that Georgette wants to look up, to look directly, emotionally at Sara but can't quite yet.

"Yes, my mother's parents," she says to Georgette. Sara never says *my grandparents*. If she thinks about grandparents at all, she thinks about Aunt Flossie in Leeds, who also died before Sara was born.

"I'm so sorry," Georgette says. Sara watches as Georgette collects herself, holding a steady counselor-of-compassion-and-concern countenance. Georgette might even put out a hand to touch hers.

"It's okay," Sara says. "My mother was sent to England. She was raised in England with her aunt who was a fabulous radical war journalist. She died before I was born, but her work is astonishing."

"So this is part of your decision."

"What?" Sara sees Georgette looks triumphant; she's clearly having an aha! moment. "What is?"

"To adopt. What your aunt did for your mother, you're doing for a child."

"Oh please, not at all," Sara says it quickly, harshly, as if she's been accused.

"Why not Sara, I think that's a good thing. Lovely. A beautiful reason to want to parent," Georgette says. Sara knows she should yield, play the move she's been given; there's obviously some bureaucratic gain in having the agency counselor a little extra involved in her adoption. But if it's to her advantage it's come up from a playing field she thought she'd fully studied, and Sara feels caught out in the open.

"A beautiful reason. But it's not *my* reason," Sara says.

⸺

"Where?" Sara asks, scanning the kitchen as if she thinks her father must be hiding, ready to pop out from the utility closet to surprise Sara. She's come to check up on him, maybe a quick dinner after a long day. "Where did he go?"

"I don't know," Carmen says, lifting plates from the dishwasher to the open cabinet. "You think your father reports to me where he's going?"

Sara puts her hands out to take plates from Carmen, and just as she expects, Carmen passes Sara the plate without making eye contact. It's an absolute giveaway that something's up—the averted gaze, the harsh tone of Carmen's response. They both know it's her father's habit, the old, careful habit of a father raising his daughter alone, to leave word of exactly where he's gone and when he intends to be back.

Carmen lifts out the cutlery basket, sorting forks first, then knives.

"Carmen," Sara says, putting herself next to the drawer. "I'm just asking if there's anything I need to know. Is everything okay?"

"What's to know?"

"Carmen, a week ago you called hysterical that my father fell and couldn't get up off the living room floor. Now he's God knows where and you act like I'm strange for asking where he's gone?"

Carmen stops, wielding a spoon in each hand, and looks at Sara full on.

"You did your job; you got him a cane. So early this morning your father and his cane walked out the door."

"Early this morning? It's nearly seven at night. Where'd he go, Carmen?" Sara tries not to sound hysterical—her father in an emergency room, her father wandering lost in the dark—she's got a slideshow of emergency images moving through her imagination.

"He's allowed a life."

"Excuse me, Carmen, are you remembering he's eighty years old?"

"He's fine. He's fine. Really. Go home, Sara." Carmen's voice is softer. "Or better yet, Sara, go out and try to have a little fun."

⸻

Sara's watching Irene Dunne and Cary Grant in *Penny Serenade*. It's all she can manage after the day she's had. It's a cheap shot, using this movie to bring on the tears. She's tried beginning her adoption autobiography but spent the evening like a high school senior trying to sound interesting in a college application. After maybe twenty calls in the last three hours, her father still isn't home. She's called down to Marco's hoping for some sexy distraction but he's gigging at the Kitchen.

She can't bear watching them, especially Cary Grant, knowing they'll lose the child they adopt.

The adoption counselor said the autobiography was the easy part. "We want to know about you, your family's history, how who they were makes you *you*. To know what matters to you. It's simple. Just tell your whole story."

Simple. Your story. What's your story? Like buzzwords she keeps hearing. Your story. What's your story? But when she starts to write her whole life feels like a cliché, except she's not sure what the cliché is exactly. She could write: My mother died when I was a child. My father raised me. He never remarried. I kept him company. My father came here during the war. On a boat. He came with his mother. My other grandparents died in the camps. I don't know anything else. Now there's even a new name, Henri Goldenman, with a daughter who seems to know more about Sara's family's past than Sara. Is this new name part of her family's story? And her own life as a translator feels cliché, translating from her father's languages, German philosophers, French poets; now she's translating Walter Benjamin. Her personal life is ridiculous. She keeps choosing married guys, unavailable but needy men. She's middle-aged and wants a child of her own. But this adoption process has touched another, even deeper need. She wants to give a lost child a new mother. And now Georgette wants to make that all touch-feely, a personal healing episode. Screw it if her choices might have been a bit more subtle, less metaphorical—but there it is. She might live in New York, but she doesn't need a fancy New York psychotherapist to tell her what's what.

Cary Grant stands in a doorway. He looks crumpled as if he needs the door to hold him up. He blinks and his dark eyes look like they might fill with tears. He blinks again and it's clear he's refusing even tears. He's so ordinary. Even his handsomeness has a terrible ordinariness. The good-looking man, the man who might have been glamorous, stuck in a regular life where terrible things happen.

"Sara," her father's whispering. "I don't want to go."

"Dad," she says, her voice too loud in the dark. She's fallen asleep on the sofa, the TV screen blue and blank. "Where are you going? What's going on. Are you home? Where were you? Do you know it's three in the morning? Are you feeling okay?" Sara's wildly alert, questions toppling out of her mouth. Already imagining the worst.

"I'm not leaving," he says, his voice suddenly sturdy. She hears him rustling papers. The sound of papers is always in the background of their phone conversations. The sounds of his desk, mounded with papers, statements, receipts, scraps where he's written numbers that might be somehow useful, the names of people he's met. Cards from every store he's walked past. The names of maître d's. A mortgage broker's number, though he has no mortgage. He's home. He's alive. That's good for starters.

"Dad, what's up with you? Where were you all day? Tell me." She's holding her breath, not sure what she's waiting to hear, afraid of hearing. There's only the sound of her father's breath rough with fluids.

"I feel fine." Now his voice is distant. "It's late. I must have woken from a dream. Sorry, honey."

"Who's Henri Goldenman, Dad?" It blurts out of Sara. It's the first question that pushes the sealed envelope since fifth grade.

"What?"

"Henri Goldenman. Your friend. Tell me. I met his daughter." She's trying her best to keep her voice steady, but she hears her betrayal. And her relief.

"What's to tell? There's nothing to tell." Her father's voice is suddenly sharp, annoyed, awake. She's gone off point.

"Then tell me the nothing." Her own voice by comparison sounds childish and apologetic for her interest. All throughout Sara's childhood, friends asked, "Where's your father from?" "Why? What's he sound like?" she'd ask. People told her he had an accent but she couldn't hear it. Never had. Only, occasionally, on a few words. *Th*-words came out as *tr*-words. Thruway. Trueway.

There's the sound of papers being moved about, the incessant piles of papers her father makes and remakes.

"Sara, you think I have nothing more important in the middle of the night than to talk on the phone about some boy I knew when I was a kid?"

SEPTEMBER 12

11:00 A.M.

Dear Mrs. First Lady,

Maybe everyone in America has a house as large as a French chateau and grand places don't even take your breath away, but when Gustav swung the car into the open gates, claiming, "I've found us an abandoned paradise," I felt like a boy on holiday. The driveway wound through a beech stand and then took us past a wooden stable. The heavy doors were swung wide and the stalls were empty. "All of us and the two cars could spend the night in there," Gustav said.

"No horse sheds tonight. I need a bed," said Marie. From my angle in the back seat, I saw her eyes close. Her nostrils flared, taking in the new scents that swept through the car as we drove through a column of cedars. "I am desperate for a bed."

Gustav spoke to her in a low voice. She began laughing, a thick, abandoned laugh that even when she stopped she succumbed to again and then again. Her head shook as if she were really trying to restrain herself. Like a schoolchild wanting to crack up at the joke of a classmate but holding back and holding back, little giggles escaping until muffled, explosive, the laughter broke the dam of restraint.

Her hair was pinned up, the black coil of it rolled in a knot that was more stylish than functional. Her head shook and I watched her hair loosen from the long hairpin, the dark coil unfastening, falling free in a slippery rush. She combed her hands through her hair, and winding the hair with one hand she fixed it with the porcelain flower hairpin then quickly undid and re-pinned it, securing the pin in her black hair with a final twist.

Every way Marie moved her head made me certain I was right to distrust her and for that alone I told myself that I had good reason to keep watching her. But that night on the drive up to the chateau with her eyes closed, her breaths coming in short flares, her neck long and corded, I watched her profiled from the back seat and thought she's like a loosed pony and then I thought she hadn't been lying about the circus, she'd been around horses a lot and had taken on their manners.

I tried to think about Marie and Gustav in the circus. Each summer I went to the circus, once in July in Brussels and on August holiday at Coq Sur Mer. When the World's Fair had been in our city there had been no shortage of acts, women hanging from ropes by their teeth, acrobats, horse jumpers, and the fire-eaters. I'd find the chance to ask her if she had been at the World's Fair, if she'd been one of the women who leapt through flame wearing a mane of feathers. Maybe they had been a married act, Gustav and Marie, the famous lion tamers.

We continued up the driveway, the car scraping against the stone paving. A tiny stone chapel hunched in a low grove of un-pruned shrubs. Everywhere there were more gardens, abundant and derelict gardens, trellised roses growing thickly, wisteria trailing like a lapdog's untrimmed hair, a gazebo blanketed in round white flowers. I tried not to watch her. But I did. Listened for any little piece of her conversation with Gustav. They spoke in Walloon.

A woman and an old man stood on the stone steps at the facade of an impressive but neglected house. They stared blank faced at us as we approached. At first I thought the woman was an old servant but soon realized the woman was neither old nor a servant.

"Money," Max said quickly to Gustav as he got out of the car, and Gustav gave a quick nod to say he'd heard. I was happy that Gustav was wrong, that the chateau was not abandoned.

"Do you want me to go with him?" I asked Max. I even hoped they'd turn him away, refuse us even the horse barn. My jealousy made me petty.

Max watched Gustav. "No, he'll be fine."

The woman picked at her sweater as Gustav spoke. I saw the unkempt, misbuttoned way about her and knew that despite the grand scale of the chateau, she would quietly take our money as eagerly as the women at the rough farmhouses.

Inside, the massive, dark furniture was dusty. A few armoire doors hung crookedly off their hinges. The needlepoint rugs were worn and soiled. The hallway smelled dank and moldy. Even still the place was vast and impressive. We were to join them at their dinner. We sat down at the table. There was a servant who looked predictably ancient. She didn't look at or speak to us but set out a white-and-gold tureen with carved tubers as handles. There were bottles of wine and water on the long table.

Have I reassured you that the Goldenmans were still with us? We'd managed to travel as a team. At the table the Goldenmans were jolly; there's no other word for it; they kept a vigorous banter going. Henri repeatedly winked at me. Our meal was a thin potato soup with sorrel and garlic, a few strips of meat littering the bottom. There was a bowl of straggly bitter greens the servant tossed with large wooden combs. I noticed Maman hesitated and then ate the sharp cheese, although there had been meat in the soup.

The woman sat close beside the old man. I'd assumed he was her father, but at the table it occurred to me that he was her husband. The old man kept the spoon at his mouth, sucking at the spoon even when the broth was gone. He played with his spoon, scraping it against the bowl until the woman took the spoon from him. The cutlery was grand: heavy, large pieces of silver, a reminder of earlier grandeur. An exotically plumed bird stamped on each piece.

The only decoration on the wall was a map, though there were marks where large paintings had once hung. The drapes were drawn and the room was dim. After a while I realized the map was local, a span of towns, lakes, and forests within the region. Clusters of red and green tacks were pinned into the map. Sometimes a red tack and green tack almost overlapped, they were that closely stuck together. There was almost a design. I thought it might have something to do with troops.

But it was Henri—not me—who asked the woman about the map. She looked up at the wall but said nothing.

The old man pushed out his chair, turned to face the wall. "The red are enemies," he said staring at the map.

"But the Germans aren't yet in France," Henri said, winking at me.

The old man stood and lurched over to the wall, laying his hands flat on the map. "Mine," he said. He put his face up close to the map. "My enemies are red. And the others are my friends." His face looked fierce and full of the effort of moving from his chair to the wall.

Gustav laughed. "Ah, I see you are a lucky man. My map, I'm afraid, would be dripping with red." The old man began laughing, too, his bent form propping itself against the wall. Suddenly, the room changed and it felt like we were at a party. The servant cleared our bowls, but everyone remained at the table. The conversation turned to Paris. The woman told us she'd been a student in Paris. She described fantastic masquerade balls. There had been a hat contest that she'd won with a hat made out of a brassiere, even a bar fight once with a girl who tried to lure away a medical student. She wound up knocking out the girl's tooth. "It was quite a world, Paris," she said, looking younger and younger, dimples emerging with her smile.

"Well, here is Paris for you again," Henri announced, folding a sailor's hat from newspaper. He'd made one for each of the ladies. Mrs. Goldenman had hers pitched at a sailor's angle. Maman took hers off, read news off the brim of the hat, and then with a flourish put it back on.

As we left the table I asked my father how much the night had cost us. "Enough," he said.

That night I shared a room and a bed with Henri. The rooms were connected by a door with a carved garland, wooden grapes and leaves trailing down the door and across the paneled walls to give, I suppose, the feeling of sleeping in an arbor. I noted the carved doors as a marker for the grandeur this chateau had once entirely equaled. But now the rooms were dank, the bedspread was worn thin, and there were only pieces of rugs left with long stringy wool connecting the islands of rug. Henri talked, and as he always did since we were boys, he fell asleep in the middle of his own sentence.

Our room connected with Gustav and Marie's room. I wasn't trying to listen to them, but I could hear doors and chairs scraping the floor and the sound of them moving about. They talked late into the night. There was much laughing, their voices rising and falling, though the thick walls made it impossible to make out many distinct words. Every sound I heard through the door caused me discomfort. I didn't want to think about Gustav with Marie. I didn't want to care about her at all. Once I went close to the door and tried to see if there was a view through the crack. I believe finally I slept.

Late in the night I woke, Henri's arm thrown over my chest. I needed to use the water closet that was down the unlit hall. It was with a certain difficulty that I made my way and once inside located the toilet. I tried to hold on to being tired, to being asleep, even letting myself sway a little. Someone tried the door but I said, "I'm in here," and the door closed. When I finished I went out expecting to find someone waiting and saw no one. I started back for the room but was stopped by a sound—unmistakable, impossible, but I heard it, the weak run of urine. I looked around. Maybe I was asleep; as a child I woke once into my own accident, to the sound and feel of my own body wetting the sheets. But I wasn't asleep; I knew that. Then I saw the shape, the old man's shape in the dark corner turned to the wall. The old man's feet shuffled, trying to step out from his puddle of urine. Before he turned, I hurried back to my room.

Then in the morning our car would not start. Gustav stood before the open hood.

"I'm afraid the car thinks this is better than Paris," he said. I looked at Gustav for the trick he was playing but saw there wasn't a trick. Gustav was jittery; he had none of his confidence, no brag to his posture.

One by one, in groups, and finally, all together, the five men stood in front of the open hood. No one knew anything worthwhile about cars. We were silent. Henri uncapped the radiator.

"What are you thinking?" Marie had entered the circle of men. She stood next to me. Her tone with me was close, conspiratorial.

"Is the railway station in the village?" I called over to the servant who stood on the stone steps watching, the rumpled shape of her like a statue slowly being worn and darkened. She didn't respond. The other men looked as if I'd asked something terrible.

I turned to Max. "It's time for a train."

"We have a car," Max said. He held his hands lifted over valves as if testing for something. My father had never been good with machines. For years in the factory he circled broken machinery, shaking his head as if he were on the verge of solving the problem. He could do this for hours, delicately unscrewing and screwing caps, announcing the problem, until Charlotte came up and patiently said, "Would you like me to have a look?" Then slowly my father would give Charlotte a little room and she would go to work while Max would dance in small steps around her announcing what was wrong with the machine.

"It's time for a train," I repeated, looking at Marie.

"What about my car?" Gustav was pacing. He stood in front of Max accusingly. "Are you saying you aren't fixing the car?"

"Have you heard me say anything?" asked Max. I saw the quiet in my father and wished my father's quiet was a kind of calculation.

Then we broke off, into our small tribes—the Goldenmans, Gustav and Marie, Max, Maman, and myself—each meeting in a tight group to make his own choice. We'd talk and then come back and see what everyone was thinking. Max said to Gustav,

"Wherever we go the offer is the same, you can come with us." I watched Marie for a sign that she'd come, that she'd argue for continuing with us, junking the car, some sharp look in her eyes to tell me she'd argue that it made sense at least to stay with the money. But there was nothing to read on her face.

The Goldenmans took barely a moment before Henri's father walked over, saying quietly to my father, "It's just a matter of a day or two. We can't give up our car. It's our car. You understand, right. If we could we'd fit you all inside, we'd do that. We'll find each other in Paris. Imagine meeting in Paris, Max. A splendid rendezvous. And we'll keep together after that." He looked embarrassed and quickly drifted away to repack their car.

Max was not quick to give up the car. "It moves, Izzy. It gives us a good chance. And it's like you've said, a car means we don't have to necessarily follow where we're told to go."

"But it doesn't move," I said. "You can see that much, Max, can't you?" I was immediately sorry for the roughness of my speech. "Papa, a train moves," I said, trying to simplify and soften the situation.

Suddenly Max changed. It was as if the idea of the train, the opportunity of the train, meant that he could entertain the possibility of riding north. "Well, I'm going quickly back to Brussels. There are things we should have. I have to fix a few things."

I argued. I forced Maman to argue with Max. But Monsieur Goldenman's idea that we would meet in Paris was absolute in Max's mind. He'd go home. Get things. More money. More gloves. Give his foreman, Monsieur Rochelais, authority with the machinery. Maybe they would hide the machinery. It would be my responsibility to look after Maman, meet the Mexican contact, Manuel, show him our letters from Ricardo, secure our visas, and then, Max said, taking Maman's hand, we'd rejoin in Paris.

"Not to worry. Not to worry," Max said, his voice suddenly light, even fanciful. There were things he said he could do for us from Brussels. Who knows, perhaps he'd send word that we should return home.

"What things?" I yelled. "What things?" Max said money and contacts and maybe, who knows, he said again, the situation in Brussels would probably be a lot better than traveling nowhere in a crowded car on crowded roads. "Give me a real answer," I yelled. And when there was no sufficient answer, I just yelled and yelled like I was a small boy in a tantrum until, between choked breaths, I looked and saw that Max was unmovable, he barely heard my shouts, and Maman was hopeful that her husband would soon be returning our family to our apartment on the Rue Rogier.

I understood my parents wanted to go home.

My father. Goldenman. Idiots! Mrs. Roosevelt, I must trust you understand me well enough by now to understand my fury. Not just old men, old ways. Though, yes, there was some of that, the way they stood about holding onto an old-fashioned world. No, it was their stupid blind hope. Such hope they had. *Quickly go back to Brussels. A splendid rendezvous.* Had we not been together and seen the empty petrol tanks, the soldiers fleeing?

I stomped away and wandered through the messy gardens, trying to work up an argument that would reach Max. I would take Henri aside and without the blather of his father he'd see that abandoning all our cars was clearly the smart choice. But really—why? I fumed. Wouldn't it be easier not traveling and bargaining with fools? I'd listen to their plans for where we'd find one another. But goodbye to them. I choose practicality, not hope.

I saw Marie and Gustav standing in the doorway of the stone chapel. In the arch above them were engraved birds open-winged as if in flight. They were stood arguing. Gustav's hands chopped at the air. Marie's arms wrapped around herself like a shawl. Only her foot moved, kicking at the stone step. How hadn't I seen earlier, the nimble gestures, the way they bent and straightened? Even the deft way each morning they strapped the bags on top of the car, balancing the great topple of valises, it was a giveaway to all their traveling, the town to town. Not lion tamers, I thought. Maybe they were contortionists. I wanted to see that. And see Gustav swallow flame or whatever it was Marie claimed Gustav did. They were fighting. And even that, Marie's hotheaded refusal to unclasp and throw her arms, Marie's snapping her head this way and that, was theatrical.

Marie broke away from the argument and began walking. I wanted to walk to her, meet up and take the two of us back into the chapel to stand inside, look up through the dusty windows of the small dome. I couldn't see where Gustav had sulked away. I didn't care. I cared about Marie's fast walk toward me. She was walking straight to me, her movements fierce and precise.

"Where's the station? Let's get out of this ugly place," she said, walking past me. She was going to Paris. With me. We were going to Paris.

Then everything—all the packing and repacking, pushing Marie and Gustav's car down to the horse barns—proceeded quickly, strange and silent as if we were in a movie and the sound had been shut off. The sound came back when Henri and his father helped us to the station and the Goldenmans drove off in their car, all of us waving and shouting, "In Paris! In Paris! In Paris!" as if we were gaily making holiday plans. Max left on a northbound train. He shouted out names for us to contact as his train huffed out of the station. Then Maman, Marie, Gustav, and myself rode the train to Paris without event and with no more than the absolutely necessary conversation.

Mrs. Roosevelt, I see I might have told this story differently, made myself sound nobler. But it was as simple as that. *Quickly go back to Brussels. A splendid rendezvous in Paris.* As simply as that you might lose your best friend, your copain, your other half since childhood. As simply as that you might lose your father.

Mrs. Roosevelt, there is nothing more to say right now. I must do a bit of pacing to exercise my legs. I hope that I'll learn something good so that I can tell you the rest. But from on shore, Mrs. R., don't forget me.

Yours truly,
Isaac Lejdel

SARA SPREADS ALL the photographs out on her dining-room table. The loose pictures she lifted from her father's office, her mother's slender album, and all the big family books her mother had made that seemed to chronicle every waking and sleeping minute of Sara's first eleven years.

Sara's mother had written captions under pictures in the albums. Mostly obvious: "Tired Papa" under a picture of Sara's father napping on a picnic blanket. Some sentimental: "Our Delight delights us" and a picture of Sara, a two-year-old with an ice-cream cone larger than her face, her fingers and arms and dress coated in ice cream. Some inscrutable and private: "After Gazebo. What was I thinking?" scrawled under a photograph of five-year-old Sara with a hula hoop around her waist. The last album tapers off as the cancer takes over, her mother and father in matching floppy straw hats, her mother looking up at the camera with an exhausted shrug. The final captions almost feel like notes, more messages and consolations for Sara to find. "Think about love." "Your face taught me everything." "I'm tired but okay." "Dearest, go on."

Mostly the pictures are familiar, her mother's parents, her childhood, but now there are also new faces to consider. She's learning things. But she's not sure what. Her father as a child. Carmen says she has her grandmother's eyes. She looks through the big photo albums and finds a photograph of herself with the same slanting upper lids. Sara holds both, looking from one to another. She lays down the photographs on her table like flipping cards for solitaire. She gathers them into a loose, rough pack and puts them into an envelope that she's marked *Baby*.

The past can be seized only as an image that flashes up at a moment of its recognizability and is never seen again, Benjamin writes. And then in the next section, *Articulating the past historically does not mean recognizing it "the way it really was." It means appropriating a memory as it flashes up in a moment of danger.*

Sundays, in the first years without her mother, they went to Marshall Chess Club in the Village. Or they went down to the smoky Russian chess houses on Thompson Street off Washington Square Park. Her father said it was good for Sara to play up, and once he'd set her with a scrawny Chinese guy with a milky eye. When she told her father the eye scared her, her father laughed and said, "Come on, my girl, just look at the board. With that eye, the chink knows he's going to beat most people."

The next Sunday he was there, hunched and skinny in the corner, and after Sara beat two college boys, the Chinese man motioned for her to play. She said yes, shuffling to the other side of the long table, looking down at the wooden bench. She kept her eyes down. She could feel the Chinese man looking at her, working to lift her chin up and meet him eye to eye. She felt her father quietly watching her from where he sat across the room playing a wild bald-headed Georgian who hummed and bit the filters off the cigarettes he chain-smoked. She wanted to look over at her father but was scared the Chinese man would tilt his head and she'd catch the milky eye, so she kept her face to the board. Even still she was down a rook, a knight, two pawns. She had resisted the eye and still she was losing. She didn't move for a long time. She had that. If he had his milky eye, he also had his skinny agitated body. She had the ability to keep still. Her father had taught her to wait. Her only advantage was waiting. She wouldn't look up. It made her see the board. Then she saw a chance and she took it. She forked his rook and his king. She heard the exhalation of his breath. It would happen. In time. She'd beat him. She wanted to look up at her father, give him a sign, a smile that said she hadn't been bamboozled by the chink's advantage. But she knew he'd try to make eye contact and so even after she won and shook his hand Sara kept her head down.

⁂

Sometimes her memory of her mother seemed like scraps. Nothing complete beyond a few whole moments. Otherwise it was only fragments. Her mother's fingers on the spine of a book. The clasp of her mother's pocketbook and a coffee candy in a gold wrapper. They were sitting in orchestra seats. The opera? *The Sound of Music*? Where was the theater? She could hear the crinkle of the candy wrapper as her mother untwisted it in the dark, but not know where they'd been, what they'd gone to see. And when she tried to conjure another marker, she saw, or thought she saw, a brightly painted leopard. Since then she'd been in so many theaters in New York and had never seen the stretched pounce of the leopard or even a large cat.

There was her father and mother with her at night on a Ferris wheel after a day at the beach. It was early, before her mother was sick, or maybe her mother was in the first stages of being sick. Sara was seated between the two of them. That much was certain because in the memory she was holding both their hands. The Ferris wheel stopped. They could see over the rollercoaster and the Tilt-A-Whirl to the beach. A bonfire and the dark shapes of people, some dancing, some sitting close to the fire. When Sara tightened her clasp on her parents' hands, her mother disentangled her fingers and said, "Let's let go and wave to the dancers. Come on." Her mother began waving and singing out, "Whoo whoo." Their chair tipped and rocked. There was a beachy night wind that pushed against them. Her father tightened his grip on Sara's other hand. Sara knew that he was afraid, more afraid even than Sara. Sara wanted to hold on but she squirmed her fingers out of his hold and joined her mother. "Whoo whoo," they sang, twirling their fingers in the air. Her mother leaned across Sara, the dark mass of her hair falling against Sara's face. "Darling," she said to Sara's father. "We're really safe up here."

"Where was that amusement park?" Sara asked her father years later. And in the silence before he answered, "Playland, up in Rye," she wondered if there had ever been such a night.

Sometimes she thought about what was lost. She couldn't remember a single time her mother had wakened her for school. Or breakfast, where had her mother sat at the breakfast table? But she could recall lipstick on a coffee cup. Sometimes the memories felt like a translation. How would she tell her own story to her child? Sapphic fragments pasted into photograph albums. A poem she's made from what remains.

SEPTEMBER 12

1:30 P.M.

Good afternoon, Mrs. Roosevelt,

In Paris I was a woman.

I wanted to walk through Paris as a young man, dapper in my double-breasted blue suit. But because I was now a dodger of the Belgian Army, because it was too dangerous, Mrs. Roosevelt, I wobbled in brown high heels down the Champs Elysées, disguised in women's clothes.

At first I tried on Maman's dress, which looked less on me like a dress than a tunic I might have worn in a school Latin performance.

"Maman, buy me a new dress." How quickly I sounded like a spoiled girl. "Try to make it something young, and maybe blue."

If I could not stroll as a young man, can you blame me for not wanting to look my best as a woman?

Maman argued that I must stay indoors and not risk attracting the attention of the police, who were arresting young men, repatriating them for service in their countries. But there was no real argument. We had much to do. We hoped to finish up our papers for a Mexican visa. We had a letter from our contact Ricardo in Mexico City. And we were trying to locate Manuel, Ricardo's cousin, who worked in the Mexican offices. We were to show Manuel the letters from Ricardo, which included the receipts for monies sent and Ricardo's promise that Manuel would secure our visas. Maman understood this was not an interaction that she could manage. She was visibly weaker, exhausted by organizing our provisions and visiting the Banque de Lyon, awaiting a word from Max. I would also go to the library to research alternate shipping routes. Gustav and Marie had stayed with us. Before he'd left, Max extended his offer to them, believing they'd protect Maman and me. He'd even suggested to them that I might secure Mexican papers for them from Ricardo's cousin.

"Try this," Gustav flung a dress through the air. It was Marie's dress. I must have shaken my head no because Marie said, "It's fine, Itzak." Blue and green silk, the dress had many tiny tucks stitched in violet that gathered at the waistband from where the silk flared into a full skirt. Marie zipped me into the dress and the sensation of the silk and the pressure of her hands at my back thrilled me. For once my ridiculous skinniness was an asset as I fastened the waist button of the matching fitted jacket. Marie's ankle-strap pumps fit my feet, which caused a bit of teasing of Marie, and even the lively suggestion that Marie should wear my suit while I wore her clothes. Then Maman handed me a pair of royal blue leather gloves with seed pearl buttons at the wrist.

"How's this?" I gave a twirl and felt the rush of air as the dress skirt lifted and settled. Gustav and Marie whistled, and even Maman laughed—a first since she'd left Belgium.

"Now walk." Gustav was suddenly full of vigor. "This is theater." His voice was instructive, professional. "Less shoulder in your gait. Less gait, more lift." Like a circus master he commanded me up and down the musty hallway of the Hotel Tulipe. If he'd had a ringmaster's crop, I think he'd have given me short lashes with the training. I was determined not to be embarrassed. I learned to his grudging satisfaction how to stand, to walk, to sit cross-legged as a woman.

"Now your face." Gustav pointed to a brocaded stool. He pulled at my cheeks. I flinched and he laughed. "Poor, poor girl, not accustomed to the hardships of beauty, I see." He licked a small brush and spit into a tub of black cake he held in his hand. He mixed the brush through the little tub, spitting and working the paint into a small frothy mix. I was determined not to give him the satisfaction of any more signs of squeamishness.

"Shut an eye," he said. I shut them both, waiting for him to press the brush to me. I could feel his breath thick against my face. "No, no," he said, "I won't get this right." And I felt him back away from me.

Someone leaned over me. I could feel that it wasn't Gustav.

"Please," she said and I felt her fingers press lightly against my eyes. "Open."

I opened to see Marie leaning back, head angled, scrutinizing my face. From her bag pots of color and brushes appeared and she began, as seriously as Gustav, to apply cream and powder to my face. I smelled on her wrists and arm the grassy perfume that I'd watched her dab against her skin. Then I caught a whiff of myself, which wearing Marie's dress was a sweet grassy scent. And when I adjusted my legs, my stockinged legs made the sound I'd heard her legs making in the front seat of the car. It was disconcerting. Though I'll admit, Mrs. Roosevelt, not entirely unpleasant.

"Keep them open," she said, when I closed my eyes. When I opened them she was right there, frowning, evaluating my face.

"Good eyes," she said, "easy to make them take a new shape." I was still determined not to be embarrassed, but I could not look at her directly and I shifted my gaze. "No, look at me," she said, and I turned to her and made myself count up to ten to hold her stare. She yanked my chin a little roughly, tilting my head, while her brush spread against my forehead and eyelids. She was playful and stroked the brush down my nose. "Now let's get to those good, full lips," she whispered, her breath warm against the chalky powder on my cheeks.

Like this, under Marie's hands, I felt myself become a woman. I became an alluring woman with a turban hat, dark sunglasses, and red painted lips, ready for the streets of Paris.

You can imagine my terrible surprise when I stood at the mirror and saw that I was hardly the elegant mademoiselle I felt myself becoming. Instead I appeared as someone's unfashionable mother.

How often, Mrs. Roosevelt, we are not what we inside feel ourselves to be.

But if I was not the dapper young man or even the fashionable woman I'd wished to be in Paris, Paris was not the Paris I'd ever dreamed of—small lit streets opening onto squares, cafés noisy day and night with the debate of serious young people, their books, musical instruments, sketchpads, everything a boisterous declaration of everything we wanted to offer a better world. In the Paris I'd planned to walk through, film stars wrapped in silk scarves might be sipping a cognac at Maxim's. I'd linger watching intellectuals huddled over manuscripts or any of the French Surrealist poets arguing with the Futurist poets. Instead it was foreigners. Foreigners choked the streets. People everywhere, sleeping and cooking in the streets, hanging their rough shirts from street posts, stringing blankets up around makeshift latrines. Crowds and police. My walks along the Seine were not the late afternoon strolls I'd imagined, holding hands with Odile or a Parisian replacement of Odile, stopping close to the Ile de la Cité to lift her creamy face like a cup in my hands.

In the Paris of this early May, the quays of the Seine were campgrounds, places where people stepped among the sleeping, looking for relatives or someone who had news of a relative. "Do you know?" "Have you word of?" was the steady refrain in German and Dutch and Russian and Polish. I heard Flemish and Italian and French and, of course, Yiddish.

If you saw Paris as a bird might, flying over to the sea, you might have thought it was a grand picnic, day after day of sunshine, the mixed-up smells of food cooking on the street, like a grand festival, a World's Fair gathered in the city, all the bright decorations of countries mingling. But from the ground you would see tired ribbons of people streaming into Paris, tattered, lost, looking over their shoulders for what we all knew was coming. It was hot. The cool spring was now an unseasonable swelter and everyone looked withered in too many clothes. Postings—polite and frantic—were everywhere. Tacked improbably on the stone wall of a quay, I read, "Cher Papa," in a child's first cursive, "Jacques and I are looking for you. We are being good. We take our nap here every afternoon."

To be fair, the gendarmes and soldiers were overwhelmed. There were huge placards posted about the city hung with destinations and routes out of the city. The tone was instructive, but it didn't take much to hear the undercurrent of panic in the officials' voices.

The gendarmes had been instructed to stop everyone and look at papers. This was obviously impossible, absurd, and so when someone was randomly stopped it was done with ferocious authority as if the officer had confirmed knowledge of false documents—as if it were not necessity that let most of the crowds pass the street unchecked, but trained intuition and efficiency. Young men in particular were likely to be stopped. We, all of us, no doubt, belonged to another countries' fighting forces. There were trucks every day taking men back to the Belgian Army.

But I was not a young man, was I? Instead, dressed as a woman, I went out into the throngs looking for some word from Henri or my father. I wished for the chance to rant and stumble, reciting verses by Baudelaire or Rimbaud. But, finally, my stumbling had only to do with trying to stay upright in Marie's high-heeled shoes.

Here, at this juncture, Mrs. Roosevelt, I shall not wear you out nor test your patience with the endless hours I spent on lines. The Paris lines were practice for later lines in Toulouse and Perpignan. Let it suffice to say I stood for hours, wobbling in the heels and itchy stockings. I was careful to talk as little as possible, certain my voice would betray me. And each day was another line. Another line, another crowd of people overdressed and pressed close together. We were refugees in Paris. It takes so little to turn anyone into a refugee. A winter coat and scarf over an arm in June, jackets worn too long in too much heat; it droops the body down. There were those who gave in, coat unbuttoned, hanging off a weary frame, hardly looking anymore like the doctors or businessmen they were just weeks ago in another city. Just the slightest indication of the old established life. Maybe a telltale gold watch, a woman's pearl-and-ruby brooch. Now they press forward, pushing to keep their place in line, hugging an oversized valise filled with family valuables. After waiting for hours we were directed to other lines or told offices had shut for the afternoon. The word on every line was that people were being routed to Bretagne on the Atlantic coast, where displaced-persons centers were already up and running. Transit visas, we heard, were routinely being denied.

"There's no Manuel working here." A clerk at the Mexican Consulate delivered this news to me. In his red ascot he appeared to find himself a most important fellow sitting behind his small desk, as if wearing a silk ascot was a kind of audacious and even brave behavior. He kept a hand at his throat, petting at the silk as though it was a child's security blanket.

"But I've been told to see Manuel," I pressed, convinced that he might buckle a bit under some pressure. My voice cracked as I tried to maintain some chance that I remotely sounded like a woman.

He knew Ricardo of the Mexico City offices, did he not? I had been promised. I had been promised, I kept repeating, wincing and saying it ever more breathlessly as though he were about soon to have a woman seizuring at his feet. He excused himself, adjusting his ascot and conferred with a woman positioned at a larger desk in the same room.

"Madame," he said, returning, his fingers still fiddling with the edge of the red silk, "Madame, there has never been a Manuel who. . . ."

I did not let him finish, raising the whine of my consternation. "But Monsieur, I have an official letter which promises that Manuel will oversee the completion of my papers." This was in fact true. Ricardo in one letter wrote that his cousin, Manuel, who worked at the Consulate would complete our family paperwork. What was not true was that Ricardo had a position, prominent or otherwise, in the Mexican offices.

"As I began to say," he said looking down at his desk, "we have only one Manuel in the offices, Madame, and I am certain that he is not the gentleman you are looking to help you."

"I should like to meet him."

"Very well," he laughed.

I was escorted up a wide staircase and brought down a hallway with several doors. At the end of the hallway was a low arch and on the other side an obese man sat on a chair. About him were a variety of buckets, a straw broom and a stick with a mop rag attached with ties to a wooden block. It was hard to imagine him ever wedging himself upright off the chair.

"Salut, Manuel," the clerk called out roughly, though with obviously smug pleasure. "Hey Manuel, this woman says she must see you."

I walked to the seated man, who seemed to keep growing wider as I neared the archway. He looked inflated. I was conscious of the clerk watching, overseeing this meeting, and I tried to take small womanly steps.

"Monsieur," I said drawing close to the huge man. The man made no effort to stand from his chair. He looked at me with a blank stare. I had, ridiculously, a moment of hope. Perhaps Ricardo had meant for this swollen man who looked as if he were hardly present at all to steal the papers. Perhaps the vacancy of his look was intentional.

"Monsieur," I said, bending close so the clerk could not hear us. "Ricardo, your cousin from Mexico City has told me you will be of some help." At first he did not seem to register that I had even spoken. I was convinced this was part of his gimmick, his act, to appear dull-witted. I adjusted my legs, crossing them at the ankles so that my stance would seem feminine. The man lifted his head—not seemingly a particularly easy task.

"I am from Oaxaca," he said, looking at me. His smile opened, a big chubby-faced smile. There was brightness now in his face. "It's a long time since I've been in Oaxaca."

He stared at me as if I might speak of his city or of his parents. I considered saying, just to make certain, "And Ricardo? You know your cousin, right?" But instead I leaned very close and said, "Manuel, it is a pleasure to meet a man who takes care to keep floors as well cleaned and polished as you do. Good-bye."

I left then, with a swish, quickly past the derisive clerk, my heels clicking down the long hall.

Outside I practically fell to the street but found a wall and backed against it. I was dizzy. Everything raced around me. We had counted on Ricardo. There had been more than two years' worth of letters, money sent, guarantees. Now there was nothing. We had nothing. We were like every other person pressed into Paris wearing too many clothes in May. What could I say to Maman when I returned that evening to the Hotel Tulipe? That we'd been taken? That my father had foolishly believed in some man called Ricardo, corresponding for two years, sending him money for Mexican papers? I would have to tell Maman that Max had secured nothing. Mexico was now as little of an option as any other place. We had nowhere to go.

I tried to gather myself and find my determination. The wall was cool against my back and I stood, letting everything rush past me. I should set off to the university, settling in the library among students, immediately addressing the task of tracing other possible shipping routes, thus beginning the process of securing other visas. I considered walking past the offices of each foreign consulate, seeing which consuls had the shortest line of refugees and making my choices based on possibility and chance rather than any planned knowledge.

But eventually I'd have to return to the hotel and tell Maman that her husband had foolishly sent away money. I knew if I told Maman that we had nothing, she'd insist that we turn back to Brussels. That even more she'd want the safety of our apartment, of the life she'd known.

I knew then I would lie.

I decided to tell Maman that the visa would take a bit longer than Ricardo had expected. Not to worry; things looked good. And to keep her spirits buoyant, I would tell her that Max had directly contacted Manuel, giving us word through him that he was delayed in Brussels only because the machinery was being transported and housed in Villevorde.

Perhaps I should have felt more caution about the ease of my lies. Perhaps I should have understood that when lies begin they gather their own momentum.

When I could finally summon the courage to move from the wall, I wandered—could it even be called wandering?—through Montparnasse, half-imagining that at the busy cafés I might be called to tables to share a bottle of wine with not only some of the intellectuals and artists we had spoken fervently about night after night in Brussels but also with my long-dead heroes of the Revolution. "Hey, Copain, I've arrived," I thought over and over. Sometimes, I fear, I spoke aloud. I know that in my head were Rabelais and Montaigne and Dumas. I practiced my arguments, how I might add importantly to the debate. I was fevered. My hands sweated inside my blue gloves. My feet were horribly pinched in Marie's shoes; I walked, mostly stumbling, the stubby heels catching in virtually every cobble.

Eventually I found myself on the edge of Montparnasse on the Boulevard Edgar-Quinet and I entered the cemetery.

I understand it will sound absurd to you, Mrs. Eleanor Roosevelt, that a boy such as I was, dressed as an ungainly and buckle-kneed woman, came to the grave of Baudelaire and recited a fragment from a poem, "Le Voyage," that my school friends and I admired.

Mais les vrais voyageurs sont ceux-là seuls qui partent
Pour partir: coeurs légers, semblables aux balloons
De leur fatalité jamais ils ne s'écartent,
Et, sans savoir pourquoi, disent toujours: Allons!

I wept. And then like any maudlin fool, I felt better and stronger, felt myself to be the sort of passionate and serious man— even in a flowered dress—I longed to be. I would not be deterred. I was young and in Paris. While I did not exactly fancy myself a poet, I was certain of my poet's soul, the unbounded freedom that was mine despite any momentary setback.

So imagine, Mrs. Roosevelt, that it was in this state, this high, undone state, that I first ignored then brusquely answered, "Why must I?" when a French soldier called out, "Madame, over here, please." It would have been better if I'd had no papers on me. But, in fact, in my hopes for a rendezvous with Ricardo's alleged cousin

Manuel, I had my *carte d'identité* inside my mother's pocketbook that hung unfashionably from my fisted hand. I attempted to re-capture myself and tried to look—poorly, poorly, entirely patheti-cally—like a most desirable woman as I angled over to the soldier. I tried to conjure up my best Hedy Lamarr. I could not look at him directly, so I cast my eyes down in something that at least approxi-mated a demure if dull-witted nature.

I cannot tell you what the soldier asked. I was that nervous. I can tell you that I kept my gaze from him, thinking if he looked di-rectly into my face he would not need to see my Belgian papers to know I was no Madame. He'd see the boy I was: Belgian, seventeen years of age, in flight from the Belgian Army. And a Jew. That too, he'd see. Even without seeing my face, I knew that very quickly it would occur to him that I was not what I seemed. I considered my possibilities. It didn't take long. There were none. I considered how I might approach the question of money. Perhaps hand francs along with my papers at the point—which was undeniably soon—that he insisted I hand over my papers.

"Is there a problem?" This I heard from behind me. The voice continued. "My wife? I'm sorry, officer. Is my wife okay?" Before I could turn to look, an arm clasped me about the waist.

"Dear, please," the voice, a man's, continued with barely re-strained anger. "How many times must I insist you not go out of the apartment without your medicine or your papers. It is hardly fair at a moment like this for our country's soldiers to have to attend to your ailments. Don't you see there are serious things going on in Paris?"

The voice, I realized, was Gustav's.

Gustav! How was it possible!

He held me very close to him and spoke quickly and as if he were an overwrought husband, tired, even a bit repulsed by his wife's antics.

"Officer, what might I do for you? Have you need to see identi-fication? We live close by and my wife often comes to the cemetery for a bit of quiet. She is—how might I put this? a delicate woman—not entirely well, and more often than I'd like to admit, a patient of-ficer like you delivers her back to our home. Today I was to take her, as I do each week, to the cinema on the street just on the other side of the cemetery, and clearly the anticipation has put my wife in an overexcited state. She's prone to seizures, but have I already said this? She adores the cinema. If you'd like I can run home and grab her papers. It would be no problem."

I kept my eyes down for fear that amazement might show on my face if I should glance up. How inconceivably lucky it was that Gus-tav had walked past right then. And how strange, given my distrust of Gustav, that it should be Gustav who saved me.

I tried to assume the role of Gustav's difficult and unstable wife. I could not resist a bit of heavy breathing, a bit of shoulder trem-bling, until his hand pinched at my waist. Gustav and the soldier had a few more exchanges, Gustav adeptly leading the young soldier into a conversation of increasing familiarity, a few off-color com-ments about the flood of foreigners. Then, soon enough, Gustav, never letting go of my waist, thanked the soldier for his compassion and guided me out of the cemetery.

"My sister has been trying to convince me that you are a bright individual and someone for me to consider more seriously," he hissed, leading me to the gate. "But clearly it is my sister's judgment that needs serious consideration."

His sister? When did Marie become his sister?

Though my heart should have been racing at the close call, at the sheer gift that soldiers were not leading me to a truck bound for the Belgian Army, I was honestly most undone by the possibility that Gustav was not fooling me, that they were indeed brother and sister.

And by the genuine prospect that I was about to see a film in Paris.

Mrs. Roosevelt, have you ever seen *The Adventures of Robin Hood*? That is where we went. I think it's a great film and not just because I saw it in Paris. More soon. There's much to say. But I have to check what's what on the upper deck.

Yours truly,
E. Flynn

She's out walking again. Today Sara angles down Broadway. Out of the question, the library. Benjamin's not a thinker you can approach feeling jangled. "I need resistance to touch his language," she explained over the phone to Helen. But that's not it. Maybe if she'd seen the young man and his alto recorder in the park she'd have been able to get to the library and focus. But she's not seen him in weeks. Mainly, weirdly, it's the New York Society Library's no-cell-phone policy. She's on-call? But she doesn't know for whom.

Sara stops to look at striking, neatly sprayed graffiti. She's noticed this graffiti showing up all around the city on brick walls, bus stops, the whitewashed sides of buildings. A stenciled outline of a man, clearly corporate, with a hat and briefcase and beneath him the bold question: *Who Are the Terrorists?* She's looking for a signature, a tag—the stencil is so precisely rendered, clearly an artist's work—but who would dare claim that now? It doesn't make her any less uneasy to think about all the reasons that people around the world might hate America. It doesn't make her feel protected that, mostly, she agrees with them.

Sara's at Broadway and 20th, almost at Union Square Park. The farmer's market is on today. Sara loves the stalls of vegetables. She could spend her day buying from each farm, tuberous yams, young garlic, fingerling potatoes. She loves to hold the damp mounds of crimson bunchy radishes, wild lettuces, and dark arugula. There are baskets of field strawberries and tiny wild strawberries. She loves the bushy-bearded Vermonters who haul down their maple syrup and pies, the organic farmers with tangy lettuce. She could wander from stall to stall for eggs and sausage, fresh fish and farm butter, a bunch of blue straw flowers. But that's ridiculous. Too much food for one person. What would she do with it? She could walk into the park, sit, read, just try to think. She might actually work better there, in the midst of the city's hubbub, another eccentric in the June park. She could try to think about the letter in which Benjamin quotes Hugo's judgment of Baudelaire: *"Vous avez créé un frisson nouveau."* Or else give over and simply watch people. Surely that's as close a connection to Benjamin and Baudelaire as the hushed library. To be Baudelaire's flaneur, to idle and watch the modern city. It's the city's array, the disarray, that pleases Sara—the Peruvian musicians, the Salvadoran women selling corn tamales and *pupusas*, the deep purple-black faces of Africans, a white man and a black man in a game of speed chess. She loves the range of skin color in this city. And language. In Union Square Park there will be the ones who have also just come for a look, tourists eager for their New York experience and the people who walk the paths over and over all day like a kind of insistent meditation. The shouters and speechmakers, they'll be there, a long tradition in Union Square Park. There's a young woman who's painted her face and hands blue and written the word *sorrow* in red across her forehead. There are the guitar players on the benches and in a sparse circle drummers and scarf dancers. There's every kind of prayer, silent and gospel, Tibetans chanting. A group of young people davening. Everyone who's come here from somewhere else, now here together. Everyone inventing a new life here still holding on to bits of their old world, a scarf, a poncho, a melody, or a story.

There, on a bench near the gated playground, she might have an easier time thinking about the word *frisson*—to leave it as *frisson* in the English translation? To consider instead: *thrill* or *shudder*?

It would do Sara good to relax on a shady bench with the weight of an open book in her lap.

But Sara sticks out her hand and hails a taxi.

"Hi," she says, shutting the taxi door. Sara regards the turbaned head. The driver is talking on his cell phone. The black phone cord dangles from the elaborate coil of white cloth. He's talking so impossibly fast it seems it couldn't be a real language he speaks. Bits of English poke up from the lilt of his chatter. Good, good, he says. His head bobbles and she watches his hand keep lifting from the steering wheel, his finger shaking to emphasize his point. She leans forward and gives the driver Rochelle Goldenman's address.

<hr />

"Forever, that's what my dad said," Rochelle says, "that it took forever, the roads were that clogged. Your father apparently kept jumping out of the car he was in and striding up and down the road until he'd find my dad and the two of them would share a smoke and wave at the French soldiers." Rochelle leans forward, pressing her hands against the coffee cup.

It's clear to Sara that Rochelle sees the road in her mind, that she's heard this story—and all the stories she's been telling Sara—so many times that by now it's her own painted memory, by now she feels she's been there on the congested roads between Brussels and France.

"Look at them in that picture, it's amazing." Rochelle lifts the picture Sara's shown her from the envelope of photographs. Yes, it's her father, Henri, with Itzak. Sara's been using her researcher skills, asking questions, little prompts to keep Rochelle talking.

"But what did your dad tell you?" Rochelle looks eager. "What about the chateau, he must have told you about that strange place? And your grandfather's crazy plans."

"No," Sara says. She was getting ready to make something up, draw from the generalized war imagery from films she's grown up on. Maybe tell a little story in the universal fleeing-on-the-road direction that Rochelle's stories have gone. Something about sleeping in a roadside field. But now she feels taken aback by the specificity of the question. "He didn't mention a chateau?" Rochelle's face shifts, not exactly a shutting down, but a reticence.

"Look, I'm sorry, really. It's totally insensitive of me," Rochelle says. "I have no business calling anything crazy. It had to be incredibly hard for your dad. At least that's what my father thought. That's why my father believed your dad almost never returned phone calls, even after your mom died, even then, after all those years, your father would make a plan with my dad and then usually not show up or he'd show up and barely stay ten minutes."

"What's hard for my father?" Sara asks. She's beyond caring that she's given up any pretense of knowing anything. Sara hasn't said anything and this woman already knows her mother's dead. She's almost beyond hearing her voice, the whiny bark, when she says, "Tell me what you know about my father."

"I don't know," says Rochelle. Her hands shift on her coffee cup.

"No, tell me."

"I guess I mean it was hard about your grandmother. Leaving her with my family. My dad always thought your dad blamed him or his parents when she refused the opportunity to leave the transit camp with them unless her husband came."

"What are you talking about? What transit camp?" Sara asks, but now it's less a question than some kind of challenge. "She came with my dad." Okay, so she, Sara, doesn't know what this woman knows about roads and chateaus, about all sorts of jokes their fathers supposedly shared as boys. But Sara knows her grandmother came to Brooklyn with her father. That's where Sahra, her grandmother, died, not too long after she'd arrived at the house of her second cousin. He may not have told her much, but he'd told her that. "She died from the war," her father had said, as if the war itself was a kind of illness they hadn't yet eradicated with a vaccine. Camps had nothing to do with her father's mother. Maybe Rochelle had heard something about her mother's parents.

"No, she was with my family," Rochelle says softly. "Sahra wasn't on the *Quanza*."

"The *Quanza*?" Sara can't figure out what Rochelle's saying. Is she trying to make a joke or is it an expression, and even then, what does the holiday have to do with anything? But Sara can see from Rochelle's surprised expression that Sara's made a mistake by asking.

"Look, my grandmother was in Brooklyn with my dad. She came here with my father on a boat."

"Oh, then I must have that wrong," Rochelle says, lifting her coffee cup, covering her mouth. "Really, forgive me. I'm so sorry."

Sara's at the library. But not for Benjamin.

She Googles. Quanza. Most of the entries are about the holiday. Quanza, celebrate with music. Festival of light. But also: *Quanza*, Portuguese steamship. And Lieberman. Joshua and Marty Lieberman lecturing at the Maritime Museum in Norfolk, Virginia, on the Quanza Situation. She's surprised. As if she hasn't honestly expected to find anything. Until a few hours ago Sara didn't know the name of the boat. Now there's a steamship named the *Quanza*. And a *Quanza Situation*. She hates that Rochelle knew the name of her father's ship. She reads through what she can pull up on the search engine. Already threads of a story. Plight of eighty-six denied entry. There's even a Quanza listing on the FDRheritage.org site. It seems the ship became a kind of battleground over refugee policy.

Sara looks to see if there's a passenger record for the *Quanza*. She can't find any listing but pulls up the ship's specifics. Type: cargo and passenger; tons: 6,473; built: 1929; scrapped: 1968. On another site there are photographs of the ship docked in Hampton Roads, Virginia. One of a large ship moored beside a two-story-tall coal pier. In another photograph men and women crowd at a ship railing. Some lean over. Some wave. In the line Sara sees a young man in a suit that could be her father. Next to him an older, small woman. His mother? Carmen said Sara had her grandmother's eyes. But even if the picture was sharper, the woman's hat wrecks any chance that Sara could identify her eyes.

She scrolls through the *New York Times* microfiche, looking for something. For more. More proof to walk the two blocks over and show her father. See. Now tell me. The papers are full every day of stories of boatloads coming from Europe. Child refugees. She misses it the first time. The *New York Times*, August 21, page 5. The headline reads *6 Drivers, Seized by Germans, Here.* The article states: "The *Quanza*, a small Portuguese liner that was taken out of her usual voyage to evacuate war refugees from Europe, arrived here yesterday on her first visit to this port with another of the unique list of passengers that the war has made almost commonplace." Sara goes on to read the *unique list,* which included the captured ambulance drivers, Dutch and Negro seamen whose ship had been torpedoed, members of the Rothschild family, a Czechoslovakian figure skater, and the French film actor Marcel Dalio. Some of the passengers were denied entry. The *Times* article mentions "lowly refugees from virtually all the countries Hitler has conquered." Of course she remembers her father mentioning Marcel Dalio. Now it seems Dalio was on his ship. Nothing makes sense. Her father certainly wasn't one of the notable passengers, but was he a lowly refugee? Her father, a refugee? Did her father get off the ship in New York? Were her grandmother and her father part of the *Quanza* Situation?

Sara goes down to the computer where she can get to her e-mail, writes the Maritime Museum in Virginia. Tries to sound like she knows something. A professor's research. An inquiry. The curator mails back immediately. The Liebermans live in New York. He gives a phone number. There's a quick flurry of e-mail; she asks the curator if she might actually make a phone appointment with him. He replies with the subject heading "I'm leaving now." The gist of the message: "Definitely. Please call. I'm around tomorrow afternoon."

SEPTEMBER 12

3:15 P.M.

Dear Mrs. Roosevelt,

Maybe Gustav's more than a little right about my lack of brains. Not once, even in all this talk of Paris, have I confirmed what must be uneasily obvious by now. There was no rendezvous with the Goldenmans. We never found them in Paris. And despite a decision to lie to Maman about Manuel, there was no actual word from Max. Every day, Maman dutifully inquired at the Banque de Lyon for a telegram and returned empty-handed. Every day she seemed more frail.

Maybe Gustav's right and they're also right on the ship when they clap me on the back, saying, "Itzak the dreamer, we'll be back in Lisbon and you'll still be hunched over your typewriter making up your poesie."

If I were more urgent and focused in my efforts, there should be no more dreamy Paris! No reciting Baudelaire at his grave. It would be better to describe the somber mood here at the railway coal pier where, despite the cold rain, we eighty-six walk the deck, restless, restless, relentless; even the waterlogged Jules Wolff has gotten up from the deck chaise where he crumpled after he was escorted back to the boat. Everyone gathers at the ship's rail, calling out to reporters. The charming Madeleine LeBeau sings out in French, "Help me, help me, help me!" and I am surprised the photographers don't junk their cameras and dive off the docks to rescue her. I should be single-minded. I should describe the crowds that, despite this gloomy rain, have begun to gather and rally on the pier. There are relatives on the lower pier: the husband of Dora Mornier stands at the edge of the planks and throws sacks of food to his wife and daughters, but one by one they fall in the water. I should describe Dora and her daughters Rosa and Lile and the funny pet names their father shouts as encouragement to them. Committees meet in the morning and then again in the afternoon to carry out ever-shifting agendas. Someone always has a new idea! It is this urgency with which I should press my fingers to the keys.

And yet, Mrs. Roosevelt, I can't help it. I am only impatient to take you back to the Hotel Tulipe, where at night I tossed my women's stockings over a chair, washed the makeup off my face, and fell into bed to sleep the unquiet dreams of a young man.

But, better yet, let me draw you into the movie theater where I sit enraptured by Robin Hood's antics. Gustav slumped in the dark next to me, saying, "Stupid kid, now we have to sit though this stupidity." But he was wrong about Errol Flynn in *Robin Hood,* don't you think? Flynn flipping and lunging into his duels, Flynn in the deep green forest convening his band. Just seeing de Havilland and Flynn, in color; I'd never seen them together.

Perhaps I am always considering the wrong thing. For instance, why didn't I question the coincidence of Gustav's rescue, his in-the-nick-of-time arrival at the cemetery? Or give much of a sober, shivering thought to the Belgian Army truck that might have been bumping me toward the motherland. I didn't even think to wonder what original plan they'd had when suddenly Marie slipped into our row and sat down in the seat next to me. She leaned across me, her shoulder knocking against my chest, and said—not privately in Walloon but in French—to Gustav, "What's he doing here? Why's he here with us?" Marie's appearance in the theater didn't even seem strange. Instead all that occurred to me was that it was different to look at her profile in the dark and consider that she was Gustav's sister. Not Gustav's wife.

On the screen Robin raised an arrow at Gisbourne, asking, "Are there no exceptions?"

"He's here now. That's it," Gustav said sharply. Marie brushed back across me, settling into her seat, her head tipping up to the screen. When Robin and his men galloped off, Marie tilted close to me, her chin resting on the silk arm of my dress. Her hand found my hand and gave it a squeeze.

"Well my good woman, how lovely to watch a movie with you this afternoon," she said, not letting go of my hand.

The three of us watched the picture in silence. She never took her hand away. I let my fingers slip between hers. Our fingers fit and refit around one another. Her fingers stroked up and down my hand. Like this we watched the film.

Maybe I should not admit this, but I was, that afternoon in Paris, very, very happy. And maybe this story is just a cheerful distraction as we linger at the coal pier, but I have learned that if there is something cheerful it is worth attending to it carefully. No doubt the difficulties that inevitably follow will demand our attention. I hope you understand.

In any case, please find me at Sewalls Point. We're not leaving yet!

I remain loyally yours truly,
Isaac of the Merry Men

P.S. I forgot to mention that when I went to the mid-deck this morning I found a newspaper. Not a whole paper. Just four pages. Folded neatly. We haven't seen any newspapers in weeks. And there—on a deck chair—four full pages from the *New York Times*. August 21. From the landing in New York City. It felt like a prize! I've been reading it carefully, savoring every word as I would a new *Movie World* Magazine. And Mrs. Roosevelt, I hope you don't mind, but I've got questions. I've got so many questions. What's Gimbels? Do you know Gimbels on 33rd and Broadway? It looks very fancy. So many advertisements for gloves and other accessories. I've even found a few really interesting things you've said in one article. Many new English words for me to learn. And there's the World's Fair schedule! I forgot it's in New York right now. It was in my city, Brussels, last. Have you been to the World's Fair? What did you see? There's so much to learn in just four pages. More later. I'll have questions, I'm sure.

"To what do I owe this pleasure, my lovely one?" Her father beams from behind the newspaper. He's dapper today, not worn out, not an old man in his old robe, he's up, well dressed, even sporting a red-and-blue-striped tie and matching handkerchief in his sports-coat pocket. "Don't get me wrong; I'm thrilled you're here, but I'm becoming afraid that you're using me as a way to avoid this project of yours, Sara. Are you running away from the library again?"

Sara laughs at her father's astute observation. It's always been hard to put anything past the guy; he's always read her. It's an old joke—*Running away again?*—the shorthand they have for the fury that erupted in Sara during high school. She wouldn't so much storm about the apartment as take to blitz-cleaning the kitchen, the pantry emptied, new shelf-lining cut for all the dish cabinets. Her father knew better than to say a word for the first manic scouring hour. Then he'd come in, hold out a knapsack and a jacket, and say, gently, "Running away again?" And even if Sara at first resisted, angrily gesturing at the open boxes of pasta, the mishmash of dishes, scowling, "Someone's got to deal with all of this mess," soon she'd be fessing up, telling him what had happened to turn her heart all topsy-turvy.

Yes, he knows her, knows how to read her. Better now, Sara realizes, than she ever read him.

"So have you come to fetch your old man for lunch?"

"No, actually, not lunch today; it's about my project, Dad."

Her father's face falls and Sara feels her stomach rise a bit, the automatic clenching against bringing her father any pain.

"I thought you could help me."

"How's that?" he asks, looking back at the newspaper.

"Some German. I think I'm missing some of the meanings that might be more time-period related. There are some things that he refers to that I thought might make more sense to you."

She hadn't really planned this approach. On the walk over she'd imagined coming in and pushing close to her father, saying, *Tell me about the* Quanza. Direct and forceful, she'd be unyielding and she'd imagined that after she withstood his hesitations, he'd yield and the story of the ship would naturally unfold.

Then she tries to say it. "Tell me about the *Quanza*, the ship you came here on. What is the *Quanza* Situation?" But she physically can't. Like her mouth is stiff. Like forcing words will actually break something. Like if she closed her eyes to push out the words she'd un-squinch her eyes and her father would be gone.

Instead she's saying, "How about we stroll down for a lunch and see if we can have some fun together looking at the text I'm currently trying to translate?"

"It's not really very good anymore, my German. Yours is better by now. I'm certain of that. You're the professor, dearest, not me. You better get back to your work," he says, grabbing up the business section. Already even the lightest push has made him pull back, grouchy.

"Now who's running away?" It's a gamble, this frontal push, one that provokes Sara more than her father. But she knows she's got to get past the usual retreat to cozy silence. For her own sake. If she wants to know she's going to have to make him speak. He's yanked the paper up so that Sara can't see his eyes.

"Dad," she says. Her voice gone all daughter-soft and beckoning. She can't bear the possibility of loss. "If one of us has to run away, take me out for a fancy lunch first so I can be seen one last time strolling with my debonair father."

⸺

Her father loved the city. He'd given Sara the city. Over the years they'd walked their way through every neighborhood, tasted pumpkin curry in an Afghan restaurant in the west 40s, bought oils down on Mott.

"This is how your mother and I fell in love," he said to Sara as they walked the narrow streets of the West Village looking for a restaurant he'd read about that served bouillabaisse.

"I know, Dad." This is the one story her father had told her countless times.

"Friends introduced us. We walked the length of New York that first day. Everything was something to look at. The carvings on the cornices of buildings, the displays of fabric bolts. Simone saw everything. She delighted in everything. We ended the date—it wasn't even really an official date—at a movie house. I knew then I had to marry her. I think Simone loved old movies even more than I did. I was older than she was so I had to be patient when it took her a little while longer of walking city streets to figure out that we were meant for a life together."

⁂

Marty Lieberman picks up the phone as Sara's leaving a message.

"I apologize; I've just come home. Really rather nasty these phone machines." She hears the southern lilt in his voice. Now Sara's not sure what she's actually called to ask.

"I'm a professor, my name is Sara," she announces awkwardly. She wants to avoid her last name so that he can't make the connection. "I'm interested in a boat called the *Quanza*, the *Quanza* Situation. I think you know something about it."

"Lovely," Lieberman says, "I'm always happy to talk to professors, especially those who take an interest in the *Quanza*. I know a bit about the ship. Our family feels keeping the story alive is essential. Not just for the family, for American history, really. Our uncle, you must know, was the lawyer who kept the ship in port. With a libel suit. A rather hefty suit of 100,000 dollars for which the court set a bond of 5,000 dollars. My uncle was gambling that it would be more of a tangle than a writ of habeas corpus, though there were a couple of other lawyers for families trying the habeas corpus route. He was right on the gamble. The captain and the on-board travel agent needed authorization from Lisbon to pay out a sum such as that. Five thousand dollars. Rather a lot in those years. Maybe you already know all of this, Miss Sara. Quite a story. I always thought it would make a quite good movie. All of the intrigue and political maneuvering that went on in Washington. Very American. But you're writing a scholarly piece? A book, perhaps?"

"I don't think so." Sara hears the question in her voice. She adjusts her tone. "Just research at this moment. But in any case, Mr. Lieberman, if you have the moment and the inclination, I'd be quite interested in your full account of your uncle and the ship."

"Oh it's not just my account. There's been a real but successful effort to keep those who were on the ship together. Quite an active group. Reunions, panel discussions, whatnot. At least among those that are left, a dwindling number as I'm sure you can imagine."

"Yes, I'd like to hear from anyone," Sara says. *Active group. Those that are left.* Both notions sting equally and entirely differently.

"Well lucky for you, Professor, this is a group of real talkers."

SEPTEMBER 12
5:15 P.M.

Dear Mrs. Roosevelt,

Who doesn't know that there are stories best left tucked away in the heart?

I hope you will see that it is not bravado but necessity that requires this unfolding. And if what I tell you next seems too bawdy a tale to tell a president's wife, then forgive this young man's indiscretion.

After the afternoon in the movies, all I wanted were Marie's hands. In my hands, on my face, pressed against my lips. Sitting in the library before shipping maps, I couldn't concentrate on the rough shape of coastlines, the linking ports and routes of escape. Instead I wanted to trace the web of skin at the base of her fingers, the bones of her long fingers fitted against mine. I had scarce attention for news bulletins of the Germans' approach, for their impending invasion. While I accompanied my mother as she sought messages from the Goldenmans or Max, I let my hands slip and linger along the dress that I wore, imagining that it was not my own leg that I touched beneath the fabric but Marie's. Everything felt heightened.

She was my Paris. Her presence to me was as if she had stepped out of a film, a starlet that sat down next to me and held my hands in the movie theater.

But there was no sign from Marie that her hands were anything I might ever feel again. She was cold. She hardly spoke with me the rest of that night or for the next few days. The four of us had moved into one room in the Hotel Tulipe to save money. She and Gustav seemed particularly enclosed, their Walloon whispered and cut short if I so much as looked at them. Or they were gone from the room all day, returning at odd hours, staying briefly, leaving without goodbye. Perhaps I should have been suspicious. What were they hoping for? I had no idea how long they intended to stay with us. But when I tried to wait up for them it was so that I might see her outline in the dark when they returned. Nights were an agony, waiting for Marie and then falling at last into a restless sleep.

Then in my dream her hands were on my face. "Itzak," she said, her hands moving against my jaw. "Wake. Wake up. We have heard from your father," she said, now pushing at my shoulders until I was propped awake and in the dark saw that it was truly Marie—not in any dream—leaning over me.

"Come," she whispered.

"My father?" I said. "Where?"

"Shh, not here." She turned and slipped out the door.

I tried not to show confusion. Maman was asleep in her bed, her breath shallow and raspy. I grabbed my pants and shirt and followed Marie into the hallway. She led me out of the hotel, ignoring my barrage of *Where is he? Where are we going? Where is Gustav?* And then I stopped asking questions and just kept a matched pace with her directed walk.

I had not once been out at night in Paris, fearing the greater risk of being picked up by patrolling gendarmes. The streets were busy, full of movement. Marie had taken hold of my arm, clasping my other hand in hers; we were like skaters on a night lake. I was not in my pitiful woman's costume. I was a man. A man on the streets of Paris walking with a beautiful dark woman in his arms. I felt a delicious and reckless ease that I didn't even try to caution myself against. We walked arm in arm in a delightful silence. We marked the appearance of soldiers by Marie slipping ever more tightly to my side until we walked with our hips fitted against each other as if they shared a socket.

We entered a bar. I expected to find Gustav there waiting for us and perhaps Max with him. Neither was in evidence. Marie led me to a table and signaled to a waiter, who brought us drinks. When I asked about my father, Marie gave me a sharp glance.

"Itzak, can't we have any fun first?" She punctuated the question with a flare of her nostrils. "Please," she said quietly.

I was dizzy. It is as simple as that. I drank a cognac and then another. We had an excited conversation, telling each other stories from our lives, though they seemed like innuendos more than anything historical. Marie was by turns sharp, even brutal, in her observations and then so delicate I felt myself about to cry. Even my own stories seemed different as I told them to Marie, as if I'd had a more serious life than the one I'd thought I'd had. It was like nothing I had tasted with the girls from Brussels or even Charlotte from my father's factory, who had kindly shown me something of a woman's attentive tenderness.

Sometimes we fell into loose silence watching a parade of characters who moved through the bar. There were doctors and dancers, a Chinese woman who sang an Italian aria. Two impossibly bony women in red sheaths danced together snake-like, their bodies still pressed together after the song ended.

People passed our table and Marie introduced me, all the while holding my hand. I loved the way she said my name but loved it better when she introduced me as her lover, sometimes her young lover, and even once as her Jew lover. Even that—"my Jew lover"— felt wonderful.

"Watch." Marie pointed while a man popped out a glass eye and swallowed it down with red wine. "It's in his pocket." Soon enough he pulled a sealed envelope from his pocket and opened it to reveal the glass eye. She laughed at what must have been the amazement on my face.

"Oh, my silly love," she said, kissing me. "People are always watching the wrong thing. That's the first lesson you learn in the circus or in magic."

My love. My love. That's what she said. Then she said it again, my love, and kissed me, holding my face in her long hands.

Mrs. Roosevelt, have you sometime had the feeling that you've arrived somewhere larger and lovelier and stranger than you'd expected to find yourself, and yet the place feels utterly familiar and recognizable?

We kissed. We danced. Marie undid her chignon and slipped the long porcelain hairpins into my pants pocket. I loved the familiarity of her gesture. Excuse me if you find this horribly indiscreet, but we did not return to the Hotel Tulipe. Marie brought me up a back staircase to a room she opened with a painted blue key. Then we made love. And the next time, when we made love again, I had the chance to be impressed with Marie's circus strength and agility.

But all night it was her difficult and beautiful face close to mine, the strands of her black hair fragrant on my cheek, the pillow of her full lips against mine that amazed me.

"So is this like your schoolgirls, Itzak?" she teased.

"You are my first, Marie. This is my first full night with a woman." I did not hesitate from this admission, thinking I'd seem too boyish. I wanted to be led. I wanted her to show me the intricacies and particular discoveries of this night.

"First!" she laughed. "Silly boy, no matter who comes next, I'll be your only woman." Already this seemed true, some way in which Marie erased not only what caresses and kisses there had been before, even Charlotte and the jam cakes she served me in her small room, but also, Marie erased whatever might occur later in my life.

"Encore," she said, sweeping herself in a single gesture above me. "Lovemaking, my love, is like any great art, there is natural talent but there is also skill and craft learned from diligent practice."

Finally we crashed into sleep, tucked in each other's arms. But I barely slept an hour. "What have you heard about my father?" I asked, waking Marie.

"Oh, you're done with me now?" she said, combing my hair with her fingers.

"No more teasing, Marie. Please tell me," I said, kissing her. She turned slightly from my mouth.

"Always you are talking about your father. Go now then. Gustav is bringing him to the hotel this morning," she said. I went to kiss her again, to protest her claim about my interest in Max over her, but this time she turned entirely from my kiss and wouldn't answer when I asked what was wrong. What had I done wrong? I pleaded with her. She answered none of my questions, responding only by saying, "You better go. Your mother will be worried."

When I tried a last time to touch her, she looked at me coldly and said, "I'm through with this, Itzak. What can't you understand?"

Perhaps, Mrs. Roosevelt, you have understood all along what this story will come to. No doubt you have seen your sons as young boys careening on bicycles, the tires wobbly and worn thin, a steep hill approaching and the boys gaining speed. You've known that even if you shouted they would not stop. Perhaps you've wanted to stop me and tell me to take a breath before I open the door at the Hotel Tulipe and find Gustav and Marie's bags gone and gone, too, whatever money Gustav found when he went through our bags while Maman slept and I was in Marie's confident hands.

Of course, Max, my father, was not there.

Maman was still asleep.

My silly love, I heard Marie say.

But she had also said, *We are always watching the wrong thing.*

The room was in disarray, clothes turned inside out, Maman's linens shaken open and left in heaps. This typewriter was left with its ribbon unwound. I cleaned up the room. Our things were mostly reorganized and folded when Maman woke, and I told her that we had been robbed in the night. She would not believe that Gustav was responsible. I showed her that every sign of Marie and Gustav was gone from the room, even the silk dress I had worn as my disguise.

"But we have been traveling with them for weeks now," Maman said.

"Don't be so ridiculous," I snapped at her. "You think they had any feeling for us?" Maman started to cry. But I was not budging. It did not matter that I was, most of all, enraged with myself, my weakness, the way, even as I cleaned the room, I kept returning to the light grassy smell of Marie on my hands. We had been idiots. There was no room left for any softness. Even my father seemed a little suspicious to me, the way he'd left us to protect his machinery. He'd made a choice, I thought. I'll make choices, too. I was to care for Maman. There were only the two of us left. I resolved to trust no one.

Things might have been worse. Maman had slept wearing her money belt, as Max had insisted she must each night. Our identity papers were safely folded inside, as was a considerable portion of our money. Maman had also sewn a money pocket into the pillow that she slept with each night. Nevertheless, we had lost half of the money that we'd hoped would make our passage possible. The silver cup and candlesticks were gone. A gold brooch. The blue leather gloves I'd worn as a woman. Perhaps, like me, you'd still wait for a day or two, return to the library, go to the train station, all the time holding out the hope that Marie would walk back into our room at the Hotel Tulipe. I imagined the difficult story she might confess that drove her to use our lovemaking as a ruse for the theft. I imagined the ways Gustav had forced her to betray me. Then she'd be back in my arms asking for forgiveness. Finally I imagined that at least she'd been telling the truth about my father and that Max might actually appear at the hotel.

There's a French expression, *Quoi faire?* What to do? Stay in Paris? There was no more staying in Paris. No more waiting for Max in Paris. No Marie and her grassy perfume as she made my face up with her powders and lipsticks. No more distractions. I wore my own clothes again. What to do? *Quoi faire?* It was time to get

Maman out of Paris while there was a chance that we could get out of Paris. There was a night train to Toulouse. But we were not allowed permits for the train. The French officials were directing all foreigners to the coast. They would stamp us for Bretagne. I asked a simple question: Where can you go from a coast? My answer was equally simple: Into the water for a swim. Getting on the train without stamped papers was certainly a gamble, but wasn't it a better gamble than getting on the correct train for Bretagne? No more listening to what others told me to believe. Trust no one. I had learned.

I told Maman that once again, through Manuel, we had received word from Max.

"Why not through the Banque de Lyon, as Papa told us he would?"

"Maman, who knows?" I was impatient with her. "I'm sure Max has a reason. A good one. But, listen, he says we're to go south, to leave Paris, to the south of France."

"But where is Max?" Maman asked.

"Manuel wasn't exactly certain." I kept my face neutral. "But he does know that Max is going south. We're to try Toulouse. Then go on to the border." I didn't stop until I convinced my mother that we should hurry so that Max might find us in Toulouse.

It wasn't until I finally quit our room at the Hotel Tulipe, leaving Paris for Toulouse wearing my double-breasted blue suit, that I understood that no one was left to be trusted. Least of all myself.

Yours truly,
Isaac

Dear Eleanor Roosevelt,

Here's the fool that I am: even now, stuck on this ship, I want to believe that something in Marie's affections was true. That it was Gustav who was the liar and the thief. That he forced Marie to betray her heart. Maybe we are all the fools of our hearts, that it leads us back over and over the same losses when there's a life right in front of us that warrants our attention. Surely my time would be better spent telling you how bad things actually looked all day right here on the ship. But I just don't have the oomph for it. Instead I went and reread the few pages of newspaper I'd found, hoping it would lift my spirits. But I felt only more hopeless. Finally I went over to the first-class dining room to have a visit with your photograph, thinking that seeing you might just help.

Mrs. R., each time I look at you in this newspaper photo there's so much that I see I've overlooked. Your face—how have I not noticed this before?—it is not only serious and determined but also, if I can say this, a little lonesome and worried.

It made me wish I could do something for you.

I wish I had a good joke to tell.

But without a joke, maybe I could offer another pair of gloves? How's red? Always cheery and always stylish.

Maybe in this photo you are thinking about your sons. Maybe you're worried about them. It said in an article in the *New York Times* that the First Lady believes that there are no exceptions when it comes to a wartime draft. Even married men. You say in the article you'd expect your four sons to serve. I bet you think I'm a bum, running off and not fighting for my country. Listen, a Jew in the Belgian Army. It's no joke. Maybe it is less of a joke than, say, a Jew in the Polish Army, but neither is any great laugh.

But that sad look on your face. And now I come to you with all my troubles. Let me know if I can be of any help to you, Mrs. Roosevelt. It would be my pleasure.

Yours truly,
Isaac

P.S. John, Franklin, Elliot, and James—those are real good names you thought of for your boys. I just know you are a wonderful mother. Maybe I should choose a simple American name such as Tom (from Mr. Twain's book) or Richard.

P.P.S. Gimbels? Is it related to the word *gamble*?

SARA SPENDS HER morning thinking about the word *recognize*—how intimate a word it actually intends itself to be. It makes her sad, which Sara knows is wholly unoriginal. Benjamin cites Flaubert in a letter of 1859, *Few people would guess how necessary it was to become sad to undertake the resuscitation of Carthage.* A clunky translation. But still it does her in.

⸙

"What can I do for you? Maybe I will cut your hair too? Please." He's standing with his back to Sara, but she can see his face, smiling and intent in the salon mirror. "I'm Mark," he says with a slight, almost formal, bow.

Mark and Tim, it's a brother-owned salon, a station for each of them on both sides of the room and a tiny Spanish woman on a wooden step washing hair in a high corner sink. The brothers are both dark, handsome—Turkish? Tunisian? "Lebanese," answers Mark, the darker, taller brother, while the woman ties a plastic smock on Helen's youngest daughter, Sophie. It's one of the many shops on upper Broadway that reflects waves of city immigrants. Chin's Chinese Laundry. Carlo's Shoe Repair. Mrs. Kim's Bright Morning Grocers. Faraz Kebab.

"No, I'm only here this afternoon as her moral support," Sara says, riffling through a *People* magazine on the upholstered bench that divides the room. Earlier Sophie, Helen's four-year-old, announced, "I'll only go with Sara. I want Sara to be my pretend mommy," and leapt into Sara's lap. Sara watched something like hurt register across her best friend's face. Sara leaned away from Sophie's flurry of kisses, "Okay, I'm done in, I'm smitten, but this is your call." Helen, a little too quickly, said, "No, by all means, take her; it'll give me the chance to actually get something done in this house." All the way to the salon, Sophie was a babble of love for Sara, creating a secret Sophie-Sara language and insisting she hold both of Sara's hands like the two of them were figure skaters on the long river blocks of Broadway.

Now Sophie starts to whimper, her delight already unraveling, claiming soap's in her eyes though Sara sees the woman has only gotten as far as spraying Sophie's hair with water.

"Honey, you need me?" Sara says, but Mark's already at Sophie's side with a folded towel. "Not to worry, princess," he says, showing Sophie how to place it protectively over her eyes. Sara turns the page of her *People* magazine, actresses now poolside, or in cafés, or pointing their toes on chaises on the beach at the Cannes film festival.

When Sara looks back up he's moved Sophie to the salon chair in front of Sara. "She has beautiful hair, your daughter," Mark says, his steady eyes on her in the mirror. "What shall we do, today?"

"Just a trim," Sara says, pleased with the assumption that Sophie's her daughter. She watches Mark begin working the scissors, fanning new layers of hair, his body leaning into the practiced, assured rhythm of his hands. It's mesmerizing, his steady precision. He lifts and measures sections of wet hair. Sophie can't quit her squirming, her restless body shifting under the black smock, but the haircutter seems oblivious, turning her chin to angle the shears against her bangs.

"It's fine, Sophie. When we're done there's ice cream for the walk home," Sara says, trying to settle Sophie so that she doesn't get nicked by the shears. Immediately it's obvious the assurance was a tactical mistake. Maybe it's the mention of home or by now it has dawned on Sophie that a pretend mommy isn't as nearly comforting as a real mommy, but Sophie escalates her whimpering to full-out crying; she's obviously admiring her own distress in the mirror.

"No crying, honey," Mark says, bending close to Sophie. "I want to make you the most beautiful princess. Like your mother, who, I hope I have permission to say, is the most beautiful mother I've seen." It's so fast, the turn, his dark eyes fixed on Sara's. She feels herself flush, ridiculous, like a schoolgirl; she doesn't know what to say or where to look. The salon mirrors are ceiling to floor and suddenly there's way too much of Sara in the mirror, almost naked in her summer dress with straps that tie in string bows at her shoulders. Even her sandals are only thin crossed pieces of leather the color of her skin.

"I'm not looking to embarrass you, believe me," he says. "I just want the chance that you'll come back. Maybe for a cut or a color without your daughter." He moves and Sara sees her bare leg slightly obscene behind his pant leg in the mirror—the two of them already touching, if only in the mirror. Sara looks away to the shelves lined with firming gels, mousses, and pomades. There are photographs tucked into the mirror frame over his station. Children—how many? Two girls, or the same girl twice? A boy in a soccer uniform. There's a family picture, four of them grouped in holiday clothes, the haircutter's arm around his pretty wife's shoulder.

"No, not mine. She's my friend's daughter," Sara says, though this explanation is not at all in the league of things she wants to say. Sara should feel annoyed, she knows; the way he's flirting is out of line. But the truth is someone else's desire always takes Sara aback, as if the very presence of need is something suddenly commanding, an obligation Sara must consider.

"Well a woman such as you should be given a child," he says, and flips on the blow dryer. It's a huge relief, the noisy whoosh of heat. No chance for any more talk. Sophie seems to have settled into herself as a princess, striking poses as Mark smooths and curls her hair with a round brush.

Sara imagines how this insane story will sound to Helen when she brings Sophie home; the way Helen will say in her taut Helen tone, "What's the big surprise? He found you like a wolf smells out the wounded deer."

⁃⁘⁃

"This baby thing isn't something you're doing at gunpoint. If you're so freaked out about a baby black market, don't do it," Helen says, working her long knife, pushing diced peeled carrots and zucchini into a pile and starting in on a red pepper.

"Helen, that's not fair. You know I've wanted a baby since we were in fourth grade."

"Yeah, I remember," Helen starts to say, but all three of her children bang into the kitchen and there's a ricochet of complaint, accusation, complaint, and need, need, need while the six hands grab up all the vegetables.

"Out! Out! Out!" Helen wields her knife, gesticulating wildly, pretending she's ready for battle. "Take it to Dad, kids. Hey Frank, are you anywhere? Aren't you on parent patrol?" Helen shouts. "Hannah, please take your brother and sister out of here if anyone ever expects to eat tonight."

"Then this counts for babysitting," Hannah says, seizing her opportunity to punch in on the time clock.

"Help Toby glue cottonball clouds in his diorama and maybe you'll be on the payroll. But really, don't you think you should ever just help because you're part of a loving family?"

Hannah's intake of breath is sharp, scathing, a *whatever* of annoyance. Her whole fifteen-year-old body a shudder of dismissive postures. "Sara, will you do something about Mom? Like a muzzle? Isn't she driving you crazy with her our-life-is-so-blessed crap today?" Then she's out of the kitchen, Toby and Sophie trailing as if riding the wake of Hannah's self-proclaimed power.

Sara watches Helen chewing her lip, dicing more carrots for the stir-fry. She comes over and stands next to her, her hand smoothing through Helen's ponytail. Helen's hair slips through Sara's fingers.

"Sweetie, fourth grade was playing dolls. This hell is what it really looks like," Helen says. "Anyway, I thought you chose this particular agency for its open and clean record of adoptions."

"But when you research deeper, Helen, it becomes clear that even with the best agency it's hard to be sure what's gone on in the host country. The UNICEF documents I've read are horrifying. Poverty and greed. There's the worst kind of manipulation of poor women. Let alone the actual stealing of babies. And sometimes I'm not even sure it's right to bring a kid here."

"Sara, nothing's certain. I just want you to be happy. The bottom line is, do you want a baby? Anyway it's almost a cliché, isn't it, wondering if it's wrong to bring a child to America."

Is it wrong that, even certain about a child, Sara's sometimes entirely uncertain? She's not scared of the daily messiness, Helen's wrong about that; it's the unknown disaster that wrecks her.

"Helen, did your parents have secrets?"

"Left field, Sara. Weren't we talking about stealing Guatemalan babies? Where's that coming from?"

"Just my dad. I'm not really sure. These days I feel like I don't really know him."

"Hello. You two practically finish each other's sentences. Your dad's just sort of quiet sometimes. But that's not news."

"But I've begun finding some stuff out that makes me think he's more secretive than taciturn."

"Look, parents have secrets. Even at forty-one you're his child. Painful Lesson 101. All parents have secrets. Mine had secrets. Massive secrets. You want a juicy secret? Here's one. After Dad died, Mom told me that he'd had a twenty-year affair with our neighbor."

"Your dad! That's impossible. He was the world's most loving husband. No way!" Sara is looking at Helen for a sign that she's making this up to make a point, something not beyond Helen's rhetorical strategies. But the way Helen keeps focused on the thin slicing of mushrooms lets Sara know this is not a polemic.

"Yes, way. And when I flipped out, when I felt that he'd totally betrayed me, my mom, us, the family, that he'd wrecked the whole fucking reality that we grew up in a happy family, Mom told me to cut it out. She'd known from year one and she never told him she'd known. She said we were a happy family. That over time she'd realized her knowing was a secret as secretive and potent as his. As far as I can tell, Sara, everyone has secrets. No matter what they say. Look, I tell you everything in the whole world, you're my best friend and I've never told you that. I've never told Frank and I don't plan on it. So what are you talking about with your dad?"

"I don't know. Nothing, really." There it is, the old bond, Sara feels it, her devotion to holding on to her father no matter what. It occurs to Sara that sometimes when she thinks of being a parent, she mostly imagines herself as a protective father.

"I tell you something I'm not ever telling my husband and you say 'I don't know, nothing?'"

"He's old. He's not going to live forever. I just think he's held things from me."

"That's the point, Sara. Whatever you know or don't know won't keep him alive."

⚬⚬⚬

It's just three blocks from Helen's to the subway. She can still get downtown and spend the night watching Marco's band. It's a pretty street Helen and Frank live on, ginkgo trees and window planters with bright-headed summer flowers. There are always people hanging out on the stoops—kids out after dinner riding too fast on bikes or falling on their rollerblades.

It's not just that Sara's happy to wash the dishes and then step out of the bedlam of Helen's after-dinner apartment—though she certainly is—or happy to avoid the contrasting quiet of her empty apartment; she loves watching him. Who wouldn't? Who couldn't love Marco gigging? She loves the lean stretch of him, the way his body goes at one long angle and his head cocks the other way. He alternates between lead guitar and traditional mountain flutes. His dark beautiful hair shakes over his face as if it is making the rivery sound that issues from him. Sometimes all that can be seen through the tumble of hair is the sharp line of his jaw and a small bit of his lip plumped against the flute. His fingers are long, too, and his hands stretch across the frets, playing their remarkable percussive riffs on the guitar. She sees the audience follow him, bend to the place where Marco is in the music. The effect of him up there is dramatic. And authentic. Nothing stagey or put on about it. He's the real deal. And the band's not dumb; they're not arguing who's more real among the bunch of five Ecuadorian mixed breeds; they'll do what sells. They've put Marco front and center when they play, because he's the money shot, he's got it, whatever it is that draws an audience right up, right into the orbit of a musician, right into the purse of his lips against the wooden flute. His body moves just the slightest, like a long cord snapping and dislocating and snapping back. Even when he has paused, his eyes closed, his head moving to the rhythms of the drummer or the bass guitarist, he's something to watch. Like he's telling the audience how to feel this music, how to appreciate what's coming at them from the band. Like his groove is the only groove you want to be in.

The long black flute he's working on this song is the instrument Sara loves best. Not because its tones are really her favorite so much as she likes the way it looks in Marco's hands. Marco nods over at Sara after he's pulled out of a riff. He lets the flute dangle on one arm and with the other knocks his fist against his heart. She wishes he hadn't done it. He's told her before, "I love playing for you when there's an audience. It's like I'm telling everyone that's my one and only baby girl." Baby girl. Come on, she's a forty-one-year-old woman. And come on, one and only? Remember that one and only wife? "I remember everything," Marco would say with patience, as if Sara couldn't comprehend the fullness of life. Sara claps along with the audience as the song ends. This has to end. It is at the end. But tonight she wants to stay in his groove, not fight anything. Him. Herself. The whole club full of men and women feeling their way into this tossing improbable fusion of Ecuadorian folk music and rock-and-roll. Drums start for a new song. She shuts her eyes. There's a place for this song low in her body. It's easy to feel it. In a soft slithery way. Marco's voice comes in over the drums. Starts like a chant, then slips into something closer to a funk lullaby. She's almost there, almost at the end. She dances with her eyes shut.

SEPTEMBER 12
9:00 P.M.

Dear Mrs. Roosevelt,

There are times writing to you that I've wished for the speed of a telegram:

Maman and I stuck in Virginia *STOP* Boat to be sent back to Lisbon *STOP* Come immediately *STOP* Much to tell *STOP* No delay.

But there are times—like now—I just want to stretch back sleepily as if sitting in the cinema dark and not even tell you my story so much as watch with you as a young man in a blue double-breasted suit walks onto the screen. This young man's in a crowded railway station. It is Paris. He stops, waits, a small woman catches up with him, and he says in a stern tone, perhaps even a little rough, "Maman, hurry." We can see that like the small woman, he's weary, a weariness deeper than the exertion of carrying the too many valises he's carrying. He turns a bit, takes another bag from the mother. He moves forward, shifting the two bags strapped against his back. But the fatigue in his face is moral. We detect a longing? Sadness? A shadow of the sentimental?

"If we miss it, we're here for the night," he says to the woman, his mother, who, walking maybe two steps for his every step, is still falling behind his leggy strides. (Let's imagine Gary Cooper, Mrs. Roosevelt.)

Then the steam spit of the engine, the hiss and crank as the train lurches into movement. The camera scans the cars. A press of faces and bodies inside each compartment. Luggage racks overloaded. Finally the camera locates the young man and his mother. Each of them holds a bag in their laps; a suitcase is wedged between the young man's legs. Can we see that he is trying not to look afraid? He's told Maman more lies. Not only is she expecting to find her husband in Toulouse where they are being taken on this night train, but also he's told her that he's received permission for them to be on this train to Toulouse. In that movie we see the shadows that play across his face and understand he's weighed impossible choices. He's lied (forgive him, a noble lie) to his mother to bring her to safety. Even the unkindness in his voice is a kind of prod to keep her moving. He hasn't cursed out loud about his father's insane trip back to Belgium. He's promised her there will be no problems.

"Max will be there and he's gotten more money from the bank. We'll be fine. We can stop thinking about Gustav and Marie and what they took." That's how he's lied to his mother.

The truth is it hurts to say her name. Marie. He can't bring himself to throw out the two hairpins he's still carrying in his pocket. Despite his resolve he's keeps finding himself drifting, tracing the curve of Marie's back before he furiously yanks himself into the present where there is no special train pass, no permissions. That's another lie. That the permissions are in his breast pocket. He's brought his mother aboard this train, though they have none of the requisite papers. He has no clever plan other than the possibility the conductor will take a bribe. He's already spent too much money, having bribed the elevator man from the Hotel Tulipe to present his French papers at the station and buy two tickets for Toulouse. He shuts his eyes. He's gotten them this far. Again Marie's back. The beautiful drag of her hair across his face when she lifts herself above him. The taste of that hair. He shouldn't let himself keep going but he's tired, he's hungry, it's hard to stop. Anyway, who's to stop him from remembering the night however he wants? By the time he's through, she'll be the one betrayed. We watch him try once, maybe a few more times, to jolt himself awake, to keep the necessary vigil, but then he's asleep and Maman sits awake in the dark compartment holding her bag, and in the first car the conductor pushes his cap off his brow before opening a compartment door to begin checking papers and tickets.

How long does the young man sleep? No doubt someone else knows exactly where in the French countryside they are when an explosion jolts the train's back car forward and the young man and everyone else in their compartment and all the others throughout the train are thrown in an instant. There's screaming. Luggage falls, crashing on the jolted bodies that struggle to pull themselves up from where they've all been tossed on top of one another. The young man is lifting his mother—he thinks it's his mother—by her arm. Slowly the car rearranges itself; no one is hurt. The men and women, it seems improbable, sit back in their seats, almost primly, as if things might simply continue, the train might lurch forward with the familiar hiss and spit of the engine. (If only this were a comedy and right now Groucho and Chico and Harpo were to push into the compartment of the train, squeezing in as if the train were the stateroom in *A Night at the Opera*, then we'd laugh and know that whatever emergency has happened is in the Marx Brothers' zany, good-natured hands.)

The information—What happened? What's happening?—comes to them in bits. The train, the last car of the train, it's been hit, bombed, a lot of people—no, a few people—no, only one man, thank God, only one man has been hurt—no, killed, poor man. Still, just think what might have been. They hear shouting. Someone pulls open the compartment door to hear more clearly. They open the windows. What is it? What is being shouted? The young man listens. He has to stop himself from yelling, "Shut up!" to the woman across from him who's crying though he does hold up his hand and mouth, "Please." Someone tries to leave the car but is pushed back by a man in uniform. They sit. Hours. Police, officials, more police pass through the car. They sit. A conductor looks into their compartment. A man comes through and asks, "Is anyone hurt?" The young man wonders if he should leave the train, flee, take his mother and run. (Oh, give him Fred Astaire's charm and leaping ability.) But where are they? The middle of nowhere. In the middle of the night. And even if he were to opt for wandering off, trying to get past all the police (even Fred Astaire couldn't twirl by police with the valises and bags he and his mother have), isn't he better off for now in here, just one among the other passengers (we're back to stowaways from *A Night at the Opera*), where no one has actually come to check tickets?

Then, without announcement, the train jolts, moves. The last car has been uncoupled. The train continues through the night and no one ever comes and checks their tickets or their papers and the young man (Gable, Grant, Astaire) and Maman climb out of the train the next morning. They are in Toulouse.

Perhaps, Mrs. Roosevelt, you recall from my early letter (way out of sequence—forgive me) about the Portuguese Consul and the secretary with the fox stole. That was Toulouse. In Toulouse we also secured visas for Morocco and Shanghai. To Maman I explained that if in ten days we did not hear from Max (onscreen: the passing days are lines of people, pages torn off a calendar, longer lines again, more pages off the calendar) then we'd continue to Perpignan on the French side of the Pyrenees, where Max would have gone directly. We'd get our Spanish transit visas and cross out of France.

How's that for a night at the pictures? I liked taking you to the movies. Bet you think I should count that train as a miracle if I'm counting miracles. Me, I think that bomb was just a little luck. Miracles are for a place after luck.

With a bow *STOP* a pirouette *STOP* and a good night *STOP*
Isaac Astaire

SEPTEMBER 12

10 P.M.

One last thing before bed, Mrs. Roosevelt. Let me give you the Daily Rumors Update:

1. There are now officially three habeas corpus petitions.
2. There is one 100,000-dollar libel suit and claims of a breached contract by Captain Harberts, the shipping company, and CL Travel Agency's onboard representative, for failing to deliver a family to Vera Cruz.
3. That all of these petitions and suits are why we've attached at the coal pier at Sewalls Point.
4. The Letter Committee will be contacting two members of your Congress.
5. You apparently, Mrs. Roosevelt, are talking to your husband.
6. You apparently, Mrs. Roosevelt, are on your way down to see us.
7. You have also been meeting with rabbis.
8. You are concerned about the children and mothers on board the ship.

9. Contact has been made with the Nicaraguan, Venezuelan, and Costa Rican embassies.
10. Only twelve of us will be permitted to leave the ship.
11. All of us will leave the ship.

Finally, I have a question. Who is this Mr. Breckinridge Long? His name has repeatedly come up. And not in a good way. Rumor is he's not a very welcoming statesman.

"Is there a passenger record?" she asks the curator on the phone as soon as they are done with the preliminary introductions by way of university credentials. She focuses the conversation on her grant, Walter Benjamin, and her translations of his work. Sara omits her last name, instead adapting Lieberman's southern Miss Sara and calling herself Dr. Sara.

"I'm not familiar with the name Benjamin with regard to the *Quanza*. There wasn't a Walter Benjamin aboard the *Quanza*," he says finally.

"No, right, I know. Walter Benjamin never made it out of Europe. He died in September. 1940." Sara realizes that only makes things muddier. "I'm really exploring at this point what were possible options and outcomes for displaced persons. Benjamin was hoping to get to Lisbon and board a ship. Hopefully for New York where he would find a teaching position. I'm trying to broaden my research. Of course I know about the terrible fate of those on the *St. Louis*."

There's a silence on the other end of the phone that makes Sara regret that she didn't stay in simple email correspondence. She can hear him trying to connect the dots.

"Well, the *Quanza* was already in Virginia by September, Dr. Sara. It left Lisbon in August."

"I know. Is there a passenger record?" Sara asks, trying to maintain an academic tone to her voice.

"But Mr. Benjamin was not aboard. Who are you looking for?" he sounds as though he's guarding the list.

"Well actually, Itzak Lejdel and Sahra Lejdel."

"Itzak Lejdel? That's interesting. He's one of the Belgians. There were quite a few Belgians. Mostly Antwerp. Diamonds and such. But Lejdel was originally from Brussels. Traveling third class. I would have imagined you were interested in the more prominent passengers. You know there were quite a number of more notable passengers aboard. The Rands were a quite wealthy Belgian family. The actor Marcel Dalio was on the ship. He'd been in films by Renoir. Later he and his wife, who was also aboard, were in *Casablanca*."

"Really?" Sara wasn't prepared for that swerve. "Well, yes, them too. But right now I'm focusing on the Lejdels." Sara realizes how absurdly concocted the whole thing sounds. She's got to establish her credibility. "I've met him, Itzak. In New York. We both live there. His name actually became Richard Leader; I don't know if you know that." Sara's hoping to throw the curator off balance with this name shift.

But the curator laughs. "Yes, yes, of course I know. Mr. Leader, he's one of our most colorful characters. Initially Richard would have nothing to with our *Quanza* project. He seemed rather inflexible. Mr. Lieberman worked pretty hard on Richard. But then Richard became quite a valuable resource. Richard's been eloquent on several panels we've had. He has quite a precise and vivid memory, which, you can imagine, is valuable in this kind of project, which is, of course, largely an oral history."

"He was at panels? You've met Richard Leader? When were the panels?" Sara feels herself spiraling. Panels? A vivid memory? The betrayal feels acute.

"It's funny you're interested in Mr. Leader; we were just together last week for a talk at Rutgers in New Jersey. It's too bad you weren't there. Mostly he doesn't like to travel. But Richard's come to ones held in Washington. He was central to the New York symposium in 2000. Interestingly he refused the *Quanza* reunion celebration. On that Lieberman couldn't get anywhere. He had some difficulty with the idea of a celebration. Actually, I think he first said he'd come to the reunion, but then he never showed up for the celebration of the *Quanza*. Well except for all the materials he sent down for the permanent archive and exhibit."

"Last week at Rutgers? When, Thursday?" Sara remembers Carmen's reluctance in the kitchen on Thursday.

"How do you figure that Itzak Lejdel has any bearing on your translations of Mr. Benjamin, Dr. Sara?"

"I'm not sure," Sara says, because at this point she can't think of a better lie. "And what about Sahra Lejdel, his mother?"

"I'm sitting here looking at the full passenger list. Itzak Lejdel traveled alone. One of the ship's young passengers traveling alone, though there were other, much younger children who came alone. It was quite a moment, the *Quanza*. You've spoken to Lieberman? It's the Lieberman family who in large part are the force that brought the passengers back together and created the exhibit. It was their grandfather who kept the ship here in Virginia. Outrageous fellow, very, very colorful lawyer, Lieberman. Drove a motorcycle. He sued the ship for 100,000 dollars for breach of contract. It was a way of tying the ship up in port; the captain and the onboard travel agent from the shipping company both had to appear. Eleanor Roosevelt, she helped them, too, you know. Breckinridge Long, Cordell Hull's man, he was determined to send them back to Europe."

Sara hates the certainty in his voice, the possessed exuberant way in which the curator holds forth. This is her father he's talking about. Her father and her grandmother's ship. She's her father's daughter, the daughter who can practically finish her father's sentences.

"I'm sorry," she says.

"Yes, the response to the *Quanza* had terrible implications for later ships and for Jews trying to enter the States. Hull and Breckinridge tightened everything after the *Quanza*. That's the unfortunate consequence of this story."

"No, I'm sorry," Sara says, "you're wrong about Sahra Lejdel. She was traveling with her son on the ship." Without waiting for a denial or confirmation, Sara hangs up the phone.

Even at 1 a.m. Sara's not afraid she's waking him. Maybe with age he naps, but she knows he's a night owl. She hears the TV louder than her father's voice. The volume turned up to adjust to her father's hearing.

"Dad, I'm struggling." It's her opening move, calculated, quiet, assured.

"Where are you? Are you all right? Are you hurt?" His voice is instantly present, ready for action.

"I'm home, Dad. I'm fine."

"What, Sara?" His voice is still at attention, trying to calm itself.

"Dad, I've been struggling all night with why Benjamin killed himself. I've always just accepted it. But now, it feels different. I can't understand his choice."

"Don't ask me. I've told you, he's your man, not mine."

"He was there. They said he was going to be sent back. But every day things were changing. He'd made it to Spain. If he'd just waited. The next day things were different. I've always accepted that he knew he couldn't physically go forward, but maybe there are other important facts." She's aware how indirect she's being, how much she's using Benjamin to lure her father into thinking they're on one playing field. She doesn't care. Or almost doesn't. Trying to give him easy blunders.

Her father is silent. She listens to his silence in a new way. Silence from a man who talks on panels she doesn't know about, who's gone to Washington to give talks on his life. A man who disappeared last week into his secret story.

"What do you think?"

"I don't think."

"But try. For me. You had to cross that border, didn't you, Dad? What was it like there? You crossed. The worst was over, right? You got to Lisbon. Sahra didn't get to Lisbon with you." She's decided not to ask it as a question. Just to begin to integrate her information into the conversation. To put her pieces out in the open. Let him see that she could play a much more offensive game. Let him know she's only going this far for now.

"What border are we talking about?"

"In France, Dad. The south of France."

"There were lots of them. You went. You hoped for the best. You made the best of it. That's all."

"But what about Benjamin?"

"He obviously didn't. That's it."

"What?"

"Make the best of it."

"That's all you've got to say?"

"No, Sara, the simple truth is that's all there is to say."

"What now?" Her father's voice is steely. "It's late; I'm watching a program."

Sara's called back, ready to fire everything at him. Rochelle Goldenman, the *Quanza*, Lieberman. His mother. Everything. She wants to be ready to say everything.

"What I want to ask," her voice trembles even as she tries to match his severity, "is why it's so important not to ask?"

SEPTEMBER 13
8:00 A.M.

Dear Mrs. Roosevelt,

Let me start right out by saying we needed Spain. For Morocco, for Portugal, for someplace I hadn't thought of yet, for anywhere out of Europe we needed Spain. Two Spanish signatures were required for a transit visa. But as you might imagine, Spaniards were hardly rushing up begging to put their names on our documents.

Perpignan is a rocky, mountain city, with steep streets that wind, turn sharply, breaking open onto narrow squares. It is the final stop in France before Spain. Even in the heat of noon the streets are corridors of shadow.

Madame Dupais liked to say *the early bird catches the worm.* In Perpignan we were neither early (thousands and thousands already on lines) nor seemingly capable of catching anything that could help us into flight. The lines that led to the wide doors of the Spanish Consulate stretched two or three kilometers. All of Europe, it seemed, was on that line. Not only Jews, there were laborers, farmers, a family of dwarves, women dressed in their furs under the spring sun. Each day the lines reformed. You would think that after a week I'd be familiar with everyone on the line. But every day there were more new faces, and when we recognized faces from the day before, they were not like new friends but sour reminders that no one was getting anywhere on the line. French soldiers swept through the streets, impossibly trying to clear people who slept there in order to hold their place in the line for a visa. Sometimes I gave money to hold our spot overnight. Sometimes I gave money to jump ahead in the line.

Maman and I stayed, as was our habit by then, on the outskirts of the city. In Toulouse we'd rented a furnished room in the home of a seamstress. In Perpignan we'd found a small hotel, El Paradis, owned by a tall, carefully dressed Spanish woman who worked unceasingly in the hotel's courtyard. Even the slightest deviation from the hordes of displaced men and women gave us greater success at finding a meal and a decent room. Maman was exhausted. I tried to convince her to rest and gather strength at the hotel. I could go into town by myself. She refused to even consider staying back.

The courtyard of El Paradis was truly a kind of paradise, hung with filigreed birdcages and large terracotta pots abundantly planted with flowers and herbs. There were perhaps forty or fifty cages with small colorful birds. Gray and blue birds, hardly songbirds so much as chatterbirds, filled a tremendous cage elaborately laced with grasses the birds worked. An orange-and-green parrot spoke both French and Spanish. There were timbales and blackmasked lovebirds. There was a red lacquered cage where a blackand-white bird with a long, elaborate tail flitted between three small jade perches. Many cages were empty, some so decorative and elaborate they seemed impossible for habitation.

In the mornings we drank coffee in the courtyard and I pretended that instead of resuming our place in line, we had actually come to Perpignan for a mountain holiday. There were hiking trails that crossed through the hotel's property, and drinking my coffee I'd draw up an elaborate plan for my day of leisure. I saw myself walking out back, chickens scattering as I walked past the garden and the chicken yard. My sack would tug a little at my shoulders, filled with a packed lunch, movie magazines, and a canteen. I'd enter the forest, quickly coming up through the stand of thin trees to the rocky trails. Perhaps along the way I might gather mushrooms to bring back to the proprietress. I'd hike and after lunch flip through *Movie Complet* until I slipped with Hedy and Ginger and Lana in my arms into a delicious afternoon nap.

In truth, I'd never even ventured out to the vegetable garden or seen where the trails began on the property.

But having the steep trails and rock outcroppings close was something I thought about, not only in the mornings but often, in the late afternoon, walking back from the unmoving line outside the Consul's office. Maman remained in town, searching the lines for a familiar Belgian face and with it a word from Max. I sat in the still courtyard of El Paradis, the flowers pulled closed against the afternoon heat. Even the birds quieted at this hour. The only sounds were the hotel owner polishing the metal of her birdcages or clipping dried leaves off her flowers. It was easy, sitting in the courtyard, to almost forget that Paris had been overtaken. France was occupied. It was easy to almost forget some of the stories of arrests and roundups that I heard waiting on line.

"I'll leave now." That's what I'd say to myself jolting back. "I'll leave in the night and walk to Spain through the mountains." I'd

imagine myself hiking, drinking water from streams, rationing bits
of food, even going without food. It was a robust image, my legs
strong and secure on the rocky footpaths. But I couldn't hold onto
this vision. I'd never been a hiker. It was a standard joke among my
friends that I was the one asking, "How much longer?" as we
climbed toward a waterfall. "Are we there soon?" I'd plead and
they'd mock me, saying, "Hey, it helps if you look up at the forest
instead of at your own ugly feet, Iz." Once at the waterfall, I de-
clined joining the group, eager to press on for a view from the sum-
mit. "Isn't this beautiful enough?" I asked, stretching out and
closing my eyes. And with the daily pain in my knees, my chance of
turning myself into a bold mountaineer was ridiculous. Let's put it
this way: if I were lucky I'd be Marcel Dalio's Rosenthal in *La
Grande Illusion*, limping over the high passes. But the option of taking off—even with the pain in my knees—nevertheless seemed, day
by day, more possible than believing we might ever secure the necessary Spanish visa of transit.

I was usually not alone in the courtyard. The hotel owner's son
often read or moved ceramic chess pieces around a board while his
mother puttered about interrupting his reading with pecking questions. He ignored her or looked up from his book and gave terse answers. She spoke to him in Spanish and the son answered in French.
I sympathized with his irritation. He was close to my age. I knew
from his mother's constant calling that his name was Roberto. We'd
spoken only once before, and then somewhat awkwardly, regarding
a torn pillow, feathers stuck each morning in my hair, and, improbably, down between my toes.

I cannot recall why it was we began talking that afternoon of June
23. Despite our age, we'd never struck up a conversation before. I was

so dispirited that I hardly wanted any conversation. Perhaps it was the Germans. Their invasion of Paris. Perhaps the imminence of their arrival in Perpignan. Nevertheless, in this dark mood Roberto and I began talking. I know at some point I asked about the hiking trails, where exactly they went, if there were actual paths that led into Spain. I must have said something about being ready to give up because Roberto looked at me from his metal chair and said, "Give up what?"

"Oh, the chance that I might ever get out of here and get through Spain with proper documentation." My laugh was condescending in the extreme, meant to tell Roberto that his clueless safety was nothing I admired.

"What's needed?" he asked. He was so straightforward that I fought momentarily against my bad attitude. Instead I maintained my condescending tone while explaining the visa requirements.

"Well, you might talk to my grandfather," Roberto said. "He's usually back by five, sometimes I suppose he comes to us a bit later, but really he's prompt, especially with my mother. Let's speak with my grandfather this afternoon."

My condescension rose to fury. Counting on the wisdom of an old man, his old grandfather, some half-brained family patriarch who doled out advice. Did he not know what was going on in the rest of Europe? In France?

"I don't think he's really much use for me," I managed to say.

"Really?" said Roberto. "But I thought he'd have some suggestions. He's the Consul. He might have some thoughts, I suppose." There was no rancor or comeuppance in Roberto's voice, just an easy, eager tone of new friendship.

It was as if suddenly the courtyard tipped. Was I now desperate enough to be hallucinating absurd possibilities? A few birds clattered in their cages. I shifted in the iron chair, trying to make the world level again. Then you must imagine that I was desperate to undo everything snide that I'd said. I tripped over myself to find what I could say.

Finding nothing, I said, "I see you have a chessboard. You play chess?"

Roberto was not a strong player. I saw quickly the few moves with my bishop and queen to bring the game to a close. But I kept the game in play, giving up (I admit with genuine difficulty even under these circumstances!) obvious positions, even blundering my rooks and ultimately my queen just to keep Roberto seated right there next to me until his grandfather arrived.

The grandfather was not the imposing man—half bullfighter, half bureaucratic copy of Franco—I'd conjured all those days waiting on line. The very opposite of imposing, he was short, bow-legged, stoop-shouldered, and seemed to keep yanking into himself even as he came into the courtyard. Stopping to embrace his daughter, he pecked at each of her cheeks, pulling back, withdrawing his neck in a manner that reminded me of a painted turtle. He fussed for a long while with two small white birds, taking them out of their cages, talking quietly in a singsong voice to them, feeding them stalks of millet. They crawled over his shoulders and hands. Taking off his hat, he placed one atop his head.

Introductions were made. Roberto asked his grandfather if he'd wait until the game ended because we had a special question for him. The man stood watching our game, one bird balanced on his head, one white bird walking over his hands.

We had come to the end game, and despite myself, I'd moved into a position where checkmate was four moves away. I was certain

Roberto was unable to see this. Looking up, I was also certain that his grandfather understood the position. At first I believed that I should let Roberto win. I must not let the grandfather know that I'd seen the possibility on the board. Then I thought of Henri and his father's hands mussing my hair—"Will I live to see my own son beat you, Izzy?"—and understood it was better to let the grandfather know my range, that I was capable of looking ahead, of calculating, of keeping a composed face. I took the four moves with speed, knocking up his pieces with a determined sound on the board.

"I thought I had you," said Roberto, laughing. "I did not see that coming at all." He tilted his head and looked up into his grandfather's face.

"Popo, this is my new very smart friend, Isaac." They spoke in Catalan. Roberto spoke in the same eager and open way with his grandfather as he had with me. I watched the grandfather, the attentive love with which he watched Roberto.

"My grandson says you are trying to obtain a Spanish visa."

"Transit," I said, "Only a transit visa. So that we might go to Morocco."

"And may I ask what is there for you?"

"My father's uncle," I lied. "He's a glove maker," I added to give a sheen of truth to my lie. The question-and-answer period continued, though I already understood that it was being enacted for Roberto's sake.

"Your father is . . . ?" He looked around. It was obvious little went unnoticed by him.

"In Belgium, Monsieur. He went back to finish some final business. I am here with my mother. She's not entirely well and it makes our passage to my uncle's extremely important. It is my responsibility to take care of business and secure visas for at least my mother and myself, though a third for my father would be fantastic."

"Difficult to obtain, I gather," he said with a slight smile.

"It is a busy time. Many people want many things, I'm sure." I said, hoping to acknowledge the demands of his position. He didn't answer, and the silence was uncomfortable.

"But here at the Hotel Paradis, we provide many services." Roberto laughed and turned to his grandfather. "Popo, I was so happy to tell my new friend how lucky he was to have met me."

"Well," the grandfather finally said, his neck pulling in, his chin tucking, "please come by my offices tomorrow morning and I will make certain that you have the necessary papers." He placed the white bird on Roberto's head. The bird put its beak down and picked at Roberto's hair. Roberto laughed and the bird flew to the grandfather's shoulder.

"Would it be possible for Roberto to bring me to your office? It is often a little congested near the Consulate and I wouldn't want to get lost or delay you in any way." I measured my voice, trying to keep things light—as if he were just the kindly grandfather of a new friend I'd met on holiday.

The grandfather walked back to the cage, unhinged the door, and let the bird step off his finger. The grandfather said there were plenty of guards who could point the way, but Roberto interrupted, saying, "Yes, of course I'll bring you, Isaac. I'm foolish not to have suggested it myself." The grandfather shut the wire door. He made his way to each of the bird cages, stopping sometimes to lift a bird from the cage or bending close to make affectionate clucks, calling each bird by its name.

We played two more games of chess. I let Roberto win both after much apparent struggle. His mother served sherry and olives. I was at the Hotel Paradis. I thought of Errol Flynn, sneaking into Prince John's court. I felt that early evening that I was him, a sly fox, a sneak, and a rogue! And when we toasted—*salut, salut*—I tilted my delicate sherry glass back like it was a jug of hearty medieval ale.

Yours most loyally,
Robin Hood

"I'm sorry, your father is again sleeping," Carmen says, when Sara lets herself in. He'd been up in the night, Carmen explains, and she's finally convinced him to go down for a rest. Carmen is at her afternoon setup, ironing in the living room, watching a game show on a Spanish channel. Her iron works in small circular movements around the buttons of Sara's father's dress shirt.

Sara makes straight for his closet. Pulling down files and the thick fortress of papers he's built here and all through the house. Carmen has followed Sara into the room, neatening the papers that mount in tilting pillars on his desk.

"He's a good man, your father, always worrying about me, about my family. You know, last year when my mother was ill, your father not only paid for me to go back to my city, but he paid for my mother's hospital in San Salvador. That is something."

Sara's listening, a barely sort-of listening. It's receipts and stock transactions from God-knows-when, bank statements, every jury-duty notice or letter from the IRS. The clutter is unbelievable. "Can you tell me that the government won't come asking for our documentation?" her father asked when Sara's mother was still alive and desperate for a single empty closet or cupboard.

"Carmen, I don't need your help," she says, hearing her own snappish, snarled sound. She doesn't need to turn to know that Carmen has stopped straightening and is watching the clumsy fury of her search. Carmen obviously has been in cahoots, helped keep things from Sara. "I don't want your help. I'm just trying to find something, Carmen. I'm looking for something but I don't even know what it is."

"I'll be out of your way. But let me ask one thing." Carmen's voice is clipped, tough. "What have you set up for this baby you're about to have?"

"Nothing." Sara isn't going to be distracted by Carmen.

"Don't you think you'll need help? You'll need help."

"I'm still filling out the million documents that stand between me and changing a diaper."

"But sometime there will be a baby, right?"

Helen's been saying the same thing. Sara needs help. Though she'll take maternity leave, it's important to have child care in place before she's got a swaddled baby in her apartment, hasn't showered in three days, and thinks walking alone through the aisles of the grocery store seems like a big-time fun outing. It's time to get set up. Anyway, sooner than she knows it she'll be back full time at the university, teaching her usual course load, hopefully finishing the translations; she's definitely going to need child care.

"So what do you suggest, Carmen?" She asks to get it over with, but as soon as she asks, Sara feels relieved. Carmen doesn't so much suggest as decree. She's always relied on Carmen, who would march into Sara's teenage room, saying, "Okay little beauty, it's time we talk about this kissing boys business."

"If you want, I'll help you find someone good for now and then, eventually, I'll help you, Sara."

"But Dad needs you."

"Until he doesn't," Carmen says in her straight, no-nonsense way.

"Ouch, Carmen."

"Well, that's exactly what I'm saying. If you could face it that he's an old man, you might be more determined to hurry up with the baby and less determined to come in and start poking and stirring up things that belong in the past."

———

Sara looks in on her father. He's sleeping, fully dressed, on top of his covers. Even though she hears his breathing, Sara can't help it—she's drawn close, rests her hand on his chest. Sleeping on his back, not a rumple in his shirt, he looks arranged. Sara sees something has fallen out of her father's hand. She picks it up, a woman's hairpin, with metal prongs and on top a small, carved, white porcelain flower. It's lovely. She's never seen it before. He must have been holding it as he drifted off. No doubt it belonged to Simone, a gift for Sara sooner or later. Sara's tempted to take it but puts it on the bedspread. The white flower rests against her father's thumb.

On the bedside tabletop, the familiar pile from emptying his trouser pockets of change, money clip, credit cards he holds together with a knotted rubber band. She opens the table drawer. It's so jammed with papers and magazines it sticks and Sara pushes it back. She thinks about looking in the old suitcase below the bed. But this looking for something is useless. Entirely. She needs to open a drawer inside her father. But standing in the afternoon darkness looking at her father's face, she hears Helen saying, "It doesn't matter what you find or don't find, Sara; death is the terrible betrayal."

———

"Lima," Carmen says triumphantly before a TV contestant buzzes and answers, "Lima, Peru."

Sara's thrown herself down on the couch, her coat and her computer bag in a heap on the floor. Sara wants to apologize to Carmen— she's sorry for being curt earlier, but she knows that with Carmen too quick an apology is seen as facile and, worse, in Carmen's eyes, not from the heart. Anyway, it's comforting in an old childhood way to just hang on the sofa, listening to the game show and the hiss of the iron's steam.

"I was always so good in geography classes," Carmen says out loud, not exactly acknowledging that Sara has come into the living room. Sara's watched her share of Spanish television. For all the afternoons she's spent on that couch watching Spanish game shows and soap operas, she ought to be fluent in Spanish, but she's not. Mostly, Sara likes letting the language wash over her, words she knows, a whole phrase, a volley between a player and the host. It's comforting, more comforting than American television. She loves languages, but sometimes she loves the not knowing or partly knowing a language, even more than the fluency she has with German or French.

The host reads out the answer—something about a yellow flower in the Yucatan Peninsula. Or maybe it's a lizard that camouflages itself on a yellow flower.

"I knew it! I knew that one!" Carmen says, lifting the iron with a victory flourish.

Sara looks at the triumph in Carmen's face, the squint of her dark eyes, the wide delight of her grin, a kind of bursting pleasure that most days gives Sara comfort.

Seeing Carmen now, shaking her head, a little extra strength in her shoulder as she leans into the iron, Sara feels the unease that Carmen's happiness can also stir inside her. For all these years, Sara just thought it was her own moody, motherless shit, her inability to entirely succumb to pure unthrottled happiness. Especially in a woman. Somehow happiness made Sara feel like an outsider. But today Sara feels Carmen's determined edge, Carmen's will for joy.

What does she really know about Carmen? It's almost a stupid question—she's known Carmen for so long, been with Carmen's large family for holidays, she and her father joining them at one or another of the sisters' houses for birthdays and parties. Her father has sponsored not only Carmen but also Carmen's two sisters and brother. Sara was actually in the wedding party last winter when Carmen's daughter, Violet, was married in a lavishly decorated hall in Brooklyn. She knows Carmen's mother is still in El Salvador. That the rest of them left at some point in the 1980s during the civil war. Why has she never known more than that? What has she ever asked Carmen about her life during the civil war in El Salvador? There's so much now Sara knows she doesn't know. She's been constructing in-complete stories, partial stories, or stories that make a literal truth. So Sara comes away from Violet's Salvadoran wedding marveling at the American mix-it-up—old world sieved through the American appetites—tortillas and tamales on the buffet table next to trays of lasagna and French fries. An uncle weeping and singing one of the old country ballads. Salsa spun with Coolio and Janet Jackson. She's seen, she's listened, but maybe it's all misread, maybe she mistrans-lates everything. Especially the sorrow. Maybe that's all anyone does. Mistranslate sorrow. She thinks of Walter Benjamin asking, *Is a translation meant for readers who do not understand the original?*

"Carmen, I don't know why I've never even asked you. What was I thinking, Carmen, all those years when I was a student protesting American intervention in Central America and I don't even know where you or your family actually were during the war in your country? Was everyone even okay? You must have thought I was a real jerk."

Carmen shifts the shirt so that she has the collar edged along the side of the board.

"No, Sara. I thought you were a young girl. Young and sad."

"Would you tell me now, Carmen, if I asked?"

The television host says something that makes the audience and the contestants laugh. He pushes the joke and the audience's laughter dims like bad canned laughter. Carmen's pleasure has been interrupted. Carmen works in short strokes, slowing the iron near the seam, turning the iron slightly as she moves forward on the collar. Carmen doesn't even look up at the television. She stalls and presses the button and there's a shot of steam.

"I'm sorry," Sara says quietly. "I'm sorry."

"It is a terrible thing, a war. There are no good sides. Little kindness. And in a large family like we have in my country a war is a terrible thing. Even what lives gets killed. That's maybe what I'd tell you if you asked. But, Sara, I'd ask you not to ask."

Sara's come back to the library for a few hours before it closes. She reads in a collection of Benjamin correspondence published by University of Chicago Press, edited and annotated by his close friends, Gershom Scholem and Theodor Adorno, that Benjamin says, *I think I have come to believe that every translation that is not undertaken for the highest and most urgent practical goals (like biblical translation, as a prime example) or for the sake of purely philological research must have something absurd about it.*

SEPTEMBER 13
10:15 A.M.

Dear Mrs. Roosevelt,

Like it or not, it's my turn to help. The Eleanor Roosevelt Committee and the News Committee have both requested my typewriter.

"Urgently requested." Leon Frankle appears, his scrawny body puffed with importance. "We'll be fine, we'll be just fine if we can just get these last pieces of support in place."

"I'm working," I say, curling my body over the keys.

"Hey, Lejdel, cut it out. Right now." Leon Frankle leans over me, pressing his hands on my beautiful typewriter. "This is not a time for foolish love poems. You want us going back? This is what you want, Verlaine?"

Like that, he yanks away my Royale. Right from under my nose. He tries to heft it into his skinny arms. Practically drops it. I grab it back.

"Whoa, whoa, careful! I'll carry it to the Committees."

I run it up to where the Committees meet in determined huddles. Theodore DeJong stands at the ship rail, one white-gloved hand rubbing the band of rail and the other stiffly placed and unmoving. He is among the contingent who stand about not actually participating but not ready to reject the Committee efforts. Theodore DeJong wears white leather gloves in September. *Un peu bizarre*, don't you think? Especially for a bodyguard. That's fishy. (Ah, Madame Dupais smiles once again.) The gloves are yellow-stained; the tip of a finger on one hand even pokes through. If he really is the secretary and bodyguard to a prince, I think he'll have to get out of those raggedy gloves. At first glance I've estimated DeJong wears a men's 8. I happen to have a good mahogany deerskin in an 8. Far more practical, the mahogany. I'm itchy for a sale. *Alors,* my father's son in the end, I'm afraid.

Once I've given over the Royale, no one has much use for me, thank God, so I've come back to my office a deck below. So please accept this letter by hand, though penmanship was never my forte. My hand cramps easily. The professors say they can hardly read the shape of my letters. I hope you have an easier time. But I need to keep writing to you. I'll not stop. I'm urgent. Not foolish.

Yours,
Me

P.S. Will you ever write me back? Here's how I imagine it:
      Dear Isaac, you'd begin.
      Or you might even write:
      Dear Son.

P.P.S.
Dear Isaac,

Isaac is an important and lovely name. Not a name, I dare say, to be thrown off lightly. Trust and honor are attached both historically and metaphorically to the name, making Isaac a name of consider-able weight. I have not always admired my own name. Eleanor, it seemed a name at once too soft and thick on the tongue. Still, in the end, it is important to remember that the names we did not choose are made ours by our actions in the world. The way we deliver ourselves or fail to deliver ourselves will change and shift the names we inhabit.

Isaac, please excuse the tardiness of this reply. I have not been inattentive to your letters. I have been deeply moved by the plight of you and your fellow passengers aboard the ship. My silence has been an indication of my busy and determined efforts on your behalf. Rest assured that Franklin has indicated that you will be brought ashore quite soon. I will not rest until you and the others aboard walk off the ship. Your safety in particular commands my attention. For obvious reasons I ask, Isaac, that you please refrain from sharing this information with any of the Committees.

You seem a thoughtful and well-spirited young man. It will be a pleasure to make your acquaintance. Perhaps we shall even go to see a picture together.

Sincerely,
First Lady, Eleanor Roosevelt

P.P.P.S.
Dear Isaac,

It is me again, your good friend, Mrs. Roosevelt. It occurred to me that I forgot in my previous correspondence to respond to your generous offer for gloves. Lovely. I'd certainly welcome a gift of leather gloves. It's most kind. I am indeed a size 8 1/2. A deep blue pair would be terrific. However, may I suggest that it is not at all in good taste for you to begin selling gloves to the other passengers detained aboard the *Quanza*. To turn such difficult circumstances into an opportunity for profit is, frankly, a lousy idea, Isaac.

Sincerely,
Eleanor Roosevelt

SEPTEMBER 13
12:15 P.M.

Mrs. Roosevelt,

You are the *bee's knees, the cat's meow, and the real deal!* It means the world to me that you wrote! And two letters! Believe me, I know how busy you are! Not to worry! Not at all! I won't breathe a word of what you said! Your secrets are safe with me! Don't think about it again! Okay? Look, from what I've told you about my lowly status on the ship, who'd believe me anyway? Let every one of them think me a foolish Belgian boy writing poems! Let them all meet in their Important Committees! Sooner or later they'll learn who was responsible for getting us off the ship! Not that I'll brag! Not that I'll brag that while they were trying to reach you, you were listening to my story and writing me a letter! No, I'm just going to keep these two letters right in my breast pocket, like a wonderful bright handkerchief! I'll listen while everyone talks about Mrs. Eleanor Roosevelt, and who they know who is trying to sit down with her to explain the situation of the *Quanza* refugees. I can sit all day listening to every Rand and Rothschild without fear that I'll be left on board! Thanks, Mrs. Eleanor Roosevelt. Really, thanks.

Yours truly,
Gimbel

P.S. And oh, by the way, Frankle has just stumbled up, practically collapsing under the Royale. So I'm back in the business.

SEPTEMBER 13

12:45 P.M.

Dear Mrs. Roosevelt,

I'm more than a little tempted to write: Dear Leading Lady. You have, I'm guessing, a pretty good sense of humor, even though you look imposing and serious in your photo. I wouldn't be at all surprised to learn that you can crack a joke that has some zing to it. But it's always a question, especially given everything that's gone on between us—how far to go?

I'll tell you who has surprised me—Marcel Dalio. I thought he'd be all cloak and posture, keep to himself and just be a big French star. But Dalio's the first to jump into the action (no, not to worry, he's no Jules Wolff), no one-man show, this guy, he's the first not only to offer a suggestion but also to volunteer, a real committeeman. Maybe it's all an act or something, but he's got me convinced.

And it seems he's taken on Captain Harberts as a kind of special project.

Harberts mostly hides out in his captain's quarters, and when he does emerge, he stands, arms crossed, refusing even eye contact with any passenger desperate to appeal to him. He stands on the foredeck like some shoddy sea captain statue while each passenger takes a turn. Men practically bowing as they approach with their "Captain, sorry to trouble you" and "Perhaps I might have a moment of your busy day?" and "Might you consider Nicaragua as another port?" and "If I might offer a suggestion, Captain, Argentina or Venezuela should be considered." Harberts stays fixed, like a child playing I'm-a-rock-and-you-can't-move-me. They continue meek and amiable. Grown men with children up in their arms groveling to stir the captain's heart. Harberts stands unmoved and unmoving.

Then along comes Marcel Dalio. And my good luck is to be on deck—practically in the best seat of the house—for a fantastic performance of live comedy theater.

Dalio walks up—this Master of the Screen—the Marquis from *Rules of the Game*—without any deference in his approach. Rather it's as if he's about to welcome Harberts onto *his* yacht. Dalio flashes a real movie-star smile, all chops, as they say, and puts out his hand. Harberts steps back, a little surprised, but then sticks his hand out (who can resist a movie star?) and Dalio clasps it with both hands, turning on a full blast of his welcome-to-my-boat-charm.

"Good, good morning, Captain." Dalio keeps Harberts's hand in motion for quite some time before he lets go. "Have you had a good night?" There are further pleasantries, salutations, a brief discussion of weather. Nothing serious, no imposing questions. Everything is real easygoing so that when Dalio lowers his voice, Captain Harberts follows with his body, leaning in, curling his shoulders as if to accommodate himself to Dalio's height (much shorter than on screen). Dalio pulls back and the captain steps closer, his stiff neck craning, his head slowly turning as if Dalio has an invisible hand moving the captain's face. Dalio moves about—a little this way and that, nothing large in his gesture, and Alberto Harberts follows every movement, like a little doll on a string.

Even close as I was I couldn't hear what exactly Dalio said. I thought to get up from the deck chair, but I knew any excess movement would destroy the scene. Then I heard Harberts say in a considered voice, "I will get back to you on that, Monsieur Dalio. That's an excellent idea. In the meantime, what can we do for you? Would your very lovely wife be in need of any particular amenities?"

The captain puts his hand on Marcel Dalio's arm. "I'm so pleased to have you aboard my ship, Monsieur Dalio," he says.

Dalio reaches across and takes Harberts's hand back in his two-handed grasp. "I'm confident, Captain, that you'll take care of things. Let's speak later, shall we?" Then he drops the captain's hand and, with great poise and elegance, pivots on his polished shoes and walks away. Harberts is starstruck, standing there, his hand still kind of dangling, watching Dalio walk leisurely down the deck as if, having given the day's orders to the yacht staff, he now needs to attend to the more pressing matters of leisure with his guests.

It was a stunning performance. Dalio's a pro. "Bravo! Encore!" I wanted to shout. I wanted to give him an ovation.

There's a real lesson in that. But I'm afraid with you, Mrs. R., I've already come tromping on stage like a shoddy vaudeville act, all big tap dance, no subtlety, and even some garish moves that risked hisses and boos, even food pelted from the audience. Not a whole lot of finesse.

But the way I see it, Dalio had less to work with in a scene with Harberts than I have, having cast you as my leading lady. No flattery here when I say I simply know you're ready for this great part.

Humbly,
Your Director, Isaac Renoir

SHE'D BEEN WRONG. This time none of their nicknames fit. Not that there wasn't weeping and buzzing in the group, not that the one couple didn't have a we've-been-here-know-it-all quality to them, but, in fact, the couple really had been there, been through it once with the adoption of their first child, and Sara today understands that none of the men or women sitting in the adoption group deserved the nasty, mocking names that she had so entirely relished in the last session.

This time it seems plain and simple. Everyone in the group wants a child. Deeply, honestly, nervously, with all the full and understandable range of anxiety and anticipation, all of them want a child. It's her own stuff, Sara's contemptuous name-calling, ambivalence (chronic, Helen would say), loneliness (married guys, a winning cure for loneliness, Helen would say), self-contempt (typical American mentality, Marco would chime in). Today, Sara, sitting fidgety in the cloth-backed chair, has a roster of names to name herself. And they aren't any of them so nicey-nice either. Sara just wants the meeting over.

And where is Diane? Her comrade, the other single mother, where is she to exchange a raised eyebrow, a yikes when Franny Spillman, a.k.a. last session's Weeper, pops right up, saying that she and her husband have decided that they can take on any physical or neurological impairment; in fact, they're strongly considering specifically asking for a disabled child. Maybe Diane has decided not to adopt. Sara thinks it's not too late; she could get up, excuse herself for the bathroom, and bolt out of the building. Sara imagines Diane talking it over with all the sisters and brothers, maybe a rallying family gathering, an August weekend at the old Cape house, long sandy beach conversations, Diane on walks, in splintery Adirondack chairs, talking and talking until, one by one, each reluctantly gives up the big family trip plan.

"Diane's called with that horrible flu that's going around," the social worker announces, just as Sara's imagining the brothers standing around the old stone barbecue waiting for the coals to stop flaming and the sisters rummaging through cabinets pulling out the blue glasses, the chipped floral plates, even the old rooster corncob holders. She imagines them gathering at the pushed-together picnic tables; they'll say grace and look affirmingly up at Diane before the raucousness of the meal commences. "She says she's really sorry to miss the priorities and background discussion." The social worker looks around with what is clearly a welcoming let's-get-down-to-business smile.

Priorities? Background? Sara realizes that everyone is holding papers, loose typed pages, a legal pad flipped to show a scrawl of writing. Sara flushes with a queasy I-didn't-do-the-homework feeling. *I didn't do it; I couldn't do it; I didn't understand the assignment.* She could say any of these and be saying the truth. *The dog ate my computer* might work.

She opts for a preemptive strike—the old teacherly approach to regain control, alter the lesson plan when necessity demands alteration.

"Can I bring something up that's been upsetting me? I've been reading about the child trafficking that seems rampant. I guess I'm concerned. How do we know if the babies are legitimately placed in these orphanages?" Sara looks around the room, hoping to secure positive eye contact. Her palms are wet. The chair creaks under her shifting weight. Could her fidgeting get anymore fidgety?

"Sara, that's an obviously important question," the adoption counselor quickly jumps in, "but I'd like to stick with the questionnaire and the work we've done. Will you start by sharing your responses to the last forms?"

"What's reactive detachment disorder?" Sara asks, trying not to look busted. "I didn't know and it really just stalled me right then and there. I started thinking about all the things I wasn't prepared for. The things I plain and simple don't know about. I suppose I should just admit I got freaked out."

There's nodding among the group members, even the Spillmans, the couple who seems to want a child with extra concerns. The discussion is passionate and complex; Sara is struck by the vulnerability and honesty of the men and women in the room. It's the kind of conversation Sara hoped for when she'd first learned that this agency required a certain number of pre-adoption meetings. But now it only makes Sara feel even more like the bum she knows herself to be since, even if the disabilities scare her, it's the background information that stopped Sara. Bum or not, she's happy to have the attention shifted off her. What could she have said? I don't know anything about my mother's side of the family beyond what I learned when I was eleven. And the one thing I thought I knew about my father's family turns out to be wrong.

The flashing light shows five messages. The first, her father calling to see if she'll meet him for dinner. The second, a long silence before her father speaks up, "You think it's smart to run around the city for all hours?" More silence. His sigh. Then a fumbling of the receiver as he puts it back into its cradle. The third is Marty Lieberman. Would she kindly call him back? He asks this in his lilting southern politeness. Something interesting, quite interesting, actually, occurred earlier that evening that he thinks might interest Sara.

Then a man's voice, "Hello, Sara Leader. I'm calling about your chairs. I was thinking about them. Things got a little sidetracked when you came for a price. We never really finished our conversation. Don't be worried about the price. Or, I don't know, be worried. Come back to the shop and let's just get them fixed up."

The last is Marco. He woke to find her gone. "My heart is desolate to be left alone in the night. But if you work hard on your words tomorrow, mi amore, even my heart can mend."

It's after midnight, too late to call Lieberman. She thinks about calling her father. Imagines him sleeping in front of the television. It was their old habit when she came in from a party to nudge him awake and sit with him for even a few minutes. Then he'd rise and say, "Well, I don't know about you, kiddo, but I suppose I'm ready for sleep now," and she'd say, "I locked up when I came in, Dad." "That's my girl," he'd say, giving her a kiss on her head.

If she called Marco now the phone would ring and ring. She can feel the draped dark of his room, the way he's rolled deeper into his bed, dreaming some distant neighbor's phone. She's ready to have it over with Marco. It is already over. She sees how it was over all the time. With him, with the other impossible men. They weren't unkind; she never picked an unkind man in her life. Just unavailable, already taken, that kind of impossibility. She sees what she's always sort of seen, taking care of her father, a husband who's lost his wife, she has become his little wife, more comfortable as the third than to have the real chance to be the center of someone's affection. Or to betray her father and find someone who was genuinely available.

———

"Are you really in love with him?" Helen once asked about Marco.

"Am I in love with him?" Sara repeated, as if the question were completely novel. She adored him. She cherished him. She was always interested in him. In what he said. In how he said it. Charmed. Turned-on. She loved watching him play music. Loved watching him enter her. But in love with him—that's out of bounds. She doesn't go there. Not even in the landscape.

"He's married, Helen."

"Like that's ever stopped anyone from falling madly in love."

"Well, I'm not mad. I'm not madly anything enough to fall in love with a married man."

"I guess if you're not doing this for love then I have to admit I don't really get it at all."

———

"Thank you for returning my call so promptly," Marty Lieberman says when she calls the next morning from her cell phone.

She's sitting with her coffee from the Greek coffee shop on the steps at the New York Society Library, waiting for it to open. A man in a linen suit passes with two golden retrievers. Very weekend-in-Connecticut. A woman in workout Lycra walks a terrier. The dog on a sparkly chain, the cell phone taut to her face, plastic pickup bags, the woman's some kind of *New Yorker* magazine cartoon. The next shift will be midday, done by dog walkers out with a bouquet of dogs, or lone housekeepers walking the family poodle while the towels are in the dryer.

Lieberman's gentlemanly cadences make Sara imagine that she's reached him down in Virginia and not in midtown New York. "Remarkably, after your call the other day," he continues, "I received a letter from a Miss Glazer from Mexico. She apparently is writing her PhD and is researching the *Quanza*'s situation in Mexico. She's been to the Mexican Foreign Ministry and gone through the immigration records. As well she's apparently found all the newspaper articles that appeared when the passengers were turned away in Vera Cruz. Suddenly quite a whirl of interest in the *Quanza*. Well, I thought that you might be very interested to find another academic who is writing about the *Quanza* affair."

"I'm not writing about the *Quanza*," Sara interrupts. This is something she sees she's going to have to keep declaring to Lieberman.

"Well, perhaps, perhaps," says Lieberman. "Anyhow, Miss Glazer wrote in her letter that the ship was owned by the Portuguese government. We believed it was a private company. Certainly our family is quite interested in any new information that might be shared about the ship and my uncle Alfred Lieberman's legal hoops. We think there deserves to be more spotlight on this event. I think I told you: Alfred delivered the lawsuit against the captain and the ship on his motorcycle. Rode right down onto the loading docks. Quite a lively and vivid man, my uncle."

"I'd be most interested in contacting the woman in Mexico." Sara hears the formality in her voice matching his. She isn't sure what this woman could tell her. She's surprised that there really was anything about the ship that's actually substantial enough for someone to include in a dissertation. But Sara can't help herself from imagining that this Glazer woman will have a list of the thirty or so passengers who debarked in Vera Cruz and Sahra Lejdel's name will appear.

"Yes, I thought you would. It will be good for your writing; I always thought it would make for a good story, perhaps a film. You could write that film, Professor Sara, you know."

"I'm a translator, Mr. Lieberman." The librarian has come to the glass and steel library entrance, working his key into the interior lock. He's like a drawing of the stern librarian: a tall, unsmiling, pale man in a pale gray suit haunting the corridors of the library, making sure no one has smuggled in a bottle of water. Sara wants to get off the phone.

"Oh yes, I'm aware, Miss Sara. I simply was suggesting that you might one day consider telling this particular story." His voice works each one of the four syllables of *particular*. "My uncle's not the only colorful character in this affair."

"Not exactly my field. I'm not too creative. But perhaps, Mr. Lieberman, who knows." Sara laughs politely. "I certainly thank you for calling with this information." She wants to get off now. There's an insistence he has with her that she's beginning to find disturbing, as if she's got some obligation to him, to his uncle, to this ship.

"Well, no problem at all, and I thank you for returning my call so promptly."

"Again, I thank you." Sara's uncertain how to put a real end to the conversation.

"I thank you." Lieberman laughs. "Well, just listen to this! The two of us are so polite we sound like we're members of the Democratic National Convention."

Dear Mrs. Roosevelt,

"No," said Maman. She'd left Brussels when she wanted to stay. She'd left Paris. Even Toulouse. But she refused to leave France without Max. By now, she thought, Max must be in Paris wandering the quays searching for his family. If we'd only stayed, we'd be reunited. She would not compound the mistake. No leaving the country, and that was that. Maman crossed her arms over her chest in an effort to show me she was fierce and fixed in place.

I reminded her that Paris was an occupied city.

I reminded her that we'd just spent ten hopeless days standing on lines just trying to get near the door of the Spanish Consulate.

I reminded her that I had promised my father that I would take care of her.

Still she wouldn't budge. I became increasingly less calm. Sometime during the evening I shouted that perhaps she might as well go north looking for father or, better yet, impale herself on a German soldier's bayonet.

But bullying Maman proved a fruitless strategy. However, leading her with baby steps, I was able to make progress. Eventually she yielded a bit and with her arms uncrossed sat on the edge of the bed at the Hotel Paradis and listened.

Was there harm in securing transit visas? We were not obliged to use them. Wouldn't Max want us to have them in place once he was reunited with us? Perhaps he'd appear tomorrow. The grandfather might provide us with a transit visa for Max. Wouldn't Max be disappointed in a son who didn't make use of an opportunity like Roberto that literally appeared as magically as Marie and Gustav had appeared with a car for us?

I ached saying Marie's name.

"Do you really think so?" Maman popped up in bed.

"Of course," I said, laughing. "And think how proud and amazed Papa will be that I've done all this without a single pair of gloves offered away."

"You really think we'll hear from Max tomorrow?" Her voice was small. It had darkened in the shuttered room. The bundled form of Maman sitting up in bed was like a child huddled in bed after an unpleasant dream. She had taken a turn for the worse since we'd arrived in Perpignan; these days on the street in lines had visibly weakened her.

I came close to telling Maman the truth.

There had been no word from Max. There had never been a word from Max.

"Go to sleep, Maman," I said instead. "Tomorrow while I go with Roberto you'll go to the bank and perhaps a letter will be waiting. Or better yet, he might arrive in the city." Whether she slept I couldn't say since I left the room. I sat through the night in a courtyard chair so that I would be ready when Roberto appeared in the morning. The birdcages were fitted with covers. Still, I could hear the birds quietly shifting inside. I found a brilliant long red feather on the slate patio and put it into my jacket pocket like a talisman. It was not that I doubted Roberto. He was most genuine. But I'd stood in his grandfather's lines at the Consulate and that gave me insight, I believed, into how his grandfather played his game. I wanted to be ready. I suspect, Mrs. Roosevelt, that you might know the game of chess. If so, then you know the terrible surprise that can await you if you don't castle your king early in the game.

In the morning Roberto and I sat together while his mother served coffee, and then we made our way into the center of the city, pushing through the crowds, the wide and ragged line of men and women. I'd worn the better of my two suits, hoping to differentiate myself from all of those who, waiting on lines, looked increasingly bedraggled. When Roberto asked, "All of them are waiting for visas?" I didn't answer and pushed us through a knot of women buying loaves of bread.

"Izzy, Izzy." I heard my name being called from within the crowd. It was a girl's voice. Despite all my determination to keep moving forward, I turned at the sound of my name. "Hey, Iz." I saw an arm, a blue-sleeved arm waving. "Sylvie," I thought, "There's my Sylvie!" Sylvie with her sharp wit, her keen artist's eye. Sylvie, with whom I'd spent afternoons trading insults and ideas in the cafés of Brussels. Once I'd tried to kiss Sylvie. Not because I liked her as a girlfriend but because I imagined I should try to kiss every girl who might kiss me back.

Then as I'd drawn close to her, Sylvie laughed, saying, "Cut it out."

"What?" I'd said, adjusting the collar of my shirt. Then Sylvie gave me a hard and deliberate kiss.

"There, Iz. Now you never have to waste our time trying to decide if you should kiss me."

Now, in the dense crowd, I saw a hand waving. I felt a great yearning to see if it truly was my Sylvie. But I didn't stop. I grabbed Roberto's arm and began asking him about his studies at school. I was advancing. The king castled. I'd sacrifice pieces if needed.

At the Consulate entrance, Roberto stepped forward. His easy banter and teasing with the guards reminded me of growing up in my father's glove shop, all the long afternoons as a boy napping beneath the work tables or tagging Henri with a metal glove form I'd lifted from the back table.

A guard appeared and spoke quietly to Roberto. We were motioned through a door and through other doors into a room with rows of tall wooden desks. The room was strangely empty. A man was stationed at each desk, seated in a high-backed chair. Those who waited on the few emaciated lines looked uncomfortable, as if once admitted inside the building they feared they'd wound up in the wrong room or the wrong building altogether.

"Your grandfather?" I asked.

"I've been told he's quite busy and won't be able to join us. But he's taken care of everything." Roberto guided me to a desk at the far side of the room. I was instructed to leave our passports and return in two hours. I insisted on waiting and motioned to one of the empty benches. But it seemed waiting was not an option.

"In any case," said Roberto, "tell me why we should wait here when I could bring you to the café where all my pretty girlfriends are waiting."

I hardly protested. The game was completed, inevitable, secured. He looked buoyant, pleased with having been able to help his new friend. I wanted to keep everything friendly with Roberto. And, I'll admit, it was great to relax, to have a friend, to enjoy a few hours of flirting with Roberto's friends, especially a full-lipped girl named Beatrice whose grandmother had taught her that thirteen kisses brought good fortune. After the first delicious kisses, I whispered, "If it's no trouble, right now I could use a double dose of good luck."

Just as we were to return to the Spanish Consulate, Roberto apologized. "I'm leaving you at the front door, my friend. It was Popo's deal, that I'd go to his sister's, my aunt Marina's, for lunch in exchange for his helping you out."

"But what if—" I started.

"No worries. It's me who should be worried. Eating stringy meat off my blind aunt's filthy plates. But you have nothing to worry about." He called over a guard to escort me in. "I'll see you back at Paradis."

I was, in fact, happy to enter the building alone. I imagined that I was Robin Hood entering the King's castle undisguised. Again the room was practically empty, despite the lines outside. I went over to the same desk at the far side of the room. The clerk had papers in front of him, as if he'd been waiting for me. They were the only papers on his desk. He pressed them to my side of the table.

I opened both passports. "Excuse me, there's a small mistake." The clerk looked right past me as if to motion the next person on line to his desk. "Monsieur," I said, trying to reclaim his attention. The clerk refused me, looking down at his cleared desk.

Suddenly Roberto's grandfather was at my side. "Is my Roberto with you?" His voice was warm as if I were a welcome old family friend. I instantly felt my luck. Just when I needed his intercession, Roberto's busy grandfather had emerged from his offices. Then, of course, I realized it wasn't luck; he'd generously come to check on me.

"Actually, I'm so glad you're here. There's a problem," I said, practically bowing to the Consul as I held out my papers. "There's only one completed visa, Monsieur. My mother's papers have no stamp or signatures." I put the papers back down on the wooden desk. The grandfather lifted the papers with the same deliberate delicacy I'd seen in the hotel courtyard as he held and petted his birds.

"Yes. Unfortunate. Though, I suspect, just a temporary nuisance. It turns out it will be necessary to wait a week, perhaps more, for your mother's transit papers. A technicality. A small one. Not really in my hands. Actually the French and the Belgians are unfortunately to blame for the delay."

He wagged the papers in front of me. I understood that the situation had turned.

"You could wait, I suppose, and go whenever we're given word about your mother's passage through Spain," the grandfather continued, waving the papers. "However, you must know that presents certain risks. The Belgians have been insisting on our cooperation with repatriation. Particularly with those eligible to serve the country. And you understand there are clear indications that changes are imminent at the border. We are not certain what that will mean for the many people who are looking to leave France. If I might offer a humble suggestion, I recommend that you make use of your transit while the opportunity is available."

He pressed the papers into my hands, began to walk away, and then stopped.

"Roberto is a good soul. However, my grandson is more fragile than I would wish. It would be in everyone's best interest that he be kept uninvolved."

Like that, it was over. It was June 24. Paris was occupied. The border was still open. Choices? I had promised my father that I would take care of Maman. I had no choice, Mrs. Roosevelt. If it had ever been a game, the grandfather might have simply called over his shoulder as he left the empty room, "That's checkmate." And then I understood that again I'd been wrong. Mrs. Roosevelt, I'd been wrong about the endgame. Even the idea of the chess game had been wrong. As if playing without sufficient caution or leaving my king unattended was really the issue.

I can't really tell you how I found my way out of the building or through the anxious and tired crowds. I can't say how I managed to get back to the Hotel Paradis. Maman was not there. I closed the painted blue shutters and sat on the edge of the bed. I don't remember thinking anything in particular. I don't think I moved. Instead it was as if, frozen in place, I could attend to only what was happening exactly then. Light slatted into the room. I heard Roberto return home and his mother working her broom in the courtyard. Little bits of their conversation drifted up to my room. The birds were layers of noisy chatter. At some point I heard a key fitted into the door of our room.

"The most amazing thing has happened, Itzak." Maman burst through the open door. She was beaming. "Itzak, I went to the bank and you won't believe what I found." Maman's face seemed strange to me since she'd not smiled for weeks. Now she was practically afire. "I've found the Goldenmans."

I said nothing.

"The Goldenmans are here," she insisted, as if I hadn't heard. "They've been here for six days. They're staying in a transit camp for refugees. Rivesaltes. It isn't far from here, they say. They say it's not bad. Considering. We'll go there. We can be with them. We'll go tomorrow morning to Rivesaltes. Monsieur Goldenman says, it is not fancy but it is clean. People there seem to be getting exit visas. And Max will be coming soon." I stared at my mother. She was brimming. For the first time in weeks there was color in her face. She bustled around the room, opening our valises, preparing to join her friends, to be back among familiar faces.

I stood up from the bed and pulled open the blue shutters. The late afternoon light turned the rocky path out from the garden golden, like a child's tale with an illuminated path leading to something magical.

We are given many chances, Mrs. Roosevelt. Chances for truth and chances for freedom.

"Maman, only I was given a transit visa," I said, beginning with truth. Suddenly I longed to tell Maman everything and then insist that we go now, go immediately into those steep mountain paths and make our way by foot into Spain. Or I'd search the city until I found Sylvie. With her artistic skill she could copy the stamp of my transit visa and we'd make false papers for Maman and the Goldenmans and for Sylvie. We'd all cross safely together.

Maman did not even raise her head to acknowledge what I'd said. "He would have never found us in this hotel," she said, as she worked the sleeves of a shirt, smoothing and folding it carefully before settling it on top of a stack inside the valise. "He'll meet us there at the camp and we'll all be together again. I'm certain now. I think we can wait all this out at Rivesaltes, where we'll be protected." Maman placed her photographs inside the valise. That's when, once again, I was supposed to reveal the truth, saying, Maman, I lied. Papa's made no contact with us. Manuel in the Mexican offices was a hall sweeper, a simpleton. I've heard nothing from Papa since he waved goodbye from the train.

"There's talk of the borders closing," I said. "Within days."

She stood away from the valise and looked at me. There was a long pause before she spoke.

"Izzy, you go then. You go across and I'll wait and leave with my husband."

For a moment I thought she could see into my heart. She knew what I wanted. But then I saw that Maman hadn't seen into my heart, she was simply reckless with happiness at finding the Goldenmans. Or perhaps in that instant we both saw and understood. Maman desperately wanted our old life back. She was too frail to keep going forward. And more than safety, absolutely more than truth, I wanted freedom. I wanted it so badly I would manipulate the simplest truths to get it.

I spoke with resignation. "No, I can't use this visa. Papa made me promise to take care of you."

"No, no, Max will be here soon to take care of what is needed. The Goldenmans are here. You should go ahead first." Maman looked up from a blouse she folded. She believed that she was forming a plan. That she was manipulating the situation. She wanted her son to be safe. She was tired of being so far from Max. Her voice was strong, buoyed with certainty. I said nothing, allowing her to declare a plan. "Actually, it makes sense for you to go ahead of us. Then we can have someone arranging things properly on that side. Everything takes so long, it will help to have you ahead of us."

Again, Mrs. Roosevelt, I had the chance to correct the lies. Instead I told her that perhaps she was right. I hadn't wanted to get her hopes up, but I'd had word that Max would be here within a week. He'd been able to wrestle more money out of the bank and would arrive with our resources a little more secure. And by then,

Roberto's grandfather would easily have transit visas for Maman and Max.

Does it sound impossible to say that at that moment I began believing myself? Max would arrive. The grandfather was telling the truth about Maman's visa. He was, after all, honest about the border. Maybe he really had our interests at heart when he encouraged me to take the opportunity to go tomorrow.

I sat on the tile floor and watched Maman empty the valise she'd begun packing, now separating and repacking the linens and clothes so that there were two distinct bundles. She counted up the money left in our belts, dividing it into unequal piles. She pushed the larger pile at me.

"Papa will be here soon to take care of everything. Anyway I'll be good with the Goldenmans. They're like family." Her voice was stronger than I'd heard it since we'd left the Rue Rogier.

When I reminded her that I couldn't leave France with more than 2,500 francs, Maman answered with a quick, "You don't think I know this?" shooing me with her hands as if I were a pesky child interfering with housework. Maman set up the ironing board and began ironing each bill so that it was completely flat without a crinkle or fold. She placed the ironed bills in rows on one half of a bed sheet. Then she meticulously folded the bed sheet over and repeated with another row of ironed money. She continued ironing and folding until she'd managed to pleat money into two perfectly folded and ironed bed sheets that she packed at the bottom of my suitcase.

When everything was bundled and knotted with cord, Maman knelt next to me on the floor.

"Are your knees hurting, my Izzy?" she asked, her voice so quiet and tender. "I should give your legs a good rubdown." Maman rubbed hot towels on my legs. She was vigorous and confident. I was persuaded that it was a good thing, her renewed energy. And under the warmth and pressure of my mother's small hands, I felt less like a liar than her good, obedient son, and I fell into an easy childish sleep.

The next morning I brought Maman on a bus to the transit camp at Rivesaltes.

Considerable effort had been undertaken to try to make the dismal buildings of Rivesaltes a cheerful place. Painted banners hung between the long whitewashed barracks announcing the children's school and the center for sport. Wooden carts filled with sacks of flour and bicycles strapped with straw moved between flowerpots on the paths. Cotton curtains hung in the barrack windows. I tried to pretend that the air wasn't rank and that many of the people weren't walking around with a look of lost exhaustion, though it was still early morning.

The Goldenmans had already claimed places for Maman and myself in the same barrack they lived in, telling us they'd even secured a job for me working with Henri at the sport center. I gave Henri a clap on his back, but I couldn't look directly at him.

"I'm sending Itzak on," Maman said. "Max will be here in a matter of days."

Monsieur Goldenman began to say something, but Maman cut him off.

"Max wants Izzy to go ahead and get things properly set up. We'll hear from Itzak just the way we've heard from Max." It was obvious how much she wanted to keep things moving at a clip. Maman touched the sleeve of my jacket and gave me four brisk kisses. Then she turned, took Madame Goldenman's arm, and went quickly into the registration office.

"So you've heard from your father?" Monsieur Goldenman asked in a surprised and accusing voice. But he didn't wait for me to answer, following the women into the official building. Henri walked me back to the gate of Rivesaltes. I wanted to insist that my best friend come out of the gate and climb on the bus with me. Perhaps he was thinking the same thing. Or perhaps Henri, who'd always been my other half, easily recognized my liar's face and understood what I'd become. But if that was true, Henri said nothing. Instead he gave me another friendly clap on the back.

"In Lisbon, my friend," he said, "we'll have quite a time in Lisbon, won't we, Izzy?" I said yes and got on the bus alone.

So finally, the truth:

I am Itzak the liar.

I am Itzak the liar who lied to my mother.

I am Itzak the liar who said, "Yes, it will be quite a time in Lisbon," climbed onto the bus, and waved a flimsy see-you-soon to my best friend.

I am Itzak the liar who broke a promise to my father.

And to you, Mrs. Roosevelt, too, no matter what I've called myself—Isaac, John, Richard—I've lied. I am alone on this ship. I left Maman, exhausted, weak, and hopeful, in a French transit camp waiting for her husband to arrive within the week. Where either is now, I'm not certain. I do certainly understand if you no longer want to help save me from returning to Europe.

With apology and shame.

Yours truly,
Itzak Lejdel

Sᴀʀᴀ's ᴛᴜᴄᴋᴇᴅ ʜᴇʀsᴇʟғ into the corner of the ninth-floor library stacks. Her papers spread on the glass-topped wooden desk. Habit has three sharpened pencils lined up to the right of her writing pad, a second legal pad waiting under her books.

Out the window the building's chimneystack rises, a sooty beige against the adjacent building's asphalt roof, where someone's left an unplanted flat of tangled azaleas. Beyond there's a slice of urban geometry—angles of buildings, bricks, pipes, window glass, housing for a fan, wooden water towers, all the chipped and resurfaced colors. She lowers the woven shade just to filter out even a bit of these fascinations.

She's producing, even if slowly. But the work has become a kind of rigorous self-investigation. It sometimes feels like Walter Benjamin has become her investigator. At every comma and turn, Sara encounters questions regarding her motives as a translator. Maybe she's doubted her skill before but never the choice to translate. Now it seems too personal, self-reflexive. It's an uneasy way to proceed with the text.

Suddenly her own invisibility in the work seems suspect. In fact, hasn't the desired goal always been invisibility? The invisible translator. Losing oneself in the other. Trying to grasp the ineffable in a work of art. Always doing work that needs an original other. Never straying from or outshining the original text. It's the unfathomable—the essential substance—that the translator is after. But now Sara's chewing a number 2 pencil, worrying how she can grasp the unfathomable in the heart of his language if she hasn't allowed herself to live fully inside her own interior grammar.

Was translation always a little about loss? Keeping a text alive? Was translation losing herself in her lost mother? In what ways has she undertaken a necessarily incomplete task? Her motivations now seem less intellectual than personal. Or, perhaps, even worse, she'd been looking at Benjamin as a way of not unearthing the rubble of her own buried story.

Sara Leader, the Translator. And the translator of Walter Benjamin because Benjamin is central to a modern understanding of literature and language. But now she's thinking about the Jew part. It's not like it's a big new idea, exactly: she's acknowledged their shared background; a section of the fellowship application dealt with her connection to him as a European Jew. But that always seemed kind of easy, grabbing the Jewish thing, as if that validated anything or gave her any special insight. Especially someone brought up in a devoutly secular home. Not even observation of the High Holy Days. Even with the history of her mother's parents and her mother's childhood in England, Sara felt a bit like a liar on the application.

As a girl Sara loved the Nancy Drew mysteries. Her mother called the yellow-spined books Sara's bon-bons, the way Sara could stay all Sunday in bed reading—sometimes two mysteries in a day. A guilty pleasure. Sara thought her mother would rather her daughter read something better for her.

Now, oddly, despite herself, she's becoming Sara Leader, the Investigator. The reluctant detective. Of what? A story she's agreed not to want to know. That her mother, it seems, wanted her to know. And suddenly people all over the city, all over the country, in Mexico, have vital information they're ready to hand over. Lieberman has sent her the lengthy document on the *Quanza* that he and his nephew have written. It's all there. Memos between Roosevelt and Breckinridge Long and Cordell Hull. The government's attempt to claim that the ship was full of undesirables; *lowly* was a term bandied about. It was important to Long that all eighty-six refugees be sent back to Europe. Keep them out of the United States. Lieberman has also sent along a glossy blowup of a newspaper photograph from the *Norfolk Virginian-Pilot*. A woman and her two children stare sadly out a ship's porthole down at the husband she was to meet in America. A yellow post-it fixed to the photograph says the two children, Lile and Rosa, are alive. One of them lives at 234 West 86th Street, just three blocks from Sara's apartment.

Sara reaches down into her workbag. Lieberman's document is there. She hasn't been able to read it all the way through. If she's a detective, she's a detective with squinting eyes.

She skims through the Xeroxed pages for her father's name. She's hoping even for her grandmother, Sahra Lejdel. Of course, it's not there. But there are names of other passengers. Prominent passengers. Rothschild. Cartier. Rand. In the article it says that a drawing of the well-known French actor Dalio had been passed around by German soldiers in Perpignan as an example of a typical Semitic thug's profile.

Sara heads down two flights to the children's room. It has hardly changed; the window banquet is still there, and although the ticking has been changed to a floral print, there are still the same high draped windows with curtains pulled partway open or closed.

She doesn't know if the library has the books, too low-brow perhaps, certainly her mother had thought so. She remembered the author's name, Carolyn Keene, but wonders now for the first time if that is really a person, Carolyn Keene, or an invented author, a front for a veritable factory of writers churning out the Nancy Drew, the Bobbsey Twins, and the Hardy Boys series. Sure enough, there it is, Nancy Drew, a shelf of old yellow-spined Nancy Drew, and new boldly designed paperbacks.

Sara pulls number 11, *The Clue of the Broken Locket*.

She wants to think that she remembers the particular episode. But looking at the cover, three girls poking under low branches, the bow of a canoe, she's not sure which of the girls is actually Nancy. Sara sits down at a child's desk and begins to read. The comfort's instant, the size of the book, the type; it all has the spell of familiarity.

The mystery's announced in the first sentence: a key placed beside Nancy's breakfast plate. Also, right away there's Nancy's father, smiling, inviting adventure. That's the thing about Nancy Drew. Her father, Carsen Drew, encouraged Nancy with her mysteries. In fact, it was Carsen Drew who asked his daughter for help solving the mysteries that emerged in his professional life as a lawyer. By the third page it's all there: Nancy's encouraging father and Nancy's mother, dead. Had Sara ever noticed this when she was younger, still gobbling Nancy Drew after her own mother had died? Had she registered the dead mother connection; the mother substitute, Hannah, the housekeeper; and the attentive father? But there the connections ended. Encouraged to be intrepid, Nancy is intrepid. Here is Nancy, insatiably curious, leaping into canoes, chasing prowlers, always eager to get at the unknown. In response to her friend's concern, Nancy grins and says, "I guess I'm just a tough old sleuth!" Had Sara loved the mysteries because Nancy was permitted to do what Sara had tacitly promised never to do?

Sara reads. Every page feels cozy. The comforting dullness of plot. Upstairs are the exacting sentences of Benjamin. Sara can't force herself back to them while Nancy cheerfully slogs through swamps discovering broken lockets in the hulls of rowboats. Lights flash in the high round window of a stone lodge, and Nancy feels certain there's someone trapped inside trying to call for help. There are burglars and intruders, proper fiancés and boyfriends. Nancy and her friends are a rush of adverbs, always agreeably, excitably, admirably quick to rush into chancy encounters.

Sara stays put in the Children's Room reading right through to the end. When the librarian hovers close, Sara looks up and gives a preemptive answer, "I'm doing research."

⁂

"You were little girls?" Sara asks, looking at the two sisters. It seems impossible. Sure the sisters, Lile and Rosa, both petite, bright-faced with almost transparent skin, look youthful, but in a well-cared-for, lived-a-good-life, elderly person kind of manner. Though she's just called, they're dressed for company, silk blouses with ties, soft wool skirts, their matching blond hair curled and pinned behind their ears. They could be twins, but they've already told Sara that Lile is the elder by two years.

"Thank you for meeting with me." Sara's told them what by now is her usual line—that she's a professor doing research on the refugee situation during the war. She's been given their names by Lieberman.

The apartment's a funny combination of old and new world. Grand Viennese shabbiness meets retro modern. Sofas upholstered in threadbare purple velvet flanked by Eames and Mies van der Rohe chairs. A massive, dark hutch jammed with figurines of chickens and cows, a peasant girl and boy with milk buckets balanced between them. But there's also two framed Peter Max lithographs above the sofa and a patterned shag rug on the parquet floors.

"Won't you have some of my bakery?" Rosa holds out a plate of pound cake and cookies that look like ruglach. Sara takes a piece of cake and she feels the women relax. Like the apartment, they're a funny mix of old world and contemporary, proper skirts and stockings accessorized with silver arm bangles and dangly crystal earrings. "I'm afraid we won't be too much help, really."

"Anything's a help, really," Sara assures them.

"Well, we were quite small. Five and seven. Mother was with us. Father was already in America. We were meeting him. We were to meet him in New York but, as you know, we were not permitted to leave the ship. When we came to Virginia, our father was waiting. He was beside himself. But he never showed it. Day and night, he was there; day and night, on the pier, calling out, trying to let us know we'd be all right."

"What was it like on the ship?"

"Well, it rained quite a bit." Lile laughs. Sara watches crumbles of cookie that catch in Lile's teeth as she speaks. "We told our mother that if it rained this much in America then we were happy to go home and we never wanted to go ashore. But more than that, Professor, it's honestly just a story we've been told enough times that it seems it might be real. There's a photograph of us with our mother looking through a porthole and our father reaching up to us from the dock."

"Yes, I've seen the photograph. It's very moving." What was Sara thinking, coming here? That those dark-eyed girls were still children? Five and seven, Lile and Rosa are New Yorkers, have been for sixty-three years and the boat is, mostly, Sara guesses, like some of this old world furniture, the women's connection to their deceased parents. Sara looks at the photographs that flank the side table. Wedding pictures. A gaggle of children on beaches, in Halloween costumes, at bar mitzvah parties. A five-picture frame with grade school portraits. Lile and Rosa are not only New Yorkers; they are clearly American grandmothers—what did Sara think she'd find?

"Something more? Anything?" Sara says. But when the women share a look with each other, Sara says, "Really, even if it seems like nothing."

"I remember being scolded for running up and down between the decks. I remember making a fortress out of deck chairs. I'm sorry. This can't be what you're looking for," Rosa says, holding out the plate for Sara to take another, though she's not yet touched the first piece. "There are others who were on the ship who were older."

"Do you know Richard Leader?" Sara asks.

"Do we know Richard?" Lile laughs. "Who doesn't know Richard?"

"You've spoken to him? That would be wonderful," Rosa says, clearly relieved that the sisters have a backup. "He remembers everything. Like he was keeping a diary. So you've spoken to him?"

"No, not yet. He wasn't available."

"Well, you're in for a divine treat. Such a gentleman," Lile says. "*Him*, I remember from the ship. Very serious, very handsome; I had my first schoolgirl crush on him. I was all of seven years old. I used to force Rosa to spy on him with me, while he was working."

"He worked on the ship?"

"He had a typewriter. He wrote things."

"What things?"

"I don't know. At the time I imagined it was all something very romantic, like love letters or love poems to the girl he left behind. When you meet him, call him Izzy. That's his nickname, short for Itzak. This Richard name is his American name. He hates the name Izzy and I love to tease him."

"As you can see, Professor, once a crush, always a crush," sparks Rosa, with a younger sister's mischief and delight.

SEPTEMBER 13

5:30 P.M.

Dear Mrs. Roosevelt,

I'm not certain how to continue or if I should continue. Though the truth, Mrs. Roosevelt, finally brings some relief. I spent these hours since my last letter in front of your newspaper photograph trying to imagine what you might say, how you might respond to me. Then I took it down from where it's been tacked up by the dining room. I've decided to carry it with me.

Here's what I imagine. You are angry, disappointed. Sometimes you turn away, muttering, "A con man, indeed."

Other times I imagine you lean toward me, saying, "It is the unspoken pledge of mothers to care for the child of any mother who is absent."

Or, with a brusque wave of your hand, you announce, "No more apologies, please. A waste of my time. I'd rather hear the rest of your story. Only from now on tell the truth, Isaac."

Truthfully, it will be hard to keep to the truth. Hard not to want to heroically turn myself back at Rivesaltes and grab mother's lashed suitcases and tell you that, despite her protests, I carried her onto the bus and skillfully navigated our way across the border with only one official stamp and signature. So if I am less fanciful, less decorative for a bit, I hope you will understand that I am reigning myself in, in the service of truth.

I will try to be vigilant.

I boarded a local bus to Spain. The bus was full, overcrowded, merchants, tradesmen, locals who made the trip regularly between the border villages. And additionally there were those like myself, foreigners, trying to fit too many belongings in the small racks above the seats.

"May I share the seat?" I said, finding a place next to two girls who looked up at me with amazing dark-lash-rimmed eyes. "May I?" I repeated and the girls kept their open stare, not budging and clearly not understanding my French.

"Forgive them," a woman said in French. She leaned over the seat and scolded the children sharply in Spanish. The girls pressed close.

"Please, please," she said, gesturing to the place she'd cleared on the wooden seat. She was also dark—dark hair, dark eyes, even the shadow from the bones at her throat was an exotic, rich darkness. She was stunning, and the beauty of her girls intensified everything, as if they were some kind of gorgeous accessory, like sparkling jewelry on the perfect wrist of a gorgeous woman. And so sitting close to the girls was like being offered the hand of this bejeweled dark creature. If it sounds to you that I am dipping back into exaggeration, know that I am mostly attempting to confess how easily I was distracted from the regret and responsibility of having left Maman and into the adventure and prospect of a beautiful woman in a new country.

But before we had driven five minutes we were ordered out of the bus into the French border inspection. It was still early morning. I stood in line behind a Hungarian family. They had so much with them—trunks, lamps, rugs, even, believe it or not, metal sink fixtures. I thought my placement was fortuitous since they had so much luggage and so many children that, in comparison, my presence would be unremarkable.

A tiny, tiny woman wearing layers of sweaters despite the heat moved in twitchy quick steps back and forth between the line and the customs officer, peering around the Hungarian man's arm. I assumed her to be related to the family—a sister or aunt—until the father threw up his hands, shouting in French, "Madame, what is your business? Why do you examine my papers! Get away from us."

The woman came in very close to the man, her face reaching only to his chest. She tilted her face up to him and said in a flat voice, "I am, Monsieur, the chief inspector."

The man instantly reddened, a heavy mustache of sweat lining his lip. He bowed. He shuffled. Pulled his youngest boy up from where he rested on top of blankets folded into a basket. With all the bowing and shuffling it was almost a comical theater act. "*Je suis désolé,*" he finally choked out in his heavy Hungarian accent. "I am so sorry." He repeated it again and again, his mustache thickening and dripping until they passed his family through.

The custom's officer was brief with me. He opened my valise. He moved around my clothes, touched the sheets Maman had so carefully ironed. The money was uncreased and silent. He glanced at my papers. I declared my 2,500 francs. There were no questions. I managed a simple "Good day" and walked back outside to wait close to the bus.

But within moments all inspections were halted. A rumor sprang up that the border had shut. It was minutes before 11 o'clock. Suddenly a band began playing. Gendarmes marched in formation right up to a statue of a fallen soldier. A boy carrying the French flag emerged out of the tight formation and laid the flag at the base of the statue. A speech was made, and then another speech. I didn't dare move closer and so could not hear what was being said. The young boy began in a high boy's voice to sing the Marseillaise. Men joined in. Many of the gendarmes openly wept. Four men stepped forward and carefully folded up the French flag.

Then it was over. The customs officers went back inside. The lines reformed. That was it. We were the last bus through before the border shut and reopened under the jurisdiction of the Vichy government. I rode out of France, now seated next to the beautiful Spanish mother. Our bus bumped down the rough mountainous roads and we were jostled into one another in not unlovely ways.

Soon we crossed into Spain and stopped at the Spanish border station.

Spain, in contrast to France, has no limits on money and valuables. Only that you may not leave the country with one dollar more than you arrived with. Imagine the commotion, the tumult of suitcases, the tearing open of children's satchels to reveal silver candlesticks and spoons. It was a frenzy as all of the hidden valuables were brought out. The bus was a glitter of precious stones and diamonds. A cheer of delight rose up from the Spanish locals when a long rope of black pearls was pulled from a child's sock. Like a magic show. To the astonishment of the mother and girls, I carefully unfolded every pleat of my two bed sheets, gathering each crisply ironed bill into my money belt, which I declared to the Spanish inspectors.

By that night I'd arrived in Barcelona and found a room in the Hotel Europa. I was alone in Spain. My mother was in France. I didn't know where my father was. Roberto's grandfather had been right about imminent change. I'd listened to him instead of listening to my father. I'd like to say that I felt lonely and scared. I'd like to say I felt like a guilty son. But I felt lucky. There's the truth. And I wonder, Mrs. Roosevelt, if there isn't always a kind of ruthlessness to luck?

Yours truly,
Your son

I T B A N G S A G A I N S T T H E back of her leg going up the narrow stairs. She can't afford what she's doing, getting the chairs re-caned, but she figures that if she goes at them one at a time she can do it, taking a break when the money gets tight or, at worst, she'll have two or three usable chairs if the money runs out. But she needs things mended. Her life in order. And if her life seems like too vast a goal, at least she can pay to get the chairs fixed. Get her life in order before a child comes into it. She's said good-bye to Marco, which wasn't as hard as she'd anticipated. He kissed her on forehead and said, "Mi carino, you are always in my heart." Then in an hour's time, she'd sat down and written the autobiography for the adoption agency. Soon she was told she would have to write the child a letter, send photographs of herself and those she considered her family. She might as well start with the chairs.

She sets down the chair at the counter. The shop smells richly of wood stain and oil. Down an aisle of stacked chairs, Sara sees the owner standing on a metal stool unhooking a ladder-back chair from where it hangs from a ceiling rafter. Until she sees him, the lean stretch of him, the tousle of his hair, she hasn't even quite admitted to herself that she'd hoped to see him again.

"Hello, hello, Sara Leader," he says, smiling down at Sara. "Looking to meet more people from your past in my shop. That was some wild moment. You should have seen yourself—like a creature stunned in the road."

"I'll just stick with redoing chairs, thanks very much." Sara laughs, happy to have a quick retort. She likes that he'd seen her, been watching, but she doesn't like being seen through so easily. "How do you remember names so well?"

"By only remembering the ones I want to remember." Now she locates the shop's clean smell of rush caning. Oil and straw. It feels good to breathe it in. She likes his smile. She's never seen him smile.

It makes her nervous, actually.

"I know you're ridiculously expensive, so I figured I'd just stretch the chairs out and do them one at a time."

He stands down from the stool and makes his way to Sara, moving chairs in his path.

"You could go the other way?"

"What's that? Pay you less?"

"Stretch out paying me my ridiculous rate but do the chairs all in one swoop."

"That seems dangerous."

"I don't know. I like the idea of you owing me. I might like that a lot."

She looks again. No ring. Doesn't mean anything. The guy works with his hands all day. Wouldn't wear a ring.

"And your name is?" she starts with an easy question.

"Will you remember?" He looks at her straight on. No play in his voice. Nothing's going to be easy with this man.

"I'm not great with names," she says. If she responds to him by saying that yes, she'll remember, it sounds too serious.

"Let's have a look." He holds out his hand and Sara's flustered, no fast comeback. What does he want to look at? Her hands? Is she wearing a ring?

"The chair," he says, as if reading her confusion. "Let me take a look at it."

He kneels next to her chair and begins moving his hands along it. He presses at the broken weave, pinching it between his fingers. His fingers are a sheened, uneven brown. He covers the perimeter of the chair, keeping his face close to the seat, as if he's listening to the chair.

"I could use a synthetic and it would be quite a bit less. But you won't like it. This one also needs re-gluing. Or you're going to fall right on your ass."

"If I'm doing it, I want you to do it the right way. So you might as well do the whole shebang and if I go broke at least I'll have one perfect chair."

"I'll do it the right way, Sara." He slips his stained hands along the wood of the legs. "And, by the way, even if you don't remember, I'll tell you: I'm Ethan." She likes the way the smile fits on his face and he can still look a little grumpy at the same time.

"Hello, Ethan." Her shyness surprises her. Formal. She's inclined to stick out her hand. As if she's just walked in the room. As if they haven't been talking all this time.

"I want to ask you to get a coffee sometime. But I watched the skilled way you put that woman off last time. Forget it, I'm too scared."

"I'd like that very much, Ethan." She doesn't try to push any of it away—not her own formality, not his interest.

"Why would I be here, why would I sitting here in this coffee shop having coffee with you if I were married, Sara? Why would I call you?" No play, no irony. The man's serious.

"Oh, come on. Are you serious?" Sara asks, making every effort to keep her voice light. She wants at least to pride herself on calling the situation before she's finished her first cup of tea. But there's Ethan across from her and he looks like he's waiting for her to answer her own question. Ethan looks at her. Hard. No trace of the boyish smile. She watches something working—a muscle, a twitch—under the skin of his face. Sara looks down into her cup. It seems impossible to look up.

"How could I be anything but serious? Are you serious, Sara?"

"I like making a useful thing useful again." That was his first answer when she asked him about the repair business.

His second answer was wood. He loved the complexity of wood that other people had cut and turned and jointed. Touching it, he loved touching it. His hands keeping whole what another man he'd never meet, another man most likely long dead, had made with his hands.

"Is that pitifully romantic?" Ethan asked. "Sometimes I worry that I'm not living enough in the present. Then I look around at what the present offers and I don't know."

When it's her turn, she tells him about the woman she'd met in his shop. She hasn't even told Helen about Rochelle Goldenman. Or her father. But she's telling Ethan.

They leave the coffee shop and walk down to Riverside Park. They stop by the Hudson River boat basin and lean against the metal fence that closes off the boatyard. There are seasonal small craft moored in the slips and permanent houseboats, each with distinct hodgepodge constructions—a wooden two-floor tower, decks, skylights, and a metal chimney for a wood stove. A light's on in the smallest of the houseboats moored there. It gives a golden glow to the boat's curtained cabin. Ethan angles sideways against the fence and looks at Sara. It seems okay telling him about her father. Beyond okay. As if with him there's nothing she'll have to edit about herself.

"It's funny that it was you there that day," she says, "like you were meant to be the witness of this shift in me."

She tells him what Rochelle Goldenman had told Sara about her grandmother and the camp. How she's looked it up. Sara's even found an Internet site, which has photographs of how the place looked. It wasn't a concentration camp, not even a deportation camp at that point. It really was a refugee camp, a transit camp. People went in and out with passes. In the photograph there were banners, some attempts to make the place look a little jolly. But she read that the conditions even then were deplorable. It seems to have been built on a mosquito-infested swamp. There's a piece of text that speaks about what went on at the transit camp. There were even classes held for the children. The trains didn't begin for a little while.

"But he brought her there. He left her there, his own mother." She says it like a confession of her own worst deed. By the end Sara had wanted her mom to die already. She'd even refused for a few days to come into the room where her mother lay when the night nurse called Sara to read to her mom. When she'd finally agreed, she read badly, in the flat tone that she knew her mother would have corrected if she'd been able to get out the words. And afterward she had never been willing to receive consolation. Hated every smushy kiss by her mother's friends.

"I'm sorry," the music teacher said, stopping Sara after class had ended and the children had thrown their plastic recorders into the instrument bin.

"For what?" Sara asked and, with an annoyed toss of her hair, rushed ahead to where her friends bumped into one another, horsing around by the fifth-grade lockers.

Ethan moves his hand against Sara's on the railing. "And why do you think you know what that means, Sara?" He's smiling now. Without mockery or judgment. An open smile.

"No, it's that I don't know." She wonders what her mother had known. If her father ever confessed it to his wife. If at some point he'd genuinely come to believe his own fabrication.

"And you think you have to know. Why? I don't understand."

"Because I'm his daughter," she says.

"And knowing will make a difference in you?"

"Because I'm his daughter," she says, as if repetition makes the response correct. But that isn't it. Because she's begun thinking that even not knowing was in the end a kind of knowing. A corrosive thing that harbors silently inside.

He leads her up from the water, lingering at the dog run, past the bronze sculpture of Eleanor Roosevelt at the park's edge on 72nd Street. Sara looks around. There's a lady sitting on a bench with two toy poodles in her lap. Another lady walks by pushing a double stroller. Across the street, where Riverside Drive curves, is One Riverside Drive. The building is turn-of-the-century, old New York, a limestone façade with rounded turrets. Once home to a prominent family, now home to the Islamic Cultural Center. At the entrance tall wooden cubbies with shoes stored and stacked while men go inside for prayer. Outside, on Riverside, a line of parked taxis.

"Where to now, Sara Leader?" Ethan asks.

"Can we keep walking?" she says, though what she means is she'd go anywhere.

SEPTEMBER 13

7:30 P.M.

Dear Mrs. Roosevelt,

Look long enough at any atlas and the way to go from anywhere to anywhere will at last make itself evident. For two afternoons I sat under the high ceilings in the library at Lisbon University and stared at maps of the Americas. The library fans clacked above my head, occasionally filling the thick pages with air. Like sails of a ship, I thought. It was a ship I sought, or rather shipping routes. I was looking for a Mexican ship that went either to Morocco or Shanghai, where I had legal visas. I wanted to create a necessary reason for a Mexican transit visa. If you recall, I'd not yet secured anything from the Mexican Consulate except for the sad exchange in Paris with the fat Manuel.

I'd not had any initial luck with the Mexicans in Lisbon. But if I could prove that I needed passage to Mexico en route to China, for instance, I stood a chance of getting transit papers. But I was more than a little glad for the chance to sit in the library. Maps have always made me happy. A map declares, makes a proclamation: this country exists, is bordered by that country. This wide river flows through this kingdom. To look at the lines, the shaded areas, is to yield—even momentarily—to a belief system. The assertion seems physical, but isn't it really political? Who controls the waterways? Who has which resources? Who gives the mapmaker his daily cup of wine? The declarations of maps are really a record of shifting political allegiances, a record of power, how commerce has defined our understanding of space.

Maybe this all sounds a little theoretical for a fellow trying to find a way to Mexico, but I suppose it felt good to sit again among other students and have a day to think the curious thoughts of a student.

It was on the crackly page of an old shipping map that finally I traced a broken blue line that swung down from Mexico, making a path around South America, dotting around the world and landing in Shanghai. Eureka! Mexico to Shanghai! I felt like Columbus. And just like many a discoverer in Lisbon showing his path to the sponsoring kingdom, I could now run to the Mexican Consulate with proof that a valid transit visa could be issued.

But I didn't rush to the port. I stopped along the marbled sidewalks on the square off the Avenue d'Liberdad, where for a few escudos I had a coffee and ten pastries. I ate all ten. Slowly I entered the heaven of crèmes and fruits. And what a heaven it was!

Then I strolled to the shipping companies and corroborated that there was a cargo ship that ran five times each year from a port south of Vera Cruz and landed in Shanghai. By the end of the next day I'd secured my transit visa for Mexico.

I'd already learned that a ship called the *Quanza* had been chartered for New York and Vera Cruz, having been rerouted from its regular South African passage. It was scheduled to leave in a few weeks. I purchased a third-class ticket from the E. Pinto Basso and CL Travel Agency. The company insisted that each passenger provide payment for a return ticket, their insurance for the risk of transporting those of us without Mexican or American citizenship.

The ticket agent looked suspiciously at my Mexican transit visa, and no amount of pleading persuaded him to drop the return fare. For a moment I considered backing away, not shelling out for the return ticket and waiting for another boat.

But the *Quanza* seemed already to have some good luck connected with it, even before it had left Lisbon. It was known that a Rothschild had booked passage. Also Pierre Lazarette, editor of *Paris Soir*. I thought somehow that this boded well for the ship—that we'd be safe with money and press aboard. My passage felt insured, as if they'd confer prestige on me.

Lisbon was a perfect place to wait. I settled easily into days of pastries on the Avenue d'Liberdad. There was a festive summery feel on the square. Each day I met people who had managed to cross at the French border and I toasted and drank to our health and safety. I asked everyone about Rivesaltes, but no one had information. The Vichy border was unpredictable—but certainly men and women were still coming into Spain.

One afternoon I watched as a man touched a woman on the shoulder. She turned and fell into his arms in a swoon. Then she stood back, disentangled from his arms, and just looked at him. She stood not speaking for perhaps two minutes. "Thomaz, Thomaz," she whispered and held her palm to his face. It was a moment out of the cinema. Every day there were dramatic moments. Between sisters, between childhood friends. It was not as if I hadn't seen people reunited in Toulouse or Perpignan. But Lisbon was different, like a relief, like a summer resort where we had all finally arrived to pass the long hot days together.

With all the movement around me, how could I not be hopeful that soon Maman and the Goldenmans and Max would appear in the square? I scripted loud, tearful scenes of reunion in my head. "Didn't save any for us," Henri's father would tease, balancing an empty plate of pastries on my head. After all the hoopla, we'd hurry over to the E. Pinto Basso and CL Travel Agency and secure tickets for everyone on the *Quanza*.

It was not all dreaming. Each day I made daily postings to Maman at Rivesaltes. I wrote to Max in care of his factory foreman. I returned to the library and charted new routes, ones that took Maman and Max through South Africa or from Spain to Africa and then on to Argentina. I could meet them in Brazil. The strategies were lengthy and hopeful, and I included in my letters, whenever possible, the names of various shipping companies.

I'd imagine our new lives. In Mexico. In Argentina. An apartment in New York City. We'd gather at our new dining table, eating off new plates. At the end of the meal we'd all agree that my leaving alone was what had finally saved us all.

The day the *Quanza* departed from Lisbon was clear. I was proud to be on a ship with so many notable passengers. Again, I enjoyed my luck, certain that I was exactly where I was supposed to be.

That first night, my easy acclimation to the sea even seemed a sign that I'd been right to leave Europe without my parents. Brussels seemed so far away. A small, provincial city. And if my parents also felt far from me, even that seemed somehow like a lucky opportunity to measure the man I was becoming, a man who would bring his parents to safety.

How easily, Mrs. Roosevelt, I'd forgotten my own rule to trust no one, especially not myself.

Yours truly,
Isaac

"I NEED SOMETHING ridiculously not me," Helen says, holding up two bottles of nail polish. "Maybe purple, like I'm playing drums in Aerosmith. The more outrageous the better."

Sara and Helen are at Kim's Salon on 94th and Broadway, sitting in big overstuffed chairs, getting pedicures. Below them two Korean women lift their feet in and out of soapy hot water. It's become their thing, Sara taking Helen out for a weekly wilding—martinis with lunch, facials in Soho. There's been talk of a strip club.

"I'm not sure a comedy club isn't a better idea," Helen says. "I'm having a hard time thinking that some gay boy in a G-string shaking over me is going to really do a lot for me at this point."

This week there wasn't time to consider strippers or comedy or the tasting menu at Bouley Bakery. Both of Helen's kids and now her husband are home with a bug that Helen says is the bug of all bugs. The hit man bug. The motherfucking bug couldn't decide whether it wanted to be the fever-and-puking kind, the stomach kind, or the snot, congestion, whooping-cough kind. So it decided to be all of them at once: Asian flu, Brazilian scourge, Amazon malaria—you name it, Helen says, it's the killer-off-the-boat-New-York-melting-pot flu.

Helen has exactly one hour. Exactly one hour, she says, to feel like something other than an embittered, furious, germ-infested, ready-to-buy-a-one-way-ticket-to-Tahiti kind of mother.

"Yes, do absolutely everything," Helen says, when the woman holds up a razor to use on Helen's callused heels. She leans close to Sara. "If there's time after my hands and my feet, maybe she'll give me a happy ending plus a facelift."

The Korean manicurists chatter continuously as they work below Sara and Helen. They speak across the room, shouts and chirps from the pedicure section to the nail tables. It's like every language Sara can't understand—sitting in the midst of it feels cozy. She knows they could be right now saying something derogatory about her, about all the customers. *What was this one thinking, putting that ass in those jeans? Look at that big show-off diamond on a woman with the face of a rat!* Or it could all be workplace complaints. About tips. Smelly feet. Cindy, who is now massaging warm cream on Sara's legs, might be talking about wanting to hurry the fuck up and go have a cigarette. It doesn't matter. Sara just likes sitting among the cadences, the rise and tilt of an unknown language, the familiarity of their unfamiliar banter.

Sara tries to concentrate on what Helen is saying to her. But given the choice between the lullaby of Korean voices and Helen's clear, enunciated fury, Sara wants to be soothed.

Sara considers the nametags pinned on the women's striped work jackets. Where did Cindy come up with the name Cindy? Susan. Cindy. Carla. Jill. Maria at the front desk. Why the suburban American names? Is the assumption that the customers are too stupid, too unwilling to manage a name like Su-Xin Kim? Is Cindy only Cindy here at 94th and Broadway? Sara had gone to school with a Victoria Pak, a Ralph Chang, a Heather Dvirsky. Children whose foreign-born parents had begun the process of making American children, the insistence on giving their American-born children

American names. Children of a new world, sons and daughters of men and women who'd arrived here every which way. Sometimes with legitimate visas. Often they arrived across borders in the night, over barbed-wire fences, fording rivers, stowed on planes or on boats. Small boats dragged ashore on every coast of this country in every season, and always the border guards, inspectors, immigration officers looking to turn them back. Men and women and children abandoned in the back of metal trucks, dead, finally, of the Texas heat. How many each year don't arrive, don't finally show up at relatives' houses in Los Angeles, in Queens, in Miami, in Houston, in Atlanta? And how many show up and say, "I'm here, like I said in the letters, I've arrived." Wave after wave of immigrants, all of whom want children holding hands over their third-grade hearts, saying with good clear accents the Pledge of Allegiance. American children. Let these children born in this new country be safely ashore. Let them learn the ways of this country. Let them blend in. Children with proper birth certificates, children of the American mall, American television, American consumption.

Helen is talking to her. Something about the stupidity of pediatricians and their germ-infested lairs. Something about buying stock in Lysol. Sara tries to give herself to Helen. Maybe she should tell Helen about this new man, Ethan. But it is so new. Nothing really going on. A coffee. A walk by the river. Helen would want to know. She'd croon over his availability. But there's even more that feels different, some change that's happening in Sara. For now, Sara wants to just keep it for herself.

"Just promise me that when you become a mother, you won't become one of those holy mothers on me, one of those humorless I-love-every-minute-of-the-whole-motherhood types. Okay?"

"Not a problem, Helen." Helen's her oldest friend, almost less a friend than a sister. She'd promise Helen anything.

"And also I want seniority," Helen says. "Even if you're suffering. Let's say both our kids have colds at the same time. I still want to be the one who needs the most TLC since I'll have been at it longer."

⬥

The split spine of the *World Atlas* cracks as she opens it. She's come to the library to gather her books from where she'd left them before meeting Helen. But first she wants to look. Wants somehow to place everyone in their rightful spot. She pushes the large heavy pages and they buckle, then hang in the air before straightening in a fall to the other side of the book. Each page makes a weighted whoosh paper sound. She passes Europe and has to flip back a few pages to find it. Rochelle Goldenman said the families traveled from Belgium together to someplace north of Paris. It had taken six days to get from Brussels to the border. Sara locates the ledger. Measures the distance against her finger. It's 264 kilometers between Brussels and Paris, 164 miles. How could it have possibly taken six days to get into France? In a car, Rochelle said, with people they didn't know. On the West Side Highway on a Friday, if you didn't slip out of the city early enough, you could get stuck for more than an hour between 72nd and the ramp to the George Washington Bridge. That was in normal rush-hour traffic. Not flight traffic. Not traffic that included those on foot or bicycle or wheelbarrow. She's a New Yorker; of course she's imagined disaster routes, and each time Sara felt the serious failure of her imagination. It became comical. People riding off on kid scooters, the tricked-out fancy jogging strollers loaded down with computers. The Sunday rollerbladers skating off with boom boxes blaring salsa. Everyone on the road hooked up with disc players and iPods.

In northern France, Rochelle said, they'd all split up. Sara's grandfather returned to Brussels by train. They'd not found one another in Paris but had reconnected in the South of France. In Perpignan. She touched the line, the light brown that indicated the mountainous border of the Pyrenees. Her grandfather was in Brussels, her grandmother at the border in a transit camp. Sara's father had crossed over to Spain. Like Walter Benjamin, her father had crossed through to Spain. Just months apart from Benjamin. Unlike Benjamin, nobody eagerly awaited her father's arrival. Nobody eagerly awaited the manuscripts he carried. Nobody was busy working to ensure him a position at a university. Unlike Benjamin, he crossed through to Lisbon.

Sara moves from the atlas to microfiche. All the editions of the *New York Times* from August and September 1940. There's the text of Churchill's speech on the war's progress and the U.S. defense plan. Trotsky's murder. An August 28 article from Vichy, France, announcing the repatriation of 1,000,600 refugees, including 390,000 Belgians returned home. The minister reported progress in the housing and care of refugees and the organization of services that helped persons separated during the exodus to find one another.

But mostly it's all the other things in the newspaper that draw Sara's attention. The schedule of the World's Fair. The Flying Eugenes present hair-raising tricks, including Mr. Solomon, the fire diver, diving 120 feet into a four-foot tank. There are lectures on "The Art of the Ages," swing bands, organ recitals. There's a trousseau display in the World of Fashion Theater. There's an official film in the Federal Works Agency called "Housing in Our Times." In one article, Bonwit Teller department store claims the pompadour as the hairstyle of the minute, with toque hats and tricornes to fit the neatly swept hair. There's hardly an article about Eleanor Roosevelt that doesn't mention what she's wearing. She arrived at the Works Progress Administration headquarters to urge the speedy signing of national defense contracts wearing "a brown flowered print dress, a brown straw hat with a wide brim, brown stockings and shoes to match." There's an entire piece devoted to the addition of six costumes and three hats added to Eleanor Roosevelt's winter wardrobe. It takes a leap of the imagination to see her posing in her new day dress of "black velvet with a Basque-type bodice."

Sara relocates the August 21 *New York Times* article on the initial landing of the *Quanza*. She reads it again, though she's been sent a Xerox of this article by Lieberman. Also, there's a small September 5 mention of a ship being turned away from Vera Cruz, Mexico. The ship apparently came from Lisbon, carrying 100 Jewish refugees with improper papers. The ship's name is *Zawoa*. Sara wonders if the name was reported incorrectly. She knows that some twenty people managed to get off the *Quanza* in Mexico. Again she feels the ridiculous hopeful surge that her grandmother was among them. She makes prints from the microfiche of these articles and the front page of the *Times* on August 20.

Everything else that she prints is random, advertisements of purses and gloves, a map of the British air war on Axis powers, back-to-school clothes from Best & Co. There are advertisements boasting a complete dinner at Childs' restaurant in Manhattan for fifty-five cents or a cape house in Beach Hampton, Long Island, for 1,290 dollars. Sara feeds dimes into the microfiche printer. She lines up the scanner. Tries to be precise. It takes four prints per page of the *Times*. Often she has to repeat a section. Still there are always overlaps.

SEPTEMBER 14

4:30 A.M.

Dear Mrs. R.

Madeleine LeBeau.

Madeleine LeBeau.

I must say her name. And because I cannot, dare not, say it aloud, forgive me, Mrs. Roosevelt, but you must be the recipient of yet another confession of my ruthless luck.

Again, and again, Madeleine LeBeau.

I should be asleep, but here I am pacing the deck, practically typing as I walk. It is somehow right that I confess this to you because it was last night as I stood holding your photograph and saying, if you will, a final good night to you, that a door swung open, light from the room spilling out, and also spilling out, practically falling on me, was Marcel Dalio's wife, Madeleine LeBeau.

"Have you been waiting long for me?" she asks. Her voice is moist and breathy.

"At least most of my life," I say without a moment's pause. Call me Cary Grant. I have the movies to thank for that catchy line.

She stood smiling and looking at me. I didn't know what to do next. I was stunned she'd spoken to me. I forced myself not to look down, not lose her gaze. She's beautiful, that hair, those eyes, exactly the kind of beautiful you'd expect to win the heart of an actor like Dalio, though I believe I've mentioned to you that she must be younger than he is by at least twenty years.

"Would you care to take a late evening stroll?" I managed when I could finally speak.

"Oh, don't be dreary," she said, slipping her thin arm in mine. "I couldn't abide another walk on the decks besieged by endless updates on our boringly hopeless situation. I want you to take me out of here."

The childishness of her request was instantly clear. Take me off this ship. I'm weary of this silly business. With her pouting face tipped up to me, I wanted desperately to fulfill her request. No doubt this was a girl who was accustomed to having her desires avidly met.

"Come," I said, though without a clue as to where we might go. I'd already tried the doors to the many empty first-class cabins, though I'd not yet found a single one open. In any case, a night in a first-class cabin would hardly be a treat for Madeleine LeBeau, who, obviously, was already traveling first class.

A group of men walked close to us and I panicked, trying to untangle my arm from hers. She refused, tightening her grip on me, pulling me behind a column. She kept me yanked close to her until the men passed. Then she let go, stood back, and turned to me. She was laughing. I must have looked scared. I was. Why shouldn't I be scared? I was a third-class passenger hiding in the dark with Marcel Dalio's beautiful wife.

"Watch this," she whispered, not taking her eyes off me. She lifted her wool scarf from her shoulders, letting it settle on her head. Then she set about wrapping it, not in any fashionable manner but in the babushka style of a peasant. At the same time her body began shifting and she managed to assume the shape of a gnarled, bent grandmother. Then she reached out her still, lovely hands and pulled at my fedora, pressing and shaping the brim so that soon I had a farmer's hat pulled low on my head. She slapped my shoulder and knocked my hip to indicate the crooked tilt and shuffle my body must undertake. Then standing back again, she took in my transformation and dragged me out so that we made our hobbled way, a crone and old farmer, down the stairs to the lower deck.

Trust me, we were hardly old under our funny disguises; we were like children. It was like playing Agents de Le Guerre with Henri. Madeleine and I snuck about in our costumes, crouching behind chairs where our other shipmates anxiously discussed middle-of-the-night angles for our rescue. We hid behind doors, covering our mouths, attempting to turn our laughter into the chortled asthmatic efforts of the elderly. At one moment Dalio came close beside us and Madeleine shrank even deeper into her hunched limp and I teetered beside her, though the tremor in my body was not any feat of the stage. *Take me somewhere,* Madeleine had asked of me. But after weeks stuck aboard the *Quanza,* it was she who took us back to being children with every possibility still before us.

I can't even brag that later, when I hoisted her lovely small foot up into the lifeboat, it was my brilliant addition to our night. Of course it was Madeleine's. The heel of her shoe poked through two fingers of my locked hands. She was deliciously light; her slender leg pressed against me, the hem of her skirt seamed against my chin.

"I won't get anywhere like this," I heard her say and then I heard the swish and a zipper and felt the rustle and sudden slipping of cloth against my face. Before I could register the feel of her nylons against my skin, her leg swung free and she was out of my arms. "Throw that skirt up, will you? And here you go," she said. A rope ladder swung through the dark from the lifeboat.

Even with the help of the ladder, I was not nearly as graceful as Madeleine in my efforts to climb into the lifeboat.

"Here," she said when I finally tumbled in beside her. "I keep these up here. It makes the boat a little cozy." She pressed something soft—a pillow—into my hands. "I find I've always needed a place to disappear."

We lay in the lifeboat among her stash of pillows and blankets and cookies and cognac. We were children in a hideout telling stories and listening to people pass below us. She fed me a piece of chocolate, something I had not eaten in many weeks. I told her about my father's glove shop, the scraps of leather and silk I'd hoard, hiding under the work tables pretending they were delicacies from China and India and that I was the only boy in Belgium who had ever tasted these treats.

"Now give me a treat, give me a treat," she said, tickling me. Then abruptly she stopped and said with real seriousness, "Give me one of your poems and that will be my treat."

Like the others, Madeleine LeBeau believed that I was a poet. Itzak the dreamer. Itzak the poet. "I'm afraid I don't. . . ." I began to confess but she interrupted me cooing, "Please, please, just one poem." What came to me then was Baudelaire's poem *Le Voyage*. I recited the first stanzas and was made to recall Gustav saving me from the French police and how that afternoon was spent in the dark beside a woman. How different this poem was to me now.

O le pauvre amoureux de pays chimériques!
Faut-il le mettre aux fers, le jeter à la mer,
Ce matelot ivrogne, inventeur d'Amérique
Dont le mirage rend le gouffre plus amer?

I paused at the irony of these lines spoken in the lifeboat of a ship stuck screaming distance from land. There's nothing original in saying that Baudelaire's poems are often brutal, an ominous howl. But when I whispered to Madeleine the three lines—

Mais les ténèbres sont elle-mêmes des toiles
Où vivent jaillissant de mon oeil par milliers,
Des êtres disparus aux regards familiers.

I felt I had entered his poems as I could not have three months earlier. I was quiet and sad and missed everyone—Maman and Max, the young freedom of my Odile. I missed Henri and our games of Le Guerre. But I was also thrilled with the night, the distances I'd covered. I felt as if I—not Baudelaire—had actually had been the author of this poem.

Madeleine broke the silence. "Since I have no more chocolate gift for you, would you like me to kiss you, Mr. Poet?" She sat up in the boat. It shook a little under the shifting weight.

"You're married to Marcel Dalio," I said, unable to yank the words back after they'd left my mouth.

She laughed. She looked so slender and young in the dark in the lifeboat. "I know who my husband is. But that doesn't answer my question." Then she repeated. "Would you like me to kiss you, Mr. Poet?"

Remember all the nights I turned the pages of my movie magazines, pressing the papery lips of actresses to my lips? How could I resist Madeleine LeBeau? Who would want to resist? Mrs. Roosevelt, my lips are puffy and sweetly sore from all our kissing. I think she'll be a great actress one day. Perhaps even greater than Marcel Dalio.

I do not want you to think ill of Madeleine LeBeau. She's assured me that these kisses do not break her marriage pledge.

I do not want you to think ill of me, though in one night I stole the lines of Baudelaire and for hours kissed another man's wife. I do not know which crime is worse.

Sometimes it astonishes me the way a day unfolds itself.

Dreamily yours,
Isaac

Sᴀʀᴀ ᴄᴏᴍᴇs ᴛᴏ the Riverside Funeral Chapel late and seats herself in the chapel's last row. She wanted to make sure she's missed any milling around, any greetings and introductions. Even still, she looks for Lile and Rosa. It's always strange, a funeral, but this is stranger, a room full of necessarily unfamiliar people. Last night she'd pressed the message play button and there was Lieberman's voice. She's begun not to be surprised by Lieberman, his messages on her answering machine, his southern gentleman's voice, like bits of bread not leading her out of the forest but deeper in.

"Miss Sara, I'm afraid to be calling to say that one of the *Quanza* survivors, Mrs. Ida Mittlebaum, has passed away. There will be a funeral tomorrow for her at the Riverside Chapel on Amsterdam Avenue. 10 a.m. Perhaps you might be interested to attend."

If spending a day at a funeral seems awful, then spending a day at the funeral of someone Sara doesn't even know seems awful-times-ridiculous-times-theatrical, but now in a navy linen shift and wide-brimmed hat, Sara looks to see if she might guess which dark suit is Lieberman. The pews are mostly full. She sees the backs of heads, yarmulkes pinned to white hair or propped on bald heads, but there's also a surprising number of young people. She settles first on one man—tall, erect carriage—but when another man looks back and smiles at Sara, she thinks maybe he's Marty Lieberman. He's seated next to two small women she recognizes as Lile and Rosa. Are there other *Quanza* passengers in the room?

"My mother. Well, what can we say about Ida?" A woman says, adjusting the microphone. "That she was a piece of work, that nothing we'll say here today can match her vibrancy? That she knew how to have more fun than all of us put together? That she loved to bake? Has anyone in this room not tasted Ida's chocolate cake or lemon tart? That my mom loved theater and loved no theater more than musical theater? I honestly considered just having today's service be tunes from *The King and I* and *Camelot*."

A woman's voice chimes, "You're forgetting *Les Miz*."

There's a nodding of heads, laughter, a free-for-all of: "What about *Annie!* What about *West Side Story, Sound of Music!*" A young man shouts, "She was crazy for *Rent!*"

Sara has suddenly welled up, tears slipping down her face. She smudges her hand against her wet cheeks.

Next the son stands to speak about his mother's nerve, her taking up singing lessons at age seventy. He steps off the last stair and a young woman glides forward quickly to embrace him. Sara sees him give in then, his shoulders heaving. He holds tight and gives an extra clasp before releasing her. The young woman moves past him, then up to the podium. She's got a streak of bright pink in her hair, which is pulled neatly back into a ponytail.

"I loved listening to my Nana Ida tell stories," she begins. "I loved the world she gave me of her childhood in France, the picnics on the canal. Nana Ida could make her childhood happen each time she told me another story. I think I've crouched next to her, behind the heavy dark drapes where she hid for hours after cutting up her mother's new blue dress because she wanted to make fancy dresses for her dolls."

Sara bites at her lip, sucking in tears that collect there. Sara hadn't thought to bring Kleenex; why would she?—she didn't know Ida. She doesn't know why she's crying. She wants to leave. Right now. But it will attract attention, leaving in the middle of things, even from the last row. Why did she even come? No one's talking about the ship, nothing directly about the *Quanza*. The granddaughter spoke about Ida having come to New York, making the city her own playground and home. But nothing directly about the passage. Ida was younger than her father by eight years, Sara calculates. A child on the ship. Closer in age to the sisters Rosa and Lile.

At least the granddaughter's coming to the end. "My Nana taught me that the only way to be alive is to live deeply in life. I think my grandmother was afraid of nothing, which I try to re-member when I feel afraid."

Sara chokes out a sob. She can't hold back the sound, which is low and childish. She's come to this funeral like she's Nancy Drew in *The Secret of the Quanza*. But it's her mother, her mother's insistent bravery, and her mother's absolute honesty during the dying that keeps rising up in Sara, wanting to be found. Sara can't stop crying.

Before she can slip out, people begin filing out of the pews. She'll wait, watch faces; if Lieberman figures out she's there, she'll pull it together somehow and talk to him. Otherwise she'll leave for the library when the chapel clears.

When Sara sees her father stand she assumes it's not him, just blurry tears or the chance angle of a man who looks like her father. She wipes her eyes. The man's wearing a yarmulke; her father wouldn't put on a yarmulke. But when he turns it is her father. If that's not enough, Carmen's with him, her arms supporting him a little as he turns out of the bench and, with the cane Sara bought, makes his way up the aisle. Sara picks up the memorial book, slides down in her seat. She's glad she wore a hat. She wishes she'd kept on her sunglasses. From the slat between the book and the brim, she watches. He shakes a man's hand. Gives a woman a hug. Another a kiss. Her father keeps getting stopped—more embraces, more kisses. "Izzy," she hears and sees Lile pushing in front of her sister to clasp him in her arms. Her father places his hand on Lile's face and, like that, they talk. Lile's gestures are responsive, girlish; her face tilts into Sara's father's hand.

As they approach the last row Sara hunches, turning her face to the wall. She tilts her hat, can't help feeling silly in this half-crouch—less Nancy Drew than Lucille Ball—and waits till they pass. She's certain someone—Lile, Rosa, Carmen—will notice her flimsy attempt at disguise.

"Thank you, I feel good, mostly," Sara hears her father's voice, bright today, charged with vigor.

"So then you'll come with all of us," a man says.

"I'd love to," Sara hears her father say, "but let me take a rain check on that."

"You still think we have so many rain checks left, Izzy." Without peeking Sara knows it's Lile, and despite herself, Sara's glad that her father refused their offer, whatever it was.

It's not Lucille Ball or Nancy Drew but, instead, noir detective Dick Powell she's channeling as Sara hides in the ladies room through all the goodbyes. Then Sara trails her father and Carmen up Amsterdam Avenue, swerving into the small shops on the avenue to keep her stride slow enough to stay behind her father. His gait is so familiar to Sara. He's barely using the cane. But there's no comfort in the familiar right now. There's this other man, Itzak Lejdel, Izzy, who had a life, who, apparently, still has a life that is unknown to her. In fact, the familiar seems suspect, a false consolation. She goes into Ottomanelli's meat store on 79th and waits at the large window until the crosstown bus comes. Sara watches Carmen steady his elbow as Sara's father steps onto the bus.

Sara waits for the next bus and takes it across the park to her father's apartment.

"Hello, hello," her father says, looking up cheerfully when Sara comes into the apartment. "I'm so very pleased to see you. Tell me about your day."

"It's been great, Dad. Just a great day." Sara looks at him for a telltale sign. The thing of it is he seems just like her father always looks—happy to see his daughter.

"Everything okay? You seem funny."

"I'm fine," Sara says.

"You sure? Work, okay? Why aren't you at the library? I haven't heard anything about the adoption in a little while."

"What about your day, Dad? What did you do today?"

"Same-old, same-old," her father says.

"Same old what?"

"I don't know, morning, papers. Are you okay, Sara?"

"Are you, Dad?"

"For an old guy, I'm okay. How about a movie I picked up? Clark Gable and Claudette Colbert. Can you guess which?"

"I can't," Sara says, though she knows perfectly well the video is *It Happened One Night,* a movie her father reliably watches to put him in good spirits.

"You know my thinking—nothing better than Claudette in the middle of the day. I bullied Carmen into saying she'd watch it with me, but she'll be enormously relieved not to have to pretend to laugh along with me."

"You look pretty dressed up to watch a movie." Sara hears the challenge in her tone.

"You're right. What am I doing in this?" he says, and Sara sees how worn out he looks, befuddled, as if he actually doesn't know why he's wearing a suit. "Get it set up, honey, while I get out of this attire."

Sara turns to Carmen as soon as her father's out of the room. "What's the deal, Carmen?" she asks, but Carmen keeps busy, down tidying the coffee table, stacking magazines. "I know where you were. I saw you."

Carmen doesn't stop cleaning, doesn't look at Sara when she says, "And I saw you too. What matters is that your father didn't see you."

"I'm his daughter."

"Exactly."

"You think your family would feel good if they realized you had a whole private world? I know Violet and she'd be furious. I'm a grown woman. Just tell me, Carmen, something about my father or about you, even one small thing."

Carmen stands, coming close to Sara. She looks fierce, staring, keeping silent, and Sara has to work to keep from averting the gaze that Carmen's got her locked in. She can't read Carmen's face at all, a face she knows so well. Just when Sara thinks that this is it, that Carmen's going to stand here in this silent blockade until Sara's father comes back into the room, Carmen begins in a hard, deliberate voice.

"We left our town on foot. The bridges had been blown up. So even if we had dared to go in our car, we couldn't go in our car. For a long time I had to see again so many things in my dreams. I hated sleeping. I don't anymore, Sara.

"There was a neighbor, a woman with two boys, and she was pregnant having twins. When they buried her they buried her with the babies inside of her. There's your small thing, Sara. Does it make you feel better?"

<hr />

"I'm glad you decided to come back; you have no idea," the hair-cutter says. He's standing behind her, twisting and pinning up sections of her hair.

"You gave my friend's daughter such a great cut," she says. "I figured it was worth the risk." It's not a lie, but it's not the reason she's come here straight from her father's. She'd thought about Ethan, calling him or showing up in the shop. She knows his voice would calm her, the way he'd listen and ask questions. Good questions. But maybe she's not ready to be calm quite yet. She's not sure she knows exactly what—but there's business here for her to finish.

"There's always risk in something worthwhile." He laughs and Sara notices the precision and ease in his declaration. She meets his eyes in the mirror. They're beautiful dark eyes. There it is, the familiar tug in her stomach. Like an undertow. The insistent desire for something not genuinely accessible. To be the third angle in the triangle. What did Helen call her? The wounded deer?

"Anyway, is risk a bad thing?" He combs her hair and begins working the scissors. He keeps looking at her and she can feel the flailing, the drowned feeling. The way her drowning has been a kind of saving. But it's also different today. Today, seeing her father at the funeral home, in his other life, she realized how complicit she's been. Coming here, she knows, is a test even if she doesn't fully understand the material.

Sara watches herself as he unclips and parts her hair. He's waiting for her next move. She has no move. Everything she might say sounds provocative, as if she has already agreed to something. As if when she speaks it will be at best a version of what he wants her to say. She lets all the easy responses pass through her unsaid. Why hasn't she seen this before? The old strategy, the chess game: the simplest move is not to move.

He works through her hair, cutting layers and combing, measuring, and cutting more layers.

"When did you come here from Lebanon?" she finally asks.

"I like that you remember this about me." He tries to adjust her question into his frame. "You flatter me. You were paying attention."

This time Sara just holds his gaze. She's able to feel curious about him. Not obligated.

"Tell me." She watches discomfort move across his face. She recognizes it now. Carmen's tensing. Her father's. A city of refugees.

"I left during our war."

"From civil war," she says, "to a hairdresser on Broadway. There's got to be some story there."

He laughs. "You can't imagine, honey."

"Would you tell it to me?" Sara's made an altogether different move than he was prepared for. He regards her in the mirror, seeing that now she's really looking straight at him, wanting something from him. And like she's seen in Carmen, she sees him measure out what he can bear to give.

"Remember that risk for something worthwhile you were talking about before?" Sara teases. He smiles a you-got-me-I-surrender smile. "Let's start with something pretty simple. Do you miss your real name?"

"Mohammed? You tell me—how's that for a hairdresser's name on the Upper West Side of Manhattan?"

"Mohammed, do you miss your country?"

He lowers the blow dryer and the round brush he's been working through her new layered hair. He meets her eyes in the mirror. Straightforward. There's no flirt now.

"Let's just say I want to be here."

"Why?"

"It's a whole lot nicer to run this little kingdom where everyday I can make people happy holding scissors and a hairbrush instead of delivering and continuing misery holding an AK–47."

SEPTEMBER 14

10:00 A.M.

Dear Mrs. Roosevelt,

This morning Madeleine LeBeau—no longer my Madeleine, my disguised lovely crone, my girl in the lifeboat—hardly has the briefest nod for me as we pass on the ship deck. She hangs on Dalio's pinstriped arm. The perfect wife. I ache at her formality.

What are my choices? To stand about filling the hour with rumors, going between committees, trying to maintain hope. Even now I see the captain having his men secure the ship. He has them polishing all the brass. It means something. But what? This morning aboard the ship, you might imagine, there are eighty-six opinions.

My other option is the newspaper. In these few pages I happen to have the Photoplays Lowes guide and screen-news articles. So many new films! American films in America! Makes me crazy to get off the ship. Bob Hope and Paulette Goddard in *The Ghost Breakers* (give me anything with Paulette Goddard! Did you see *The Women*?). It's playing at the State and at the Paradise Valencia on 83rd Street. At the Metropolitan Fulton Street (do you know it?). Mickey Rooney and Judy Garland in *Andy Hardy Meets Debutante*.

I'm all for Mickey Rooney, but I'll pick Paulette over Judy any day. If you haven't already, want to see *The Ghost Breakers* with me when I'm able? My treat.

I find new words each time I read through these same pages: hair-trigger, obloquy, decked-out, grosgrain, vinylite. It's exciting. Soon I'll speak like a socialite and not a barfly or a kid fresh off a ship.

After reading all the advertisements I'm thinking that there's an overemphasis on hats and not enough mention of gloves. I may just have to follow in Max's footsteps after all.

Maybe that's how I can get close to her. I'll work my way over to Madeleine and Dalio. Sit on the cushioned arm of his deck chair. First I'll compliment him on his good work yesterday with the captain. Then I'll make him a present of red suede gloves for his lovely wife. All aboveboard. All proper. A chance to be near to my Madeleine's lips. A chance for her to look at the poet in the light of day.

Yours truly,

Isaac

SEPTEMBER 14
10:20 A.M.

Dear Mrs. Roosevelt,

I know you're busy, busy as a bee. And with all the meetings you are having on my behalf, it must be tough to have even a minute to fit in a letter. But I just know that if you could, you'd say the movies is a dandy idea.

I bet with all he has to do in a day, Franklin is seldom inclined to spend an evening in the cinema. Sometimes, I'd guess, you even go alone. So a companion would be lovely. Here's my guess on your favorite actors. Okay, Cary Grant—an obvious choice for a woman, and I just bet you especially adore Clark Gable in *Too Hot to Handle.* Then probably Mickey Rooney and James Cagney are actors you're wild about.

Even if you had a moment to write, I know you'd have to keep it brief. But I bet you'd tell me that from everything you've told Franklin, he says I sound like a most interesting young man.

I think also you'd want me to know that you've begun inquiries to locate Maman. Everything will be fine, Isaac, you'd say in your note. Though I'm guessing you might scold me a bit, suggesting that Mrs. Dalio is not entirely the best object of my romantic affections. Then I think you'd sign it: Love, Mother Roosevelt.

And so in closing, I'll close in the following manner:
Love, from your new American son.

"REALLY?" IS ALL Sara can think to say. The photograph of her baby has come. Her girl. A baby girl from Kazakhstan. "We'll download the image and send it over," Georgette, her adoption counselor, says. "I just wanted to call first so you don't get surprised when you go online. It's sooner than we thought. And Sara, it's okay to be nervous." Sara doesn't like the way Georgette assumes she's nervous. Even though she is nervous. Could she have read it from Sara's "Really?" when Sara was conscious of making her voice sound all chippy and enthusiastic?

"What am I supposed to do after I see the picture?" Sara asks. She's not ready to let the counselor get off the phone. "Should I be doing something?"

"Maybe print the photograph. Carry it around. Tape it to your fridge. I suppose the best thing you can do is look at her picture a lot. Feel whatever you feel."

When the counselor hangs up, Sara walks around her apartment. It's probably not there quite yet, the photograph, since there wasn't time already to download it, so it's not bad that she isn't rushing over to turn her computer on.

She fights the idea of calling Helen to come over. She doesn't want to open it alone. But she wants to want to open it alone. Have it be a special moment. She could wait. Open it in the morning. Just because it will be on her screen doesn't mean she has to click on it. Not *it,* Sara corrects herself, the photograph of *my* daughter. She's always felt that the adoption process was a kind of gestation. She even wondered if all the bureaucratic baloney was just put there to make the whole thing take time. Metaphorically let the child take shape inside her. But now it's arrived. The baby's there. She wonders if that's what pregnant women think—a moment when they bolt up out of sleep and, holding their huge bellies, ask themselves, "But really, how is this thing going to get out of me?" Or when the doctor says at a checkup, "Well, the head is fully engaged and you're 80 percent effaced, so it will be happening soon." And the woman thinks, "No way. Not yet, I'm not ready." Pretend this is the water breaking. Not the part where she's supposed to push. But opening the PDF file will be important. Her first moment of seeing her daughter. The photograph of the child she's going to love. She knows she's not supposed to feel love right now. Georgette has said that repeatedly in group. That it's normal not to. But she wants to. Just take her in. Take in this baby's being. Her personage. Whatever of her spirit can be found in the photograph.

<hr />

Sara's startled by the phone. She grabs it before she thinks about whether she wants to talk. If it's Helen then that will be a sign that everything's okay. With Helen she'll be ready to look at this, her first picture of her baby.

"Sara. Ethan."

Sara's silent. Doesn't know what to say.

"Sara, it's Ethan. You there? Everything okay?"

"I'm about to have a baby."

"Whoa! Right now? I was just calling to say your first chair's ready. I want to come by, bring it later today and pick up another. But if you're having a baby, maybe this isn't the best moment."

Then she's laughing. Hard-from-deep-inside laughing. Ethan laughs, too, with her, with the sheer force of her laughter. She can't even stop laughing long enough to explain about the photograph and the baby and the adoption. It doesn't matter.

"Yes, bring the chair," she manages finally to say. "How about in the late afternoon. About five." It feels good to laugh this hard. With this man.

———

Benjamin asks the question, *Is a translation meant for readers who do not understand the original?*

And later in the same essay, "The Task of the Translator": *One might, for example, speak of an unforgettable life or moment even if all men had forgotten it.*

———

Her father has his suit jacket draped around his shoulders. Sara called, saying to meet her at the coffee shop—she has someone important for him to meet. He keeps looking around for someone to join them until Sara takes the computer picture from her bag. Her father looks and looks, saying, "Kazakhstan?" Now he's propped the pixilated image of the child against the menu board.

"This is way too much for me," her father says, when the waitress sets the milkshakes and burger platters down.

"Eat what you want; it's not a problem, Dad." He looks shrunken in the coffee shop booth. Sara feels large across from him, protective.

"I haven't thought enough about being a grandfather," he says, pushing the pepper shaker up like a clip to fasten the picture in place. He straightens the paper, which has started to curl over. "What can I do?" His voice is genuinely interested, eager. "Are you sure about this, Sara? About doing this alone?"

"Why didn't you marry again after Mom?" Once again, it's not at all the question she wanted to ask, was determined to ask. But suddenly there it is.

"Why would I? I loved your mother." Her father's voice is steady, unsurprised. As if he'd been waiting for her to ask this all these years.

"Weren't you lonely? Didn't you want company?"

"I would have been lonely for your mother if I'd have married again. Our marriage, that was my marriage. Then I had the finest company in you. But maybe I was too selfish. I held on too long to my wonderful companion."

Selfish? She's berated herself plenty that she'd been unable to let herself leave her father. But never that she'd been captured by him. Her father, selfish? But she'll think about that later. For now, he's answering questions and Sara's not about to miss the opportunity.

"Why Richard?" Sara asks. "Why did you change from Itzak to Richard?"

"Who has a name like Itzak?"

"Someone whose name is Itzak." She thinks of the girl at Kim's Nails, Cindy, who held her feet.

"Please. Don't be ridiculous. In America?"

"Mohammed, Gilberto, Sung-Yi. People have names. Why didn't you at least change to Isaac?"

"I thought of Isaac. Richard was easier. I thought it wouldn't hurt to be a little more American. Is this now a crime?"

Now's the time. Stop playing it easy. Maybe slouch, sleuth style, against the chair, and fire back the tough questions: *Funny you should mention crime. What else did you do because it was easier? What did your mother think about your changing your name? What else did you change, Dad? What happened to my grandmother?*

"I forgot how delicious this is!" Her father touches his lips to the plastic straw. The coffee shake fills the straw, overflows; there's a milky froth on his lips.

"Dad, you asked what you can do. There are still more forms before I can go for the baby. Georgette, the adoption counselor, she told me. . . ." Sara stops, tries again to form the question. But she's undone by the careful effort her father makes with his food. He eats his burger as he always has, removing the bun and cutting the meat with a fork and knife. The fork trembles in his hand. It's as if it takes every ounce of concentration for him to get the food to his mouth without bits of burger dropping back onto the plate.

"Sara." Her father looks up, his gray eyes moist. He puts his fork down and touches Sara's hand "If you really want this baby, be careful. You don't know her, this Georgette woman. You don't know who's finally giving the stamp."

There's a passage from one of Benjamin's letters that rises up in her. *I fear that those who have been able to extricate themselves from it will have to be reckoned with one day.*

She tries to see the young man in him. But it seems her father has always been old. He eats the last of his burger. The slackened skin of his jaw. His full lips. He'd been old and now he's older. The same-old same-old, her father. But now the same story's different. Same actions, different meaning. He has good reason to be suspicious, Sara thinks. This is a man who abandoned his mother and held on tight to his daughter. It's a stark formulation. She tries to really look at her father in a new harsh light: an untrustworthy man, a liar, a betrayer, a man capable of saving only himself. A selfish man. But she can't. He looks like her father always looked. Like the one who hadn't abandoned her. That parent. And not just the parent who attended teacher conferences and gave out curfews. He'd taken her for her first bra to the Town Shop. Wasn't he the parent who brought her an electric heating pad when her adolescent periods came with relentless cramps? The parent who stayed alive, that's who he was.

"I wish I was strong enough to go with you, honey. It's not always so easy traveling alone."

There's an opening. But Ethan's question comes to her. Maybe she didn't have to know. The daughter's desire to know the story that lived behind her. Ethan's wrong; she needs to know. But maybe she doesn't have to make her father go back there with her. He's come to believe his own story. There's no other forgotten story left to remember. Perhaps he won't ever understand that part of why he's held his daughter so close to him is because he once knew how far a child might choose to let go.

"Not too shabby a job with that burger, Grandpa." She watches him smile, a delighted smile. "Like that, Grandpa?"

"I'm stuffed; I feel more like an old cow." Her father laughs. Satisfied. Like he didn't know he still had it in him. "Maybe you'll stay around and watch a movie with me?"

"I'll stick around for a while," Sara says.

But after the stroll back from the restaurant, it doesn't take long for him to doze off in front of the film. He stretches out on the sofa, his hands holding his stomach, as if the burger platter has knocked him flat. As if his daughter, the detective, has slipped him a mickey since she doesn't have a proper search warrant.

⸻

"I want to know." Sara sits forward on the chair in Rochelle Goldenman's living room. She's come right from her father's, ready this time, she thinks, to hear and learn what she can. "Please, I really want to know everything now."

"More tea?" Rochelle asks. She's clearly tentative, as if lifting the floral pot or even the question itself might upset Sara. Sara can hardly blame Rochelle after the way she, Sara, practically stormed out the last time they met.

"Rivesaltes, I've looked it up. It's on the Internet. There were pictures. A kind of makeshift classroom. It seemed, at least at that point, in May 1940, pretty benign. Did your father or your grandparents ever talk about the transit camp?"

"What about?" Rochelle clearly isn't willing to make any mistakes.

Sara wants to get to it, to Sahra, her grandmother, she wants to stop wasting time, but she sees how skittish Rochelle is and she doesn't want a conflict.

"What about your father? You say that he and my father were close friends." Sara thinks this, a friendship between boys, is probably a good place to start. Bingo—Sara hit it right on. Rochelle's face opens and Sara thinks, let her lead.

"My father adored your father. Always did. Even all those years when they hadn't been in touch. God, my father would lapse into routines that your father and mine did when they were boys. Slapstick kind of stuff, like Laurel and Hardy playing soldiers."

Sara recognizes longing in Rochelle's voice, the eagerness to talk about her father, to tell the living stories of the dead. Sara settles back in her chair. She wants to make herself look easy, look willing, let Rochelle relax into her story.

"My father was a ridiculously funny man and he says your dad was, when they were children, the more cautious one. But as they got older that changed. Your dad was ready to bust out. He thought Brussels was a backwater. I remember your father, Sara. Twice I met him. Once he came to shiva at our house after my grandmother died. My father walked around the living room holding your father's arm like he was a boy holding a new puppy, or like a celebrity had visited him. Like he couldn't believe his remarkable luck. I remember thinking my father was happy when he was supposed to be sad that my nana had died. Like I said, I already knew who he was, your father; he was sort of larger than life to my dad. Your father's appetite was legendary in our house. To the point that when I was little, if I really, really wanted seconds on desert, I'd say I was pulling an Izzy, and my father was sure to crack up and cut me a big piece of cake.

"Later, before I went to bed, I came to the door of the kitchen and heard a man crying. I thought it was probably my dad crying for his mom, but it didn't sound like Dad. It turned out that it was your father. My dad and yours were at the table with a chessboard in front of them. They were smoking cigarettes and my father didn't smoke cigarettes. Your father was crying. My father shooed me out of the room, but I stayed just by the door. I couldn't believe this man was making my father smoke. Do you want to hear this, really?"

She's come to learn about her grandmother, about Rivesaltes, but here, now, the possibility of her father crying in a kitchen she's never known about, among people Sara never met, feels worse than impossible—it feels wrong. Where had her father told her he was going that night? And cigarettes? Her father never smoked. Now she's being told he's responsible for another man smoking. She has to refrain from saying to Rochelle, "I don't think you're right. My father doesn't smoke either."

"Yes," says Sara. "I do. I want to hear everything." Sara picks up the teacup, though she's not sure she can get herself to drink.

"'I'm sorry,' he said. He kept saying he was sorry. I thought he meant that he was sorry that my grandmother was dead. Or that he was sorry that he hadn't visited my father in all those years. I couldn't see him from where I'd hidden on the other side of the door. But I could hear him scraping the metal chess pieces along the board in just the way that my dad told me would scratch the board. I thought my dad would tell him to stop. That he was being polite and I should go into the room and tell him to stop. But then your father's sobbing became really strong. When he could finally speak he said, 'Henri, I thought I'd be able to find her. I thought I'd get somewhere and then send for her.'"

"My grandmother?" Sara makes herself hold her gaze when Rochelle nods yes. She wants to feel journalistic or like a translator who can console herself that the devastations of the primary text are not her own. "Tell me what you know about her. At Rivesaltes."

"They all said she was determined. It's that simple. She was weak, actually she was pretty sick by then, a kind of respiratory thing, if I'm remembering correctly. But when there came an opportunity for them to leave, she refused. She was determined."

"Determined?"

Rochelle looks at her. At first Sara can't understand the look—fear? impatience?—until she realizes it's something closer to sadness or pity. She sees that Rochelle is considering retreat, considering that she doesn't want the responsibility. Sara keeps herself from even the slightest turning away from Rochelle's look.

"Determined?" Sara repeats so that Rochelle knows that she wants to know, no, needs to know, that Rochelle doesn't have a choice to tell or not to tell. It's Sara's right.

Rochelle breaks the stare first, replenishing the tea in their cups, offering up the milk pitcher and the sugar bowl, though Sara had refused both for the first cup.

Finally Rochelle says it quietly, in a matter-of-fact tone. "Determined to wait for your grandfather."

There's silence then, both of them lifting and lowering their cups. Sara feels it again, the desire to not know, to unknow even this much, to not press forward.

"They fought. But your grandmother wouldn't budge. She would wait for her husband. Apparently my grandfather accused your father of having lied to her, of having brought her to Rivesaltes for selfish reasons. He even said he was pretty sure your grandfather had been killed or put somewhere, that Itzak had made up all the supposed contacts. Your grandmother wouldn't listen. But in the end she said it didn't matter, that, in fact, by the end she'd guessed Itzak hadn't heard from Max. But that she was waiting for your grandfather because she wanted him to bring her back to Belgium. She didn't want to go anywhere new. She wanted to go home."

"I need to ask you something else." Sara is pushing herself to this last question that she doesn't want to ask.

"Wait, let me ask you something first, Sara." It's clear Rochelle isn't waiting for a green light from Sara. And that she's guessed the question and she's refusing to let Sara ask. "You play chess, don't you?" Rochelle says.

"Do I play chess?" Sara's aware she keeps repeating things, but the question comes from so far in left field. Sara had prepared for the worst, some challenge about her relationship with her father, some way this woman here with all the knowing is going to use it to prove her relationship with her own father trumps Sara's. "Sure, sort of, I play, but I'm no chess master or anything."

"When my father was teaching me chess he'd tell me about your father's game. He said that he wanted me to be a player like your dad. He said it all the time, 'I'm nothing to beat. I just got to teach you to beat Izzy.' After my father died, Sara, I called your father. He took me to lunch."

"My father took you to lunch two years ago?" Sara can hear the shrillness in her own voice. Rochelle clearly doesn't want anyone going ballistic near the landscape of her father's death. "I'm sorry, it's just surprising; I keep pretty close to my father's schedule."

"I met him at his apartment. He showed me a few photographs he had of him and my father as kids in Brussels and on holiday. And then we walked to a small place around the corner. We talked a little about where he'd grown up."

"My father talked about Brussels?" Sara reminds herself to breathe, to keep her voice down.

"I'd gone to Belgium with my parents a few years earlier. My father had wanted to show me where he'd grown up. Your father asked how it all looked, what had changed on their streets. If the apartment buildings were the same. I had to tell him that my father had walked us around the neighborhoods for hours and that, forget about apartments, neither street was there anymore. Only their school was left, but it wasn't a school anymore."

"What else?"

"Well, I wanted to give him the present my father had picked up for him in the flea market over there. But when I showed it to him, your father refused to take it. There was that present and what my father left him in his will." Rochelle turns, walking to the fireplace to lift a mounted metal piece from among the objects arranged on the mantelpiece. "Here, this was the present. You should have it."

Sara can't figure it out. It's a large bronze hand and forearm, flattened—a kind of art deco sculpture? Rochelle hands it to Sara. It's heavy. Sara turns it in her hands. On one side there's an etched stamp: 9 1/2 R. Pelletier and Jaminet, Rue de Crimee, Paris 19e.

"What is it? What's it mean?"

"My father said it was exactly like the molds in your grandfather's glove shop. Your father wouldn't take this, but he went home with what my dad left him."

"Which was what?" Sara's ready for anything at this point— metal glove molds; her grandfather made gloves—each foray she makes keeps bringing her to places she didn't know existed.

"A small folding chessboard with painted metal pieces. The board they played on when they were kids. It was maybe the only thing my father had from his home in Brussels. Even though my father left it for yours, I loved that board. I wanted to keep it. I challenged your dad to a game. The winner got to keep the board."

Dear Mrs. Roosevelt,

I'm surprised! It's not that I haven't been asking for exactly such a moment. It's not that I entirely thought Frankle was wrong when he said things looked good for us. But still, I'm surprised.

I guess somehow I thought you'd send word to me first. Even if you needed to keep it on the quiet, you'd let me know. But now I'm figuring out that since time is of the essence, you sent these men right on board to start things going.

I'm right, right?

I always knew you'd take care of this. I never doubted you. Never.

You know this Mr. Patrick Malin? Right? Says he's been sent from the President's Advisory Committee on Political Refugees. From Washington. That would be you, that Committee. He's come with three inspectors. They've set up at two tables in the first-class dining room and they've called in four passengers for interviews. All very closed-door.

I suppose it would have looked a little suspicious to start right away with me. Don't worry, I understand.

You gave them my name, right?

Guess I'll be seeing you very soon,
Isaac

THIS TIME SHE doesn't wait for the bus. Or a taxi. She runs, practically throws herself across the park again, armed with what she's learned from Rochelle Goldenman. And wielding the metal glove mold. That's how it feels, armed. As if she's got the AK–47 now. And there's no stopping her. She's going to do something— raze the village, take hostages—ready or not, here she comes.

"I don't care," Sara huffs, holding the glove mold up like a salute when Carmen says, "Quiet. He's asleep." But when she storms past Carmen she's not prepared for what she sees. The office is clean. Cleaned out. No piles of papers. No overstuffed legal folders and legal files. Like it's someone else's office. Tidy, pared down, a place for everything and—forget about everything—there's not much of anything in drawer after drawer that Sara pulls open.

"Where did all his mess go?" Sara barks at Carmen. "When did you do this?" She's aware her voice sounds accusatory. An interrogation. She pulls on the closet door, standing back, prepared for a sudden topple of boxes and papers, her father's childish effort to clean up. The door swings open and the closet is empty or mostly so, a few boxes, neatly labeled, stacked and pushed to the corner of the large walk-in closet.

"Why? Tell me why!" Sara struggles to keep sounding tough.

"It was time," Carmen says gently.

"Time? Time for what?" Sara is standing inside the closet. As if there's something she'll find—a trap door, a hidden safe.

"It's enough, Sara," Carmen says, moving with certainty through the ordered room. "Here. You're looking for something. This is all there is." Sara makes her way next to Carmen. Not even lost in among the tax boxes and statements, the jammed-to-the-ceiling closet but right there on his cleared-off desk, like an ancient clay pipe that has floated up on the tide, or the tip of a pyramid exposed by the steady erosive elements of wind and rain, there's a large sealed envelope. In her father's crimped script: *Quanza.*

Sara starts to rip it open.

"Please, not here," Carmen says. "Not with your father in the house."

"What?" squints Sara. Carmen doesn't answer. Crosses her arms across her chest. "Fine," Sara says, turning to go. She gets to the front door. Turns back. "Tell my father I picked this up for him. Tell him he forgot to bring his gift home." She says, banging the glove mold down on her father's empty desk.

She's barely home and here's Ethan at her door; the chair held out in front of him, a dozen bright pink roses leaned against the new rush caning. Between the adoption and the envelope, she's completely forgotten to expect him.

"Were you expecting someone else?" There's no barb in the question. Nothing coy. Nothing even needy.

"I'm not sure," Sara says, wanting him to come in.

His hands smell like oil and wax. He's touching her face. It didn't seem particularly attractive to tell a man who'd brought her flowers that she wanted to be a mother.

Earlier she'd felt shy explaining the choice to adopt. She wanted to keep it simple, even a brusque *because I want to*, but instead she'd spoken about the ways sometimes in a dream her mother is back, alive, or strangely dead and alive at the same time, and when Sara wakes she's amazed by the completeness of her mother in the dream, the exact way her mother's eyes slant, the slight scar above her mother's lip, the way the upper lip curls tentatively before breaking into an open easy smile. Even the feel of her mother's arm, the skin so soft and hairless. Things she wouldn't have even thought to remember were there in the dream.

She said, "Look, I'm not trying to prove anything by doing this alone." She wanted to stop, but now she couldn't stop. She knew she should keep it simple but there she was, admitting that she's afraid, afraid she'll be lonely as a single parent, afraid she'll never get the chance to make it work with a man. But when she'd finished talking and looked up, Ethan was right there, looking at her with the most steady and considerate gaze. And his eyes were wet. She tried to make herself not turn away from him because of her shyness. But she stood up and began adjusting the roses in the vase, bunching them tight and letting them fall open, filling the vase. Sara pulled off a leaf that had browned along an edge.

Then he came to where she busied herself and began this touching of her face. There it is again, the deep scent of wood oil on his hands. She remembers the last thing he'd said the day they walked the new pathways along the Hudson. *It feels good to care for what needs care.* She almost can't bear the confidence and inquiry of his fingers on her skin.

"I'm not looking to give you some pitiful motherless child song and dance. It's less complicated that any of that hullabaloo I was droning on about," Sara says, wanting to pull her face from his hands, from their pressure against her jaw.

But he's lifting her face in the V of his palms.

"I'm happy you haven't gotten the baby yet," Ethan says, bringing her face so close Sara feels his breath against her mouth. "This is incredibly forward to say but I'm happy that in some way maybe I might get the chance to be around."

"Here it is." Sara holds out the picture. "The baby." Then she corrects herself, saying, "This is my daughter," trying it out for the first time. *My daughter.* Ethan takes the picture from her hands, holding it almost as carefully as if he were really holding a baby.

"She's perfect," Ethan says and they quietly look at the baby together.

"Well, you did a little more than just the re-cane," Sara says, admiring the fixed chair. It is re-sanded, re-glued, and oiled.

"Just trying to prove the enormous price tag is worth it. Get you to hand over the other wrecked chairs."

Sara laughs, "Yeah, right. Anyway, thanks for taking the extra time."

"Sure. I admit, I liked it. Gave me extra time to focus on you."

Sara looks up, embarrassed.

"I decided I was wrong, something I said before, about your father. I was wrong challenging you."

"What's that?"

"I asked you why you had to learn everything. Why knowing mattered. What was the big deal about the past. But while I was working on the chair, I kept hearing your voice, its grain, if you'll forgive my own corny metaphor. When I'm with you I can't help mostly hearing your professor confidence thing. But working I heard the chipped, splintered surface below. You should go there. Find out what you need to."

"Where?" Sara watches the way he keeps his hands in motion, smoothing them over the wood.

"To Virginia, To that museum that's there, sweetheart."

"Oh, forget that. I already spoke to the guy," Sara says, purposefully tough against his endearment. "He didn't really have very much to say."

"But you also said there were things sent down for the exhibit. Something your dad sent there. You need to go and see and touch what's actually there."

"But it's probably nothing," Sara says. "I should really just stay here and finish up my work. Anyway I haven't had the chance to open it, but I've just found an envelope that I think will tell me something."

Ethan moves his hand from the chair to Sara's face. Again his gaze is constant, intense; she'd like to wriggle out of it. "It's time to move on, Sara. You're about to become a mom. You should go to Virginia and look at what your father sent there. It will free you up, Sara, and I think that's what you actually want."

Later they come to the kitchen with hunger, searching out something easy to eat. But there's nothing much in her refrigerator, just a tomato, half a red pepper, a small piece of goat cheese, eggs. A late or early breakfast, depending. Depending, Sara thinks, but she doesn't know what it depends on. Sara lifts the wooden spatula from the pan.

"You probably planned for something different than this," Sara says. She feels Ethan sitting at the table enjoying her move about chopping pepper and tomato, slicing the cheese, whisking the eggs.

"Did you?" he says.

Sara doesn't know how to begin saying the things she did know. She's used to limitations, no, she'd chosen them. But Ethan's open, ready, it seems, for whatever she puts before him.

"Do you really get that I'm about to adopt a child?" She skims the spatula over the vegetables softening in the pan. The tomatoes hold their sliced form.

"Did you know what you'd be making before you came into the kitchen?" he asks.

Sara waves her spatula—ta-da—as if the rest of living could be that easy.

"No, really. I gave up planning," Ethan says. Sara turns to look at Ethan. His face is so serious; it surprises her, that seriousness. "It's like the shop. When you're a repair shop you can't ever anticipate what gets brought up the stairs."

Sara needs the whole crowded, jostling train ride from New York to Virginia to be alone. She can hardly believe she's doing it, actually leaving her work at the library and going out of the city to track her father down. And there's the night she's just spent with Ethan. There's the photograph of her daughter in Kazakhstan. She hasn't even had the chance to open the envelope Carmen gave her. She brought it along. But there was something convincing, even practical, in Ethan's saying, "It's time to move on." It seemed so immediate, an invitation more than anything else.

The man next to her is fully rigged for the serious work world: laptop open on his tray, his newspaper folded on the NASDAQ, a cup of coffee, and a jelly doughnut. He keeps pressing a button, saying into his cell phone, "What's Lou say? What's the situation now?"

Sara tries the phrase in her own mind. *What's the situation now?* A whole life and what does she know? What does she know? Isn't that what the detectives do? That's more essential than the situation. Go over the gathered information; try to see what they haven't seen before.

Start with her father's story.

That her father's a liar. That's jumping ahead. That's a conclusion. She can't get emotional with her data.

Just stick with evidence. *What's Lou say?* What is said is a kind of evidence. Whether true or false. Well, let's start at the beginning, Detective. She'll hold off on the envelope until she's gone over what she's already learned.

Earliest piece of evidence: her father's claim. That he and his mother arrived in America together on a boat.

Second: she was told her grandmother died soon after arriving in America. "From the war," he said, when she asked how her grandmother, Sahra, had died in Brooklyn. And because he was so quick to turn away, back to the business at hand, Sara never dared challenge: "So the war's an illness?"

Was there any fact at all in this evidence? That her father said it to her. That was true. That he came on a boat. That was true. His name was on the *Quanza* passenger list. She'd learned that from the curator. That her grandmother died. True. That, however you looked at it, she died from the war, was also true.

The rest of it: came together on the boat, died after coming to Brooklyn. Fact: that they were said. But untrue. A fact that was a lie.

And the rest? The untold, that was evidence, wasn't it? All that. The plight of the *Quanza*. Her father had been on a ship sent away from two ports. That the boat was ready to send eighty-six people back to the German occupation of Europe. Untold by her father: how he got between Brussels and this ship, the *Quanza*, that left from Lisbon.

Evidence: that her father did not want to tell her this story.

She'd lived that piece of the evidence.

Could untold history be a lie? Didn't he have a right not to tell his story? Certainly Carmen thought so. Helen too.

But now she had other stories.

First: everything she'd learned from Rochelle Goldenman. Did Rochelle's elaborate story trump her father's meager telling? An unknown couple had given her grandparents and her father a ride from Belgium in exchange for food and lodging and gas. The families had stayed together until somewhere north of Paris. Goldenman thought Sara's grandfather, Max, had taken a train back to Belgium. There had been a failed plan to rendezvous in Paris. And then surprisingly, amazingly, really, given the masses of displaced persons, they'd found one another in Perpignan. Her father had left his mother at a camp, telling her that Max would be meeting her there. Her grandmother stayed on at the camp after the Goldenmans left, waiting for Max.

Then there's everything Rochelle said during this last visit. The grandfather's shop and the glove molds. The chessboard that had recently surfaced in her father's house.

Sara had to say, yes, this was evidence. But were these stories true just because she'd been told them by someone willing to talk?

Then there was Lieberman. It seemed more days than not Sara came home to a phone message or a new document Lieberman had sent in the mail. The Lieberman clan seemed devoted to preserving the memory of the work of their relative driving madly on his motorcycle from the courthouse, papers ready to fly out of his leather satchel. They'd organized reunions, panels. She'd learned her father had participated.

The man next to Sara folds his laptop, pushes the tray up, and locks it in place. "Want a coffee?" he asks, pulling himself out of the seat. Sara realizes she's been gesturing at something with her hands. She's afraid she's been muttering out loud, she's been so lost in the wrangle of her own mind.

"Thanks. Sure," Sara says, reaching in her bag for money. The man shakes his head and waves a hand. "I'm going there anyway. It's fine." And before Sara can press a few dollars on him, he's moving down the aisle, walking with a practiced wide gait to hold himself on course and unaffected by the train's rock. Sara's so glad to have the seat to herself that she doesn't care if it's her own rantings that drove him to the club car.

But curled against the train window, Sara isn't sure she hasn't started inventing. Hasn't she already started making up his story? She's suspicious. What academic hasn't heard of the researcher so driven by the possible theory that he warps or even creates evidence—the jawbone that locates man's origins in Mongolia or Kenya, the extant tribe, the language of eels? Hasn't she been guilty of hoping she'll trip upon some last unpublished words of Benjamin's? Not simply the notes and research for the other parts of his Baudelaire project, hidden in the Bibliotheque Nationale, but something that sheds new light on his suicide at the Vichy border.

Sure she's suspicious. Of herself.

"Sugar?" The man is back, balancing cups of coffee in a cardboard tray. "I grabbed a bunch of packets just in case."

Sara shakes her head no. No thanks. It's funny but she doesn't want to open the last piece of evidence, the envelope, now that the man is back. Like he'd care? He's busy with Lou. With his situation and numbers. Like he'd care about a kid in 1940. There's enough in this world, this week's bullshit, that he's measuring. The hurricane's effect on juice prices. Should he get in on Del Monte, figuring that after the tumble and dip, people are still going to want their fucking canned peaches?

Did her father want her to have this envelope? Leaving it out for her on his cleared-off desk. Or was Carmen intervening? Her way of saying what Ethan said, "It's time to move on."

Sara slips the contents of the envelope out onto the fold-down tray. The man in the seat next to her doesn't even glance over. There's not much inside. It's disappointing; she's been expecting more. First a *carte d'identité* for Itzak Lejdel issued May 1938, giving simple information: where he lives, his age. Then there's a Belgian passport. She goes through it page by page. In it—clipped, pasted, stamped—an array of visas: Shanghai, Spain, Morocco, Portugal, Mexico. France. A stamped sixty-day temporary U.S. landing visa, which states under status: Political Refugee. Child traveling alone. Signed by Patrick Malin. She closes the passport after flipping through successive blank pages. The last item is a small sketch of a young man wearing a hat ripped from what seems like a laboratory notebook. The drawing looks noticeably like the photograph on her father's *carte d'identité*. Also like the picture she's been carrying around of her father and Henri. In a playful hand someone has penned *Toujours Le Bon Vivant*, and below the name *Sylvie* is written with hearts on either side of the name. Who is Sylvie? Why did he keep this, a drawing? Sara goes back to his passport again. Looks at all the stamps. Transit visas and stamps. Shanghai? He was going to Shanghai? Mexico? The ship docked in Mexico. Why wasn't he permitted off the boat? She goes more carefully through each blank page. On the last page Sara finds two folded, yellowed pieces of paper pressed into the passport. They're cracked along the seams where they've been folded. Sara unfolds them but they're so thin she has to work carefully to keep the paper from falling apart. On the first sheet, a few lines of text made with the irregular pop of an old manual typewriter:

```
Chère Madame Eleanor Roosevelt,
Est-ce que vous aimez des histoires?
```

And on the second sheet Sara reads:

```
Dear Eleanor Roosevelt,
Do you like stories?
```

SEPTEMBER 14
12:48 P.M.

Dear Mrs. Roosevelt,

The interviews move so slowly. They're still in there with the same four passengers.

   Not that I doubt you or anything, but you gave this Mr. Malin my name, right? And just a reminder, if you put me down the list as Isaac Leader, or Fred or Richard, my name on official papers is Itzak Lejdel.

Isaac

1:37 P.M.

Dear Mrs. Roosevelt,

I'm not worried or anything, but none of the inspectors has called me in yet.

1:45 P.M.

Dear Mrs. Roosevelt,

Quick question. When they call me in, should I present gloves for
their wives?

2:22 P.M.

Dear American Mother,

Here's how it's gone so far. First the inspectors called in the Rand
family, Madame Lucien, Theodore DeJong, and the Steinrichs.
Then Dalio was called in with Madeleine. I tried to catch her eye
with a yearning, don't-forget-me glance. But latched to Dalio, she
looked straight ahead. The rest of us are waiting, trying to figure
out what happens next. Someone heard Captain Harberts report
that only thirty passengers will be released from the ship. Someone
said that after these initial people have been interviewed, only children would be called. Mothers and children.

You've told Mr. Malin that even though I've turned seventeen, I
should still be allowed off the ship. Seventeen is still considered a
child, right?

I've looked for you on the pier with the others. I hope you are
coming to meet me. The pier has a carnival feel: both the upper
railway and the lower docks are full, people shouting encourage-
ments, many promises called out to relatives. The reporters call up
to us, asking if we are hopeful that that we will be allowed off the
boat. I think it is best not to shout anything back.

Please come. Are you coming? Are you coming, Mrs. Roosevelt?
Are you coming, Mother?

Isaac

P.S. I understand if you are angry with me about Madeleine being married. I'm sorry. Don't hold it against me right now. Let's talk about it later.

P.P.S. I know I haven't even told you about what happened in Vera Cruz. I promise I will as soon as I get off.

"I'd like the chance to wander through and formulate my questions," Sara says, declining the curator's offer to walk her though the show. He's still in his summer suit in mid-September. Sara wonders if he's dressed up and put on his seersucker just for her visit, or if every day he wears a suit to this empty museum when he could be wearing pajamas for the amount of traffic it looks like this place gets. Sara saw in the exhibition log that the last visitor was days ago.

She notices the way the curator lingers, reluctant to leave her in the room. And even when he finally goes into his office, she imagines he's watching her through the louvered shades. Hanging up on him obviously hasn't made a good impression. He doesn't trust her, that's for sure. At the entrance he'd shaken her hand. "Just call me Tom," he said after she'd maintained formality by introducing herself as Professor Sara. There's not any good reason for keeping up the front that she's come down to supplement her Benjamin research with successful escape routes. But she's not ready to supply her story. Funny, what was it her father said the other day about not trusting people with too much information? She's her father's daughter.

Sara moves slowly through the single-room exhibition. If she told Tom who she was, she could get right to what her father has sent to the exhibit. Instead Sara wants to go through the room methodically, starting with the show's title placard: Saving of the SS *Quanza* Refugees: A Prelude to the Holocaust, accompanied by a poster-sized photograph of the ship docked at the high pier at the railway coal piers at Sewalls Point in the port of Hampton Roads, Virginia. Next is an enlarged copy of a hand-written letter: *Dear Moische, With a worried heart I write you this letter.* Sara reads the letter slowly. *I must not give up hope. We still do not understand what went wrong in Vera Cruz. We were lined up ready to disembark. Hopefully there will be another port.* And then the letter closes: *We send regards to Mr. Berner and his wife.* The cordiality makes Sara think of Benjamin's later letters, the way that even in his increasingly desperate scouting for paths of survival—New York, Switzerland, Havana—his intellectual pleasures poke through. *Have you read Faulkner?* he writes to Adorno in a letter from 1940. Sara also thinks of a colleague she'd spoken with at a translation conference in Vancouver. He'd published a book entirely composed of letters between undocumented Central Americans in the United States and their friends and families back home. These men and women— cooks, maids, gardeners in Southern California—had brought him paper grocery bags and Toys R Us bags filled with letters. People he'd never met showed up with letters. Translating the letters, he'd been surprised at the endless discussion of little things—an uncomfortable but pretty new pair of sandals, a dumb joke being retold, crushes on boys. All the *give my regards* that peppered every letter home. At first he thought it was avoidance, how little time most people spent telling what happened between Guatemala City and Los Angeles. There was, he told Sara, surprisingly little recording of the desperate and harrowing circumstances. The difficult crossings and recrossings. Initially he interpreted it as turning to the trivial instead of recording the dire. Eventually he realized he'd been an idiot. That he was just another gringo with a gringo's appetite for third world horror. That the talk of shoes and pop lyrics, the talk of Weber barbecues was not just comforting denial. They weren't even little things. They were what made up the good in a person's life. Noticing flowers, commenting on the good weather in spring, a cousin's wedding, were ways of acknowledging the spirit's appetite for life. They were forward motion. Sara had smiled at the colleague, considering him a bit flakey, a reductionist. But after this summer of translating Benjamin, she thinks her own smugness was a kind of denial.

Sara goes on to a wall filled with mounted photographs. From her research, from the information Lieberman sent, she recognizes the entire cast of characters. At the end of the wall Sara sees an enlarged newspaper photograph of Eleanor Roosevelt, a triple strand of pearls around her neck, her hair pinned up under a tilted hat. But before she can begin reading the text beneath the first photograph of Secretary of State Cordell Hull, Tom reemerges, positioned in the doorway of his office. "Since you've called I've been researching Walter Benjamin a little."

"Yes," Sara says. He's letting Sara know he's blown her cover. A Benjamin scholar doesn't belong in Virginia at this *Quanza* exhibit.

"Quite a sad final story."

Sara chooses not to engage. This curator hardly matters. She's come to Virginia following Ethan's advice to learn and move on. So far, it doesn't seem like there's anything really new that she hasn't seen online. But looking at the blown-up photograph of the ship and reading the dry description of it as a passenger and cargo ship, built in

1929 in Hamburg, Germany, registered that same year in Lisbon, Portugal, owned by the Companhia Nacional de Navegacao, Sara imagines for the first time her father actually aboard the ship. And Lile and Rosa. Even Marcel Dalio, who only three years before appeared as the injured Rosenthal escaping from a prisoner-of-war camp in *The Grand Illusion*, winds up stuck on this twin-engine ship.

"What do you want to find here?" the curator says. He says it quietly, still at a distance from Sara, as if he's letting her know he's used to people showing up here with ulterior motives. He's waited out their reluctance and heard some stories in this room.

He was only seventeen, her father. A refugee. A child traveling without parents, it says on the U.S. visa. Maybe Richard Leader, all these years, has been trying to make that boy Itzak feel safe. Or maybe Richard has abandoned Itzak. A kind of Hammurabian punishment for the abandonment of Sahra and Max.

Either way, in this room she feels for the first time just how scared he must have been. Alone on the boat. Hardly a bon vivant. Whatever seventeen-year-old bravado he'd once boasted worn down so that he's now just a tired, scared boy reckoning with having run off. The boat ready to be sent back. He thinks he's being punished for his betrayal. He's relentlessly going over and over the choices he's made. Maybe he did the leaving, but now he feels lost. If only there were someone now to whom he could tell everything. He wants to sit at the kitchen table with his mother chopping vegetables. "You'll understand, Maman," he'd say, "once you know the whole story." He wants to watch her face yield its stern set. First to curiosity, then to forgiveness.

As Sara turns to address the curator, let him know to back off, she's not someone who's going to be handled, she sees, at a small table, a portable typewriter. A gray typewriter fixed in its heavy case, *Royale*, in raised letters above the keys. Nothing so portable about these old portable typewriters. That's what strikes Sara first.

"Itzak Lejdel," she says. "This is what he sent, isn't it? You said he said he sent things down. Does it work, still?" she asks and hears the curator's feet crossing the room.

Tom says. "They called him Itzak, the poet. A dreamer, the other passengers said. Gave people a real laugh when they saw this machine at the reunion. They were apparently constantly trying to confiscate his typewriter for the good of the ship. There were letters they wanted to send off to get help. You can imagine that given the ship's circumstances, a typewriter was a tremendously valuable commodity. They say they practically had to wrestle him down for his typewriter. In fact nothing got off the ship. All the communiqués by the eighty-six passengers were held aboard the ship by Captain Harberts; I actually have many of them here in the archives."

"May I try it?" Sara asks, looking for the first time directly at the curator. "Please."

Before he can answer, Sara opens the passport and unfolds one of the thin, yellow sheets. She's afraid it will crack as she turns the rubber roller. But she pushes the carriage return until the paper is aligned.

The poet? That's what Lile and Rosa thought. That he was writing love poems. Sara thinks of the sketch she's carrying, *Toujours Le Bon Vivant*.

Sara knows Itzak wasn't writing poems.

He couldn't spare his typewriter. It was right there, in the envelope she's been carrying, the answer. Maybe nothing was getting ashore. But he was way past caring about that. Maybe there is no whole story. But he'd keep going. Those two sheets of paper. First French. Then English. His first tries. He still believed in the power of language. He's got to tell someone who he is. It's his only chance. He wants a mother on shore, a new mother, American, a woman who might actually save him.

Her fingers have to press hard on the keys. Below the salutation that has already been typed, Sara's letters form with the same uneven jump.

```
Dear Eleanor Roosevelt,
Do you like stories?
```

"He's your father?" the curator says, though it's less a question than an offering. A commandment. *He's your father.* As if he might actually be introducing Sara to a parent she's never met.

"Itzak's my father," Sara says, her fingers fitting in the indentations on the typing keys.

SEPTEMBER 14

Dear Eleanor Roosevelt,

I know you don't want to look like you're playing favorites, but I'd feel much better if they'd call my name soon?

Dear Maman, Dear Sylvie, Dear Paulette Goddard, Dear Papa, Dear Mother, Dear Robert, Dear Henri, Dear Madame Dupais, Dear Monsieur Goldenman, Dear Manuel, Dear Myrna Loy, Dear Odile, Dear Judy Garland, Dear Mrs. Roosevelt, Dear Eleanor, Dear Mrs. First Lady, Dear Ginger Rogers, Dear Marie, Dear Baudelaire, Dear Claudette Colbert, Dear Charlotte, Dear Errol Flynn, Dear Richard Leader, Dear Maman.

Dear Sylvie,

I'm sorry I didn't look over when you called out to me in Perpignan. I've sent your portrait of me to the President of America's wife. She says you are a real talent and wouldn't be at all surprised if you wind up famous like so many of the French painters.

Dear Max,

I'm sorry I left Maman with the Goldenmans. I know what you said about taking care of her. I hope you understand. Things will be all set up for you and Maman as soon as you arrive. I'm doing great in this country. Great opportunities for gloves in America. I think I'll have everything set up in a week or two at Gimbels and Lord and Taylor's. Soon the President's wife will be wearing your gloves. She's an 8 1/2.

Dear Madame Dupais,

Is it right to say I tried "to catch her eye"? I've been in all the New York bars and no one thought I was "fresh off the boat."

Dear Odile,

Your hair. Your face. I want to hold your face in my hands.

Dear Charlotte,

I hope you've forgiven me for not coming to your room to say goodbye. It was, you must understand, a quick decision to leave Brussels. Did you see Papa when he came back? Sometimes on this boat I've thought of your room and the way the river sounded as we sat at the table by the open window.

Dear Ginger Rogers,

I am your fan. You are the most beautiful of all the beauties.

Dear Rosalind Russell,

I am your fan. You are the most beautiful actress. You are the bee's knees. I need your help.

Dear Paulette Goddard,

I am your fan. You are the most beautiful beauty of all the actresses. Please, can you help me?

Dear Madeleine LeBeau,

Please, please, turn around and say, "That young man must come with me." That would be a gift.

Dear Baudelaire,

Je te hais, Océan!

"I THOUGHT MAYBE. I really wasn't sure. But I couldn't figure out why you were being secretive."

Sara shrugs. Too hard to begin explaining. What would she explain?

"Anyway, then when he called before, I—"

"What? He called? Here?"

"He seemed to know you were here. I said you were just outside and I could get you to the phone. He said no, he only wanted me to give you a message."

"My father called while I was here? Today?" Sara feels so disoriented. Tries to balance herself on her fingers, which haven't left the typewriter.

"Just before I came out of my office," Tom says. "Just five minutes ago. He told me to tell you that since you've come all the way here, he wants me to give you something."

"What do you have?" she says, looking at Tom. She's underestimated him, or it's not exactly that, she'd dismissed him as irrelevant and now, she has to take him as more than just a small-time curator of a rinky-dink maritime museum.

"Honestly, I don't know," he says. Sara sees how awkward the whole situation is for him. Her false information. Her father's phone call. Now his involvement. Tom looks at a large envelope in his hands. The same kind that Carmen handed Sara. "He sent this right after the exhibit went up. He sent it with the clear instruction that it be kept in the archives but never opened. In perpetuity. I argued with him. Wanted to either send it back to him or let it become part of the open historical record. But you know him; he's not the easiest person to persuade. Finally I agreed."

Sara reaches for the envelope, but Tom doesn't respond. Holds it close.

"Now apparently he's changed his mind and he wants this back. He wants me to give it to you. To bring it back to the city when you go back. But he's wants you to know that he doesn't want you to open this envelope. He doesn't want the contents read."

"It's something to read?"

"Apparently so. I told him I'd put it in the mail. But he said to give it to you. I'm sorry, Sara." He hands her the envelope. She expects it to feel weighty. Like a book. But it's lighter, and softer. No binding. No spine.

Dearest Maman,

Not to worry, Maman. Maman, I have all the photographs in a careful place. I have the bed sheets folded as you fold them. I hope the Goldenmans have taken great care of you. I've been staying in Brooklyn, NY. I have a place ready for you and Papa. I can't wait to see you. Don't stay any longer than you must at Rivesaltes. Papa has made contact with me and he's told me to have you come to New York, even without him. He'll meet us here. And Maman, Times Square is just as fast and beautiful as it looks in the movies. I'm sorry, Maman. Forgive me.

Dear Maman,

I should have picked you up in my arms just as you picked me up when I was small boy who refused to come indoors for lunch or a bath. I should have picked you up, brought you on the bus, bribed our way over the border. We would be together. I'll find a way. Forgive me.

Dear Maman,

When I arrived in Barcelona I stayed in a small hotel. The man who operated the elevator whispered to me in Yiddish, "You are a Jewish boy?" I didn't answer. Then he whispered the blessing over bread, even though we were in the elevator. He asked me, did I have dollars to trade? Please be careful, Maman. There are many people who under the present circumstances are thinking only about themselves and it leads even good young men to make decisions they will regret. Forgive me.

Dear Maman,

I don't know if I'm coming off the ship in America or coming back to Lisbon. When you get this letter, please check for a message at the Banque de Lyon.

Dear Maman,

forgive me dear maman forgive me dear maman forgive me dear maman forgive me dear maman forgive me dear maman forgive me dear maman forgive me

Dear Mrs. R.,

Ever see *Too Hot to Handle?* All the crazy situations that Gable as Chris Hunter kept cooking up? Remember the girl holding the dog while in the background the bombs fell on thatched huts? And it was all a fake. One and all, those news guys were fakers. That was great! Walter Pidgeon was pretty smooth as a faker. But Gable, he was something in that movie—rakish and honorable, making sure that Myrna Loy got her brother back from the jungle. Risking everything and still having a ball. Not to mention getting Myrna Loy in the end. I love Myrna. Anyway, I invoke *Too Hot to Handle* at this moment just to say that I've realized not everything is exactly as it seems. I'm not suggesting that I think you're about to show up in Virginia in some voodoo costume with a grass skirt or anything. But I have a notion that I better have a good look around. It wouldn't be right—would it?—with all these other people wanting to come to America—the First Lady shows up on the pier just to welcome me.

I'll keep your secret secret.

Isaac

Sara ignores the knocking on the motel door. She's sitting on the orange bedspread, been sitting on the bed for hours; she doesn't think she could stand up to open the door even if she tried. She's not sure what's left of her after crying like she's been crying. Sure, she knows she's made of something like 98 percent water but, still, who knew there was actually that much water inside anybody?

She's sitting in front of a tied folder. Ditched the big envelope hours ago. The folder's elaborately tied, so she can't get to what's inside, which looks like a manuscript typed on the same thin paper she found in her father's passport. If she pushes up the corner of the folder, she can read random words, some phrases. In English. A flip book of words. But random, without connected meaning. The paper is so crumbly, bits of paper keep shedding from the folder. She keeps starting to untie the string. Has even gone so far as pulling the bow out. Then retied it. Did it all again. A lot of times. Now she's just playing with the string, twisting it, half hoping the string just unwinds, disintegrates.

At first she couldn't believe he'd do it. Put it in her hands like this and then demand loyalty. Put them in that kind of opposition. Loyalty to him or loyalty to herself, to her right to know. But was that it? Sitting these hours with the yellow brittle pages right in front of her, she wasn't even sure that was the correct equation. She thought of the Marshall Chess Club, the guy with his milky eye. She'd put the glove mold on his desk, announcing she knew things, that he was in check. Was her father just getting himself out of check with an aggressive risk, putting himself right in her face? Letting her decide what winning—if there is a winning move—really will mean.

And there it is. Her decision. To open this string, open the folder, and read what her father doesn't want read. She'd learn what there was to learn. But lose him in learning it. Either decide that he didn't have the right to have privacy. Or carry his privacy back. Hand it over to him.

She's never read a turn like this in any Nancy Drew mystery.

"This is the wrong room," Sara manages to shout to the persistent knock. She hopes that's enough to let whomever—the lady with her full ice bucket who's forgotten her room key, the kid who's been down in the game room—whomever—get the message.

It doesn't pass Sara by, the irony, Benjamin's translator in a motel room with a found manuscript given to her by a man, a refugee, a survivor, who wants it to remain unread. Benjamin says, *The past can be seized only as an image that flashes up at a moment of its recognizability and is never seen again.* There's a whole life she doesn't know, won't ever know. Stories she'll never grasp. Maybe whatever is on those typed, crackly pages is not even the real story, only the one he could let himself tell, inventions that helped him live. "I'm a lucky man at making my luck," was something her father was fond of saying. She'd never given it much thought. Or the way he'd say to Sara as a child, "Let yourself be lucky." He kept going. No matter what. Inventing luck. Inventions like translations.

Translations, Sara thinks, a way of adapting the text to a new language, a new existence.

⁓

"Sara. Sara. It's me." She realizes she's been hearing it for a little bit, her name, her name being said over the knocking. "It's me, Sara. Tom. I've brought something for you."

Tom? It takes her a second. The curator.

Sara finds the large envelope and slips the folder inside.

"Hang on a second. I'll be there in a second," she says, opening the door even as she speaks.

"I'm sorry. I know it's late. But after you left I remembered this was in back. I thought you might want to go through it before you leave." He's holding a large box out for her to take. But she can't even lift her arms. She's exhausted from everything and wishing, right now, that she could be back in the time before she knew anything, before she had to choose how far to go. Now there's a folder of unread papers on the bed. Now she's being asked to consider this box. Instead Sara moves from the door, letting Tom cross into her motel room.

"He sent this down. After the show had been mounted, along with the envelope I gave you. But this box was meant for the open archive. The show was already up. I never got around to looking through it. It got put in back. I'm sorry if it's late but I didn't know what time your train left in the morning."

Sara stays close to the door, looking at Tom holding the box in the middle of her room. She sees it is marked *Richard Leader/Itzak Lejdel*. Her father, the list of his identities, the stretch of his appositives. Tom puts the box down on the motel bed. Clearly he doesn't know where to put himself so he stays standing, swaying in the space between the two beds.

She wants him to leave so that she can approach the bed, like someone who's been bit reapproaching a dog. Take her time, come at it alone. But she sees his curiosity has been engaged; he might even use his directorial position to claim the right to be present.

Sara lifts the box a little off the mattress. It feels as if there's nothing inside. And for a moment she thinks that this is her father's next strange contribution—an empty box. The empty archive. The only evidence, emptiness. Sara shakes it a little more and hears the jostle of papers. Something rolls. She's nervous. But why? Of what? Hasn't everything already happened? Even the idea that her father had gathered whatever was inside the box and sent it to the museum. Maybe it isn't much. To be kept, safeguarded. But also to be known. Even a little. The man who said nothing, had, almost despite himself, wanted also to be known.

"It was never catalogued," Tom says apologetically.

"Should we do that? You need us to do that?" Sara notices her relief. Always safety in a professional task.

"I don't know if it really matters," Tom says and then, perhaps considering the implied insult, "but we probably should."

———

"A pair of red leather gloves," she says, and Tom writes down, "red leather gloves."

It seems random what Sara pulls from the box, almost like a grab bag—red gloves. Then Sara remembers her grandfather was a glove maker, had a factory. Maybe these are her grandfather's gloves. Beautiful leather, supple. Small pearl buttons at the cuff. The cuff is scalloped, stitched with white that matches the buttons. Clearly well made. Classy. Sara puts them on.

"Beautiful," says Tom.

"My grandfather made them," Sara says. The gloves feel great. She thinks of Ethan saying, "You want to go there, Sara, and touch what you can touch." She leaves the gloves on as she reaches into the box and pulls out a French magazine. *Film Complet*, April 1940. A picture of Clark Gable on the cover. Sara flips through. Laughs. Myrna Loy. Bette Davis. Claudette Colbert. Starlets galore.

"What's that?" Tom says, his pen poised to write down what Sara says, but she knows he means, "What's so funny?"

"I've spent my whole life watching old movies. Who knew I was being ruled by a teenager's fantasies?"

Next she holds up a bright scarlet feather.

"And this?" Tom says.

"I don't know. Bird feather?"

Sara pulls a torn stub from the box and translates from the French what she can from the faded torn ticket stub. "I'm not sure, exactly. But it's from a movie theater. He loves the movies," Sara says, and hands the ticket over to Tom.

Next there's a porcelain hairpin.

"When did he send this?" Sara asks, looking at the white porcelain flower. It's the one she'd seen her father holding while he slept that day in his room.

"In 2000, just after the anniversary exhibition went up." Sara tries to make sense of this. She'd thought the hairpin was her mother's, a piece of jewelry that one day he'd give to Sara. But this one is here, part of the *Quanza* archive. And it appears to be a match to the one he'd kept. Whose hairpin? Not her mother's. Maybe his mother's?

There are two pieces of newspaper. On one there's a Gimbels department store advertisement, a bouquet of line-drawn hats and purses and gloves selling for $5.95. She tries to make sense of the other piece of newspaper, but it seems to be the middle columns of an article about a bridge repair. Then she turns the brittle paper over and sees there's a photograph of Eleanor Roosevelt. Beneath the photo the caption reads, "Mrs. Roosevelt champions children's rescue from Britain."

Sara's saved for last a collection of envelopes tied together with the same string she's been touching on the folder. It feels good just to untie it. She's wanted that satisfaction for hours. She spreads the envelopes on the bed, surprised at how many there are. They've already been ordered by postal dates, spanning 1940–1948. Mostly they look official. The Red Cross, the Banque de Lyon, the City of Brussels, the Director of Rivesaltes.

"Why don't you drop this all off in the morning before you catch the train," Tom says, and Sara realizes she's just been staring at the letters for a long time, not moving.

"Are you sure?"

"It's all right, Sara."

"Thank you, that's kind."

After Tom's gone, it takes Sara a long time to begin reading. She returns instead to each of the objects she's pulled from the box. She takes off the gloves. She fastens the flower pin in her hair. Takes it out. She turns the pages of the film magazine, careful not to let the old pages fall apart.

Then she begins reading. Letter after letter of almost the same thing. The Banque de Lyon has no current information on the whereabouts of Max Lejdel. No one has left messages or come to retrieve messages. There have been no withdrawals of funds. The Red Cross is sorry to inform him, but they have no information on Max Lejdel. Nor the City of Brussels. There are later letters from the Red Cross, from the White Cross, from other agencies after the war, all of which state they have no current information on either a Max or a Sahra Lejdel.

Sara takes from a simple cream envelope a piece of stationary without any official agency heading. Lovely thick paper. A watermark. It's handwritten. She skips to the closure, holds her breath. She can't believe it.

SEPTEMBER 20, 1940

Dear Mr. Leader,

What a kind and moving letter I've received from you. It is, of course, unnecessary to thank me for my efforts on behalf of the *Quanza*. I am, rather, so glad that I could be of service to those of you who have faced such difficult circumstances. These are astonishing, troubling times and we must assist those in need with whatever efforts we are capable. I am honored when you say that during your stay on the ship, you felt my presence, that you felt yourself in communication with me, and that it gave you strength to endure the uncertainty.

I have sent along your parents' names and hopefully we will be able to reach you soon with good news of their whereabouts. You must know that communications are not at the present as speedy as any of us would like. Though you are rightfully concerned, try to be patient.

Finally, I'd like to thank you for the lovely gift of gloves. What a perfect royal blue color. You say they are from your father's factory in Belgium. You must be proud of his fine work. They are, incidentally, a perfect fit.

I hope you are, despite the uncertainties you still face, beginning to settle in the United States. I think you will find it quite hospitable. Clearly your letter indicates a nice command of our language. Our country has much to recommend it. I believe as a mother I can with some certainty say that your parents would be most relieved to have you engaged and always forward looking with your life. Do that for them. In the meantime I shall continue to do my best on behalf of all the displaced children.

With all good wishes I am,
very sincerely yours,
Mrs. Roosevelt

You felt my presence and you felt yourself in communication with me. Sara reads the line again. Itzak, the poet, the scribbler of love poems, the dreamer, they had to practically wrestle him down for his typewriter. Sara looks over to the envelope with the unread typed pages. To be unread in perpetuity.

Now it's time for the four letters Sara hasn't touched, stamped from Rivesaltes. The first is dated October 19, 1940. It is from Monsieur Goldenman, saying that they have received Itzak's letter and that everyone is glad he has arrived safely in the United States.

They have finally been given word about their papers and hope to be out of the camp within the week. The situation in the camp has changed, he writes cryptically. It is a good time to be leaving. However, he wants to tell Itzak that he is concerned about Sahra, who shows no willingness to consider leaving the camp. She insists on waiting for Max. "Honestly," Monsieur Goldenman continues, "I am not confident that your mother is physically strong enough anymore to make a trip." He will continue to plead with her. Itzak should hope for the best. The second letter is four sentences long. "Dear Izzy, Everything you say about New York sounds wonderful. I am feeling fine. Not to worry. Soon we will all be together again. Love, Maman." The third, dated February 11, 1941, is from the director. He apologizes for the delay in his response and, by way of explanation, says how swiftly the camp is growing in size. It is difficult, he says, to attend to all the many essential matters in a timely fashion. His French is formal but a little elegant; Sara believes she can detect a plaintive tone in the sentences. He is very sad to have to convey the following information. His mother, Sahra Lejdel, has, the director states, died at Rivesaltes. The date of death is December 23, 1940. The cause of death is heart failure. A certificate of death shall be sent upon request. Finally, he has no information that a Max Lejdel ever came through Rivesaltes. The fourth letter, without a note included, is the certificate of Sahra's death.

There it is. What finally happened. Her father looked for seven years. Even after he's held his mother's death certificate. He kept looking for her and Max. He contacted every American and European agency that people used after the war to find missing persons. He'd lost them. He'd left them, but he hadn't planned on losing them.

She thought of the remarkable penned letter from Eleanor Roosevelt, her declared commitment to help look for Sahra and Max, her motherly command to continue forward in his life.

Somewhere a child—in Sierra Leone, Eastern Europe, Indonesia, in more countries than not—will soon join those who have crossed borders and become an American child. Soon Sara will go and bring her daughter home. Her daughter will become an American child. The story of that passage will be part of their new story. "Sometimes circumstances make keeping a family together impossible. Maybe they believed this was their chance to give you a better life." Is that what Sara will say to her child, when one day Sara's asked how parents could abandon their child, leave their child in an orphanage? Sara wants to think she'll be brave, tell the truth, even if the truth is *not knowing*. But what is the truth for a child of four and for a child of seventeen? For a forty-one-year-old woman? "Let yourself be lucky. It's okay." Will she say that to her daughter? Sara doesn't know, won't ever fully know about her father, her grandfather, her Grandmother Sahra whose name she shares. She won't know what Carmen's seen in her war in El Salvador, or what impossibility Benjamin finally saw, or even what the baby she's adopting felt in the first moments against her mother's exhausted body. She thought she needed to find everything out. What's the everything? There's this pile of letters, a response to her father's continued search. An unread folder. That's okay. Sara knows she knows enough. She wants to go back to New York.

"Ethan." Sara hears herself saying his name though she barely remembers lifting up the motel phone.

"I'm glad you called."

"It's me, Sara."

"I know, Sara. I was just thinking about you."

"My father looked for them, Ethan. Even after. After he knew."

"Are you okay?"

"I think I am."

"Can I do something for you?"

Sara's quiet then. She's tired. As if she's been traveling for days on end. Tired but still restless, as if she can't unwind.

"Ethan, will you stay on the phone with me. Just talk to me. Say anything. Just a little more till I'm ready to drop asleep."

Dear Eleanor!

Tricky, tricky, tricky. I figured it out! I see you out there, Mrs. Roosevelt. I just figured out who you are. You are something else! The bee's knees! Madcap, madcap, madcap. Very tricky. Good job of disguise.

Oh, it's all very screwball comedy. Wasn't I just thinking about *Too Hot to Handle*? People expect disguises from Myrna or Carole or even Claudette. But who'd considered Eleanor Roosevelt? This is dandy. Not to worry; I won't blow your cover. I'll keep it my little secret.

Who would ever think to recognize you on the dock in that policeman's uniform! Talk about a feather in your cap, for this costume.

But hey, how will you recognize me? Are you sure you even know what I look like, which passenger I am? I'm afraid I've spent too much time describing my knees and not any time at all describing my face.

Wait, just to make sure, here's what I'll do. I'm going to go up to the main deck. I'll come all the way forward. You'll see me at the prow of the ship. Then you'll see me lean forward. I'll be in the double-breasted blue suit, holding a sheath of papers. Can you see me? I'll lean a little more. Yes, Mrs. Roosevelt. Yes. Mother, that'll be me.

Wait, I'll do better and give you a huge, unmistakable sign. Here's what I'll do. First I'll lower my arms. And then, with a big send-up, a big whoosh, I'll toss up the letters, all the letters, our letters, Mrs. Roosevelt. Airborne. They'll be airborne. Look. Look. Look. You won't be able to miss them. All that terrible thin paper floating and fluttering. Catching the wind. Page after page, scattering, lofted, drifting. All the Dear Mrs. Roosevelt letters, every one of them, sailing forth.

Who could miss that? Look. Everybody for a moment will look up. Like these are streamers announcing the moment of debarking. The pages of the letters hold the air for a moment and it is almost as if they are waving, like white waving hands, like every glove in Max's factory set free. Then you'll settle your gaze down to the young man who tossed the pages. That'll be me. Empty-handed. I'll be waving, too. Who cares about the letters anymore? Who cares about my story? Look, if you're interested, I'll tell you every last thing when I'm ashore.

See me now, Mrs. R? Here I am, your boy. Waving and waving.

And those news reporters. I think they'll catch that on camera. Everyone will see me, right? They'll see me with my Royale (I'm not tossing my typewriter! Not ever!) and I won't walk off this ship some nobody kid from Brussels, I'll walk off a movie star. Like the other passengers with relatives who've grown weary all these weeks and days of waiting, you'll run forward and embrace me. A boy coming home to his mother. But I guess, since you're a cop, a boy coming home to his father. Someone will catch all that on film.

It's a good story for the movies. Starring Richard Leader and Mrs. Eleanor Roosevelt. Our own touching, screwball comedy. Some story this will be. Maybe I shouldn't toss the letters; I might need them for Hollywood, for the film script. But you know, Mrs. Roosevelt, the way I'm thinking right now, all the stories I've told you hardly matter at all anymore. What matters is that I'm coming ashore. Together we'll find Maman. We'll find Max.

I'll make you proud.

Isaac Richard

NOW IS THE moment, the end of this story. This is her last stop before she catches the train back to New York.

It is morning and the passengers are finally coming ashore.

It is September. Maybe not the fourteenth of September, exactly, but close enough that Sara thinks they are breathing the same turning air, warm but without any summer humidity left in it. Late summer. Early fall. Changing air.

She's come to the railway pier, the lower wooden pier where Sara imagines the relatives waited. Locals have shown up. Church groups welcoming the refugees. The synagogue has organized homes for the *Quanza* refugees to spend the night. The reporters down from Washington and New York; local Virginian newspapermen slouch, already a little bored with these couple of days of hanging around the same story, the same port. There was talk that Eleanor Roosevelt might actually come to greet the refugees. That would be news. But she's not here. The photographers see the opportunities are limited. They try to perk up. There's the man waiting for his wife and daughters. He's slept at the pier these five days. There's already been a photograph in the *Norfolk Virginian-Pilot* that showed his plight, his dark outline, and above him, in a ship porthole, the faces of his children. The family torn by war. Readers responded. Now a family reunion picture would be good. There's a film star aboard, but who is he? He's not anyone Hollywood. So who knows him? Which one is he anyway? People disembark, wobbly with possessions. Sara waits, men and women, more men and women. Then, finally.

Sara sees Itzak. One of the last. Finally. She was beginning to worry. He's walking down the boat ramp. There's nothing graceful about his walk. He looks like a colt just let out of his stall—still awkward on his long legs. With a suitcase, two large wrapped bundles, and a portable typewriter, he's barely managing. Around him there are shouts, names being called, more names, big hugs, someone saying, "Here, I'm over here." He stops. His body swivels toward the voice. Lost, yes, he looks a little lost, expectant too, but also something else. It's childishness, Sara sees. He looks like a frightened kid. A camera, suddenly, so close to his face—pop and flash—so that he stumbles a little, and when he regains himself, hoisting a bundle, re-gripping a suitcase, he looks back up for a moment but it's too bright to clearly see. "I'm here," he hears again a woman's voice, and he looks across the crowded pier. It sounds like Maman. He's been desperate to see Maman. He bumps into someone who grabs past him. He stops, puts one bag between his legs. Looks around. There are two men embracing. Someone hoists a young girl up onto a man's shoulders. He thinks he hears someone say his name. But there's so much commotion. Everyone hugging. So much shouting and excitement. She's such a small woman. He can't locate where the voice came from. "Maman," Itzak says.

Sara, there on the empty railway dock, lifts her arms to the boy who has just come ashore alone. She waves and waves. Hoisting his suitcases, he continues walking. Behind him Sara can see there are more. One after another, after thousands, stepping alone onto shore from their passage. History's children. By plane, by ship, by truck, by foot. The children who have been brought or bought or smuggled in or snuck aboard. All ready for futures. Ready to be an American child. They look around, lonely, dazzled, expectant, hungry, afraid. Sara waves like a mother reassuring her child who's just realized he's wandered off too far at the busy World's Fair. She's walking toward him, the child. "Here," Sara calls, "I'm here."

NOTES

While the *Quanza* was an actual boat, and several characters in the novel are inspired by or based on actual people who were either aboard or associated with the *Quanza* situation, I have extended, invented, and altered as needed for the novel. *The Border of Truth* is a work of fiction.

The personal and historical knowledge of several people has been helpful in my writing of this book. David and Stephen J. Morewitz have been indefatigable in researching the history of the *Quanza* and in championing the efforts of attorney J. L. Morewitz to save its passengers. Stephen J. Morewitz's "The Saving of the S.S. *Quanza* in Hampton Roads, Virginia on September 14, 1940: A Prelude to the Nazi Holocaust" is an informative survey of the ship and work done on behalf of the refugees. I am also indebted to the insights of Francine Goldenhar whose father, Dr. Maurice Goldenhar, was aboard the *Quanza* with his parents and sister. Above all my gratitude goes to Irving Redel whose generosity of mind and memory was essential.

Though my character, Sara, is a translator by profession I am not, and I have happily yielded to existing excellent translations of Walter Benjamin's writings. I encourage readers to investigate these remarkable books:

Walter Benjamin, Selected Writings, Volume 4, edited by Michael Jennings and Howard Eiland. Translated by Edmund Jephcott. The Belknap Press of Harvard University Press, 2003.

The Correspondence of Walter Benjamin, edited and annotated by Gershom Scholem and Theodor W. Adorno. Translated by Manfred R. Jacobson and Evelyn M. Jacobson. The University of Chicago Press, Chicago, 1994.

Illuminations: Essays and Reflections, edited by Hannah Arendt. Translated by Harry Zohn. B Schocken Books, New York, 1969.

Stanzas are quoted from Charles Baudelaire's poems "Le Voyage" and "Obsession."

ACKNOWLEDGMENTS

Thanks, first, always and again to my father, Irving Redel, who has been kind enough not only to answer every question I put before him but for giving me his blessing to make everything up. I could not bear the simple but often terrifying task of sitting with myself required to write if it were not for the daily happiness, continuity, talk, and friendship of the tribe of family, writers, and friends I am lucky to have so richly in this life. To each my love and thanks. Thanks to Gabriel and Jonah who are particularly well suited to the task of returning me to everyday necessity and joy. Thanks to Sonya del Peral, Martine Vermeulen, Melinda Fine, John Brainard, Katherine Mosby, and Honor Moore who were kind enough to read and discuss this manuscript at various stages in its development. Thanks to Jessica for her sharp eye and the Bergman brothers who provided me the necessary retreat by the river and the rocks. Thanks to Vilma Lainez for her essential help and her knowledge of El Salvador. I am truly grateful to my agent, Ira Silverberg, who, with enthusiasm, encouraged me to go further. All gratefulness to my editor, Amy Scheibe, who nurtured this book with intelligence, generosity, and humor. Thanks to everyone at Counterpoint for their efforts on my behalf. I'm deeply indebted to Bill Clegg for his encouragement and vision. And always and ever to Stanley Kunitz. I am grateful that he opened a gate to the garden and welcomed me in.